A Gentle Calling

A GENTLE CALLING

DONNA FLETCHER CROW

VICTOR BOOKS ®

A DIVISION OF SCRIPTURE PRESS PUBLICATIONS INC.
USA CANADA ENGLAND

Cover art by Ken Call, showing Catherine and Phillip
in Finsbury Square off City Road. White building behind
the carriage is the Foundery.

Library of Congress Catalog Card Number: 87-81032
ISBN: 0-89693-353-9

VICTOR BOOKS
A division of SP Publications, Inc.
Wheaton, Illinois 60187

To Betty Waller

Librarian, Teacher, Friend
who inspires all who cross her path
with a love of books.
I'm thankful our paths crossed.

The Perronet Family

Vincent Perronet, youngest son of David and Philothea Perronet, born in London, in 1693. David Perronet was a native of Chateau d'Oex in the canton of Berne, a protestant who came to England about 1680. Philothea Perronet (nee Arthur) was from Wiltshire.

Charity Perronet, daughter of Thomas and Margaret Goodnew of London, married Vincent Perronet on 4 December 1718. They had twelve children.

> **Damaris,** called Dudy
> **Edward,** called Ned, married Durial
> **Catherine**
> **Charles,** called Charl
> **Vincent Jr.**
> **Elizabeth,** married William Briggs
> **John**
> **David**
> **Henry**
> **William**
> **Philothea**
> **Thomas**

The Cambridge Collection

THERE ARE SO FEW PEOPLE now who want to have any intimate spiritual association with the eighteenth and nineteenth centuries . . .

Who bothers at all now about the work and achievement of our grandfathers, and how much of what they knew have we already forgotten?

DIETRICH BONHOEFFER, *Letters and Papers from Prison*

DONNA FLETCHER CROW brings a lifetime love of English literature and history as well as intensive research to The Cambridge Collection—her historical series on the work of the Evangelical Anglicans. A former English teacher, she is now a full-time writer. She and her husband, Stan, have four children.

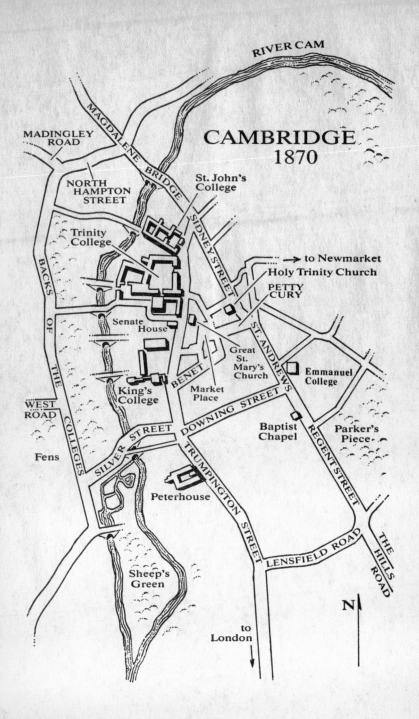

· *1* ·

"NED, YOU'RE BLEEDING!" Catherine Perronet rushed across the room to her brother. "What happened?" She took his arm to lead him to a chair, but he drew back sharply.

"Don't touch it, Cath. It may be broken."

"Broken!" This was too much even for Catherine's usually unruffled calm. "Were you attacked by a mob again?"

Edward Perronet smiled weakly. "I attempted to sow the seeds of truth to a crowd at Brixton. Shall we just say they were stony soil?"

"Apparently. They found plenty of stones to hurl at you." Catherine turned to fetch a bowl of water and some rags. "We must call a doctor for your arm, but I shall wash your wounds first. If Durial should see you in your present state, I wouldn't vouch for the safety of your future child."

"Pray, do clean me up, Sister, though I would guess that Durial will be more distressed for her chair cover and carpet than for our child." He looked at his boots caked with fresh mud from the April rains.

Catherine directed a servant girl to bring a fresh roll of bandages and sent the stable boy into Greenwich for the doctor. When she had staunched the blood from the worst of her brother's head wounds, and had cleansed all the caked blood and mud from his hair and face, she paused in her labors. "I must say, Ned, this is a fine way to make your homecoming after three weeks absence. I suppose the family of an itinerant preacher should become accustomed to such behavior; but still, you could have sent us some word of your progress in Wales. Were you beaten there too?"

11

Ned raised his tall, lanky body straighter in the chair, moving carefully to protect his damaged arm. His expression became suddenly serious, far graver than it had been over his physical injuries. "Sit down, Catherine. I have news I didn't want to put in a message. I fear it may distress you."

Catherine sat with quiet dignity. "In that case, let us have it quickly."

"My stay in Wales was extended because I attended the marriage of Charles Wesley to Miss Sally Gwynne." Catherine stared at her brother. She heard the words, but her mind refused to make sense out of them. "Charles is married? Charles Wesley?" *My Charles?* "But I thought . . . I hoped . . . I was almost sure . . ." She forced a little hiccup to cover what wanted to come out as a sob.

"Forgive me, Ned. I fear I have been indulging in foolish fantasies. But after you told me of the list of women John Wesley thought would make eligible wives for his brother . . ."

"That was most unwise of me. I should never have told you."

"On the contrary, the information provided me many happy fancies with which to wile away dull hours. You made it quite clear that there were three names on the list and that Sally Gwynne's was among them. I fear that I simply relied too much on the fact that Catherine Perronet was first on the list."

"And lest you hear from another and think me a traitor, I must also tell you that the letter I carried to Mrs. Gwynne from our father was instrumental in winning that reluctant lady's approval to the match."

"You and Father both? And what of our own Charl? Surely you knew he had spoken of a fondness for Miss Gwynne too."

Ned nodded. "Yes, I am fully aware that many hopes will be disappointed."

"If you carried a letter to Mrs. Gwynne, you must have known what was to take place. Why didn't you tell me?"

"I had an idea it was likely. I knew Charles hoped most fervently. But I also knew her parents had not consented and might not, so I wished to spare you pain in case nothing came of the matter."

He rose and crossed the room to take his sister's hand. "I'm sorry to be the bearer of news that wounds you so deeply, Catherine. But I thought it best to come from one who loves you. I wish I could say something to ease your pain."

She shook her lace-capped head of rich, dark curls and forced a trembly smile. "It's nice to know someone loves me, Ned." She withdrew her hand and resumed her composed posture. "Now, I think you had best finish what you've begun and tell me about the lady . . . at least that she is worthy of so great a prize."

"That comfort I can vouchsafe you. Sally Gwynne is a fine musician and a beautiful young woman. And she is from one of the first families in that part of Wales."

"Fah, that is not what I wish to hear. Will she make Cha . . . the Reverend Mr. Wesley a good wife? Will she keep him comfortable? Support his work? Make him happy?"

"Yes. As far as it's possible to predict such things, I believe she will do all that. She is much younger than he, by twenty years I should think, but she has the heart of one much more mature. When Mrs. Gwynne tried to make Charles promise never to return to Ireland where he was so nearly stoned last month, Sally jumped to her feet and said, 'Indeed, I shall go with him!'" Ned paused before driving the final nail. "And Charles is much in love with her."

Catherine nodded, then turned slightly away so that her brother should not see the tears that persisted in brimming in her eyes, no matter how staunchly she ordered them not to. "Thank you, Ned. I am content. At least, I shall be soon." She stood, shook out the panniers under her wide blue skirt, and checked that the fine lawn fichu at her neck was in place. "I believe I hear the wheels of the doctor's carriage on the gravel. I shall prepare my sister-in-law for the shock of receiving her battered husband. But do not forget to put on a clean jacket before you present yourself to her."

Durial Perronet was resting in her room upstairs, her curtains drawn against the midmorning sun, and a cloth of lavender water folded on her brow. It was indeed fortunate that the Perronet fortunes were well-endowed from their family estates in France, for no mere itinerant Methodist preacher could afford to keep such a wife as Durial. "Am I disturbing you, Sister?" Catherine asked.

Durial sat up, carefully laid the lavender-water cloth on the marble stand by her bed, and arranged the neckline of her sprigged cotton dressing gown. "I am happy for a visitor. What is all the coming and going I hear below?"

"Ned is returned from Wales."

Durial pulled back her sheets without care for wrinkling them. "My husband home, and I not told? Oh, where are my slippers?"

Catherine produced the slippers from under the four-poster bed.

13

"He will join you in a few minutes. But I must tell you first, there was an altercation . . ."

"Oh, no." Durial sank back on her pillows. "Was he stoned again?"

"I fear so. But he was quite unharmed—except for his arm. The doctor is with him now."

"Doctor! Oh, why won't he give up this dangerous enthusiasm and take a settled parish? I don't ask him to stop preaching, although I could wish he gave more time to his hymn-writing; but why can't he be a respectable vicar like his father? Your father has been settled at Shoreham for thirty years and your mother didn't have to bear any of her twelve children while in fear for her husband's life."

Catherine was still doing her best to reassure her brother's wife several minutes later when Ned entered, his arm in a sling. "Edward," Durial said, "if I weren't so glad to see you, I should give you the thorough scolding you deserve. If you don't take any thought for your wife's nerves, at least you might think of your son." She put her hand to her waist where evidence of new life was just beginning to show.

"If you will excuse me, I shall leave you two to sort this out. I must get to work. The children should find their teacher in her place." Catherine crossed to the door.

"Cath, you aren't going to the Foundery today? Not after—everything?" Ned turned away from Durial. "I'll send a message that I am unable to drive you. The wrist is not broken, still . . ."

"Fah! What does that say to anything? Our father taught me to drive when I was twelve years old. One of the stable boys can accompany me." Ned started to protest, but she stopped him. "Please. I would much rather be alone."

She tied a broad-brimmed hat of leghorn straw firmly under her chin, drew a bottle-green wool cape around her shoulders, and proceeded to the stables.

Catherine had never been more thankful for her work with the Methodist Society than she was at that moment, or of the long drive from Greenwich to Moorfields which would provide her the solitude she desired. Whether the emotion was joy or sorrow, Catherine had always felt deeply. But in spite of the depth of her feeling, or perhaps because of it, she wanted to be alone today, to experience the fullness of her sorrow and examine the true state of her mind. She did not want sympathy or company; she wanted uninterrupted time. Whatever was to come to her, she could find the strength to face it; but she must understand her feelings first.

"You will sit up in back, Joseph, and be very quiet."

"Yes, Miss." The lad scrambled up on the box, and those were the only two words Catherine heard from him.

Old Biggin knew the way to the Foundery as well as Catherine, so she could give her full mind to Ned's report. The fact that her dear Charles would be happy was a consoling thought; but all her dreams of being the one to make him happy, of sharing his work in close companionship, of singing his hymns with him. . . . Well, she would simply have to amend her dreams. After all, it wasn't as if Charles had ever offered any concrete encouragement for such fancies. But the dreams had been so real to her . . . .

No, they had been more than dreams—or, at least, she had believed them to be. Certain this was God's will for her life, she had often claimed Psalm 32:8: "I will instruct thee and teach thee in the way which thou shalt go; I will guide thee with Mine eye." But how could she believe the Lord was guiding her when a beautiful young girl from Wales could shatter everything?

Catherine picked up one of the books she had brought with her, *Pilgrim's Progress*. It was her favorite book next to the Bible, and she always found it helpful in times of struggle. She held the reins in one hand and left Biggin to plod down the country lane toward the Thames. With less than half an eye on the road, Catherine let the book fall open to its most read passage and again took in the account of Christian's conversion:

> . . . just as Christian came up with the Cross, his burden loosed from off his shoulders, and fell from off his back, and began to tumble, and so continued to do, till it came to the mouth of the Sepulchre, where it fell in . . .
>
> Then was Christian glad and lightsome, and said, with a merry heart, "He hath given me rest by His sorrows, and life by His death." Then he stood still awhile to look and wonder, for it was very surprising to him that the sight of the Cross should thus ease him of his burden. He looked, therefore, and looked again, even till the springs that were in his head sent the waters down his cheeks . . .

She laid the book down. Today that joyful scene brought cold

15

comfort, for it enlivened in her mind her own conversion; and although the joy and exultation of the moment was still alive in her soul, her heart couldn't disconnect the spiritual experience from the earthly; her mind mocked her heart with the fact that it had been Charles Wesley's preaching which had brought her to that sublime experience.

Doubly sublime because she had met her Saviour and Charles at the same time. Of course, no child of the godly Vincent Perronet could be far from a knowledge of God or a desire to do right; and Catherine, always grave and thoughtful, always wanting to do right, had from her earliest days, striven to keep the commandments, and to please God and man. But the trouble was, she was never *sure*, never completely satisfied that she had done enough to please God. Her parents and numerous brothers and sisters were quick to tell her in no uncertain terms if she failed to please them: "Cath, you forgot to lock the gate and the cow could have gotten out." "Catherine, you tore your skirt again." "Your sums are all wrong, Catherine." Not that such occasions happened often or that her family was overly hard on her; but her sensitive nature remembered each misdemeanor with a gravity far beyond the seriousness of the childish crime.

But God was not so direct. How could she be *sure* she would someday hear, "Well done, My child, enter into My rest"? And so for twenty-one years Catherine had prayed and read her Bible and toiled to do good to those around her, hoping to find salvation.

Until the glorious summer day when Ned took her to hear Charles Wesley preach in the fields near Oxford. Charles had prayed with Edward when he had received the faith a few days earlier, and Ned was anxious for his sister to find the same assurance.

Catherine could still see the daisies bending on their slender stems in the long grass, feel the gentle sun on her head, and smell the fresh beauty of God's earth whenever she thought of that meeting. They had sung Charles Wesley's hymn,

> Jesus, Thine all-victorious love
> Shed in my heart abroad;
> Then shall my feet no longer rove,
> Rooted and fixed in God.

Catherine was certain she had heard an angel sing along with

Charles' sweet voice leading the crowd in the fresh air.

And then the words of his sermon brought such joy and comfort to her soul, and now she *knew* she was God's child. The warmth of the sun on her head and the warmth of the Son in her heart had fused in an ecstatic moment of light to drive all darkness of doubt from her mind and soul. From that moment she had never doubted God or her acceptance by Him. And from that moment also, she had never doubted her love for Charles Wesley.

For a few minutes, her attention was claimed by her driving, as she guided the gentle horse across London Bridge that was lined with shops and bustling with traffic. Then she returned to her reminiscing. There had been three wonderful years of growth in her assured relationship with God, and in her friendship with Charles—working with him and the others of the Methodist band at the Foundery, attending his meetings when he was preaching in London or when she could get Ned to take her to a nearby area, singing with him when he visited in their home.

Since her conversion, she had made her home with Ned and his wife so she could work regularly with the Methodist Society. And last year, she began teaching in the day school with twelve infants in her charge. She had not made the move just to be closer to Charles, though the pleasure of that circumstance did bear in her mind. Her supreme reason had been to find opportunity to express more fully her joy and her thanksgiving to God for His perfect salvation; she wished to labor more usefully in the vineyard, as so many Society members were fond of saying. She wanted to fulfill the purpose God had for her life. For with the assurance of her salvation came also the assurance of His guidance, and she had never wavered in this assurance . . . . Not until now.

How could she be sure of God's leading when something so important—so fundamental to the foundation of her life—could go so devastatingly wrong?

But no matter how wrong the world was, she still had her duty. God was in His heaven, and there was work to be done. Her students would be gathering for instruction in their letters and she must be there. She clucked to Old Biggin and urged him to a faster pace along City Road toward the Foundery. The large white building had been an abandoned foundery in ruinous condition when John Wesley purchased and reconditioned it as a galleried chapel holding seventeen hundred people, as well as a smaller chapel to the back, a day school, private apartments, and rooms for many other Society activities.

Catherine left the carriage to Joseph's care, crossed the cobbled courtyard, and entered the deserted schoolroom, checking that each bench was straight and that the floor was spotless. The Foundery school educated sixty poor children under Headmaster Silas Told and two other masters, along with the help of two female teachers. The children began their day at five o'clock with preaching, and attended classes from six until twelve; after a mid-day meal, they returned to their studies from one until five in the afternoon. Catherine instructed the younger students in reading and Miss Owen supervised the girls' needlework, which was sold to benefit the school. A frilled shirt brought two shillings, a plain shirt one shilling. The remaining instruction, primarily of writing, casting accounts, and studying Holy Scripture, was in the hands of the masters.

"Good morning, Miss Perronet." Her first pupil had arrived. Red-headed Isaiah Smithson took his seat on the front form and the others filed in behind him.

Teaching reading was usually Catherine's greatest joy. Opening young minds to the wonder of language, giving them the skill to enable them to read God's Word. Of the sixty children attending the Foundery school, fewer than ten paid their own tuition; the others were so extremely poor that they were taught, and even clothed, gratuitously. Catherine looked at the small heads before her bent over their books. What chance would any of them have for a knowledge of the Saviour or of a better life if it weren't for the work of the Society? But today the job seemed unendingly tedious.

After a review from their abecedarian, Catherine instructed her pupils to take out their primers. "Isaiah, will you please read the first lesson aloud." Isaiah stood and rubbed his freckled nose with the back of a grubby hand. "Christ is the t-t-tr. . ."

"Truth," Catherine supplied.

"Truth. Christ is the l-l-light. Christ is the way. Christ is my life. Christ is my — —." He came to a complete stop.

"Saviour," Catherine suppressed a sigh of impatience.

"Christ is my hope of gl-gl-glory." Isaiah finished and Catherine reminded herself of John Wesley's admonition to his teachers: "We must instill true religion into the minds of children as early as possible. Laying line upon line, precept upon precept, as soon as they are able to bear it.

"Scripture, reason, and experience jointly testify that inasmuch as the corruption of nature is earlier than our instructions can be, we should take all pains and care to counteract this corruption as early as possible. The bias of nature is set the wrong way; education is designed to set it right."

Catherine looked at Isaiah's bruised jaw and scabbed knuckles, undoubtedly won from scrapping with ruffians in the street, and she breathed a prayer of thanks that he and his brother and sisters were all in the school, no matter how tedious it was to listen to his halting reading.

She moved on to the lesson in moral precepts. The students read silently and then responded to the printed dialogue following the brief table. "What is the usefulest thing in the world?" she asked.

"Wisdom," they responded.

"What is the pleasantest thing in the world?"

"Wisdom."

At last, when Catherine pulled out the watch tucked in her waistband by a gold fob, she saw it was time to release her students for the midday meal and prayers. Each child placed an abecedarian and primer on the table and filed from the room in an orderly fashion that demonstrated the school's success in instilling that meekness which John Wesley prescribed for young minds.

All except Isaiah Smithson. He shuffled his feet at the end of the line, hands behind him, eyes on the floor. "You shall miss your bread and pease porridge if you don't hurry along, Isaiah." Catherine tried not to sound impatient.

"Yes um, Miss Perronet. I jest wanted to say good-bye."

"Well, good-bye, Isaiah. I shall see you tomorrow."

"No, Miss. That's not what I mean. I'll not be comin' back."

"Isaiah, what are you talking about?" She saw the glisten of a tear at the corner of his eye.

"Me da lost his job at the docks. Me and Esther and Samuel got to sweep."

Catherine's mind drew a sordid picture of what those few words meant. The two older children would spend their days and most of their nights sweeping horse droppings from the dusty street crossings, in hopes that fine ladies who wanted to cross without soiling their skirts would reward them with a farthing. Isaiah was smaller, too small to defend his place at a crossing against a bigger child who wanted to sweep, and small enough to be sent up a chimney to sweep. Altogether the children might earn a penny or two a day to supplement what their mother could make taking in washing. Catherine could only hope that the little bit wouldn't be spent on gin by an idle father.

"Isaiah, we shall see what can be done about this. Perhaps the Methodist Lending Society—I shall look into it."

Isaiah's blank look told Catherine he had no idea what she was talking about.

"Well, I shall tell you good-bye for the moment only. Isaiah, if I give you a primer, will you promise to take very good care of it and have Esther help you read in it every night?"

"Oh, yes, Miss. I will."

Catherine wished she could feel as sure as he sounded, but she must do something to keep the flicker of knowledge burning in this young mind. She placed the small brown book in his hands. "Isaiah, if you persist in your reading, you will find all that's necessary in here—the Creed, the Lord's Prayer, the Ten Commandments, even a chapter on manners."

"Miss Perronet. . ."

"Yes?"

"You sure are pretty." And he ran out the door, leaving the echo of a sniff behind.

In the empty room Catherine suppressed a desire to cry out, "Why, God?" Instead she straightened the already tidy tables before crossing the courtyard to the small chapel at the back of the Foundery. Even at midday, the room with its small windows and dark wood was cool and dim. Kneeling at the altar, she thought again of Charles, of Isaiah, and groped her way through her own darkness.

Her one solace was her teaching, and now she was to lose her favorite pupil. She had been so happy to feel she was helping bring about the will of God in the life of Isaiah and his family. But now that was to be taken away from her too.

If God was leading at all, was He leading in another direction? Maybe she was to leave the Foundery? Maybe she should not make her home with Ned and Durial? Nothing seemed to be working right for anyone in her life. Maybe, maybe. She didn't know, couldn't even guess. She felt as if she had nothing to care about. Her hands on the altar clenched with tension as she sought something to hold to.

She must care about something, if not Charles, if not her teaching, at least something, someone. And as soon as her mind formed the question, her heart answered, "God." She must care about Him, believe that He cared about her. That was the still fixed point in her universe. If God dissolved into the maybe, she would be truly lost.

Perhaps she had misunderstood what she thought was God's way for her. But wouldn't the Shepherd be capable of making the sheep understand? Wasn't faith in understanding an essential element of faith in guidance?

So, maybe . . . maybe . . . her thoughts slowed, groping for the idea . . . maybe this was all part of the process. Maybe the Shepherd was lovingly leading her through a dark valley where she couldn't see the path . . . .

As she unclenched her fingers and relaxed, she became aware that she was not alone in the chapel. A tall, gaunt form was kneeling at the far end of the altar. His black suit and hose told her he must be a preacher; his pale blonde hair was not powdered, but tied back neatly with a black ribbon. It was Phillip Ferrar whom Ned had introduced to her, just before his trip to Wales.

Catherine supposed she should leave Phillip to pray in solitude, but she was caught by the earnestness of his posture and countenance. Ned had told her that he had held a curacy somewhere in Sussex and was now seeking another living. Curious, Ned hadn't explained why he left his position and was now doing itinerant preaching. The normal thing would have been to stay in Sussex until he found something else. She couldn't help thinking that the position he left couldn't have paid very well—he didn't look as if he'd ever eaten a really full meal; and even in the dimness of the room, Catherine could see the patch on the elbow of his coat, and the holes in his shoes.

As if suddenly aware of her observation, he ended his prayer and looked her way before she had time to bow her head discreetly. They regarded one another for a moment, and then both walked silently from the chapel. In the courtyard he paused, "Miss Perronet, may I hope you recall our introduction some weeks ago? I must ask you to forgive my intrusion on your prayers."

"Indeed, I remember, Mr. Ferrar. But I'm afraid it was I who intruded on you."

"No." He put on the tricorn hat he carried under his arm. "I had nothing more to say."

The forlornness of the words struck her, because that was just how she felt. She looked at the hollows under his deep blue eyes. "Mr. Ferrar, my brother has just returned from Wales, and I believe you were about to make a journey to Hereford when we met. Won't you come to dinner tomorrow night? I am sure you and Ned will have much to talk about."

He accepted her invitation with a formal bow, and with such gravity of manner that she abandoned her usual reserve. "Mr. Ferrar, you appear much troubled. Mr. Wesley admonishes us to bear one another's burdens. Do you wish to speak of anything? I should be happy to pray for you."

Again he bowed slightly. "I appreciate your care, Miss Perronet. But the problem is not a new one. I went into Hereford in hopes of securing a living I had been told was open, but was turned down without an interview because of my Methodist enthusiasms. I shall, of course, continue my itinerant preaching if that is the way God chooses, but I do yearn to shepherd a settled flock." He paused. Her silence encouraged him to continue.

"It is always the same. There were many converts after my meetings in Hereford, but then I was forced to leave them. Lambs who had just set their feet on the path I had to abandon to all the wolves the devil can send. God knows my desire is to stay among them, nurture them, watch them grow. But it does not seem that it is to be.

"Forgive me, Miss Perronet, I did not mean to weary you with my troubles. It was most kind of you to concern yourself with me."

"I assure you, I am not at all wearied, Sir." Indeed, she felt she would like to know more of this strange, stiff man with the kind, troubled eyes. "My brother will be happy to receive you tomorrow evening."

Phillip watched Catherine cross the courtyard to the stables, her wide blue skirts just brushing the cobbles. He turned and walked slowly through Bunhill Fields toward his furnished room, upstairs back in Mrs. Watson's rooming house. He climbed the dark stairs to his room. The "furnished" part of the arrangement was an iron bed with sadly sagging springs guaranteed to produce a backache, a washstand with a cracked bowl and miniscule, blackened mirror, a creaking straight chair, and a chest. There was a window for fresh air, if one could pry it open, and a fireplace for warmth, if one could endure the smoke.

In the months he had lived in the room, Phillip had done nothing to relieve the starkness, perhaps because it was comforting in its likeness to the orphan asylum he had grown up in. Yet, compared to the orphanage, Mrs. Watson's boarding house bespoke opulence. A small shelf of books was his only concession to making the room his own. Other than those few volumes, the space between the four whitewashed walls was as cold and impersonal as if Mrs. Watson still had the *To Let* sign in the window.

Only once in his thirty years had he really taken possession of a place by putting something of himself in it, and that had brought disaster. He put everything he had, heart and soul, into his curacy in Midhurst, his enthusiasm carrying over even into furnishing his cottage. He had polished a Jacobean table he found in the attic under the thatched roof, and then had so praised the pot of flowers the housekeeper set on it that she prided herself in always keeping it full, if only of holly sprigs in the winter. And she saw that the rag rug on the hearth was shaken every day and the teacup on the little dropleaf table by his chair was kept freshly washed for the young curate when he sat by the fire at night to complete his day's reading.

That so much contentment and peace should have ended in such bitterness and hurt left a scar that Phillip no longer expected to heal. But at least he had learned to live without leaving anything of himself about—without putting down any roots that could precipitate such an emotional amputation. As he had just been refused for yet another vacancy, it appeared he might never be faced with the temptation to put down roots.

If the longing in his heart for a settled parish was from God, as he believed it to be, was he wrong to cling to the Methodist tenets that barred him from such a life? But what would be the good of having a congregation if he couldn't really share the Gospel with them and lead them in the way of salvation to knowledge of a personal God? No, as long as he had breath in him, he must proclaim God's truth as he knew it. And that meant another preaching tour next week. With such a schedule there was no danger of his putting down roots, even if he were inclined to try.

· 2 ·

AFTER AN UNUSUALLY violent bout of morning sickness, Durial was more than happy to leave the ordering of dinner for her husband's guest in the hands of her sister-in-law. So the next day, Catherine was able to fulfill her wish of setting a really full meal for the painfully thin Mr. Ferrar.

But Durial joined the party to do her duty as hostess and serve from the top of the table. The Perronet household had readily taken to the new "French ease" method of table service whereby the master and mistress carved and served the dishes that were before them at each end of the table, before the guests helped themselves to the other dishes set on the polished mahogany table. "May I cut you another slice of beef roast, Mr. Ferrar?" the hostess asked.

Phillip declined the sirloin, but accepted another serving of oyster loaf, and Edward served Catherine a slice of boiled turkey with prune sauce. "You are doing very well with your injured wrist, Ned."

"Yes, thank God it wasn't broken. What a nuisance that would have been. Afraid it will take awhile for some of these bruises to heal, at that." He gingerly touched a swollen spot on his forehead.

"Pray, don't let's talk of such unpleasant things," and Durial averted her eyes from her husband's wounds. "Tell us of the more pleasant aspects of your trip, Ned. What of the wedding?"

Edward hesitated, not wanting to distress his sister. "Yes, Ned. Tell us." Catherine's voice was composed.

"Charles had kept it so quiet we were all rather surprised to learn that he had been courting Miss Gwynne almost since he first met

25

her four years ago when he was holding service with Howell Harris near her home in Garth. She attended that day with her father, Marmaduke Gwynne who, as magistrate of the county, came with a warrant in his pocket to arrest the irregular preacher. But Gwynne was a fair man, and wouldn't arrest a man without hearing him preach first; as it turned out he was converted."

"And his daughter?" The lace lappets of Catherine's ruffled cap fell across her shoulders as she leaned forward.

"Oh, the whole family was soon converted and, it seems, all quite smitten with the younger Wesley brother. All except Mrs. Gwynne, who holds the accounts in the family, and had someone of a higher station in mind for her eldest daughter."

Durial swallowed a delicate bite of fish. "La, is that why it took Mr. Wesley four years to bring it about?"

"There were many hindrances, his lack of a settled home, her age—she's twenty years younger, you know—the fear of causing trouble in the Society . . ."

"Trouble?" Durial asked. The conversation had now become a dialogue between the host and hostess with Catherine and Phillip giving their full attention to the stewed venison.

"Yes, John especially feared that the many disappointed hopefuls for both Sally's and Charles' affection might cause dissention in the Society." Edward showed his discomfort at stating that in front of his sister and rushed on. "But Charles provided an acceptable marriage settlement from his book sales, and our father's letter seemed to soothe away some last minute problems."

"How enchanting to hear such a charming story, my Love." Durial smiled across the candlelit table. "And now everyone is blissfully happy."

Edward gave his wife an uneasy smile and turned to his plate.

Catherine, relieved that the painful topic seemed to be at an end, looked at their guest across the table and realized that he had spoken hardly a word during the entire first course. Indeed, instead of the felicitous effect she expected her excellent meal to produce, he seemed more tense and drawn than before. This made his nose seem even larger, and his dark blue eyes darker yet in startling contrast to his pale hair. She would have dearly loved to say something to put him at ease, but her own reserved nature could find no light words for the occasion. At Durial's direction, the servant removed the first course and replaced it with another pattern of dishes bearing anchovy toasts, potato pudding, strawberry fritters, and jam tarts.

When the serving was completed, Edward turned to their guest. "And what of your work, Ferrar? Is the life of an itinerant suiting you?"

"If it suits our Master, I shan't complain."

Ned smiled and shook his head. "You're a man of few words. I should like to hear you preach. I think you might easily avoid the trap of tediousness John Wesley admonishes us to abjure."

"Would you truly, Edward?" Phillip raised his fine, surprisingly dark eyebrows in question. "I should be most happy of your companionship on my next tour. Someone to lead the singing would be more than useful, as my abilities in that area are woeful."

Ned opened his mouth to reply, but Durial spoke first. "Indeed not, Sir. My husband is not yet recovered from the treatment he received at the hands of the last mob he sought to evangelize. If the rabble insists on going to the devil, I cannot see why you shouldn't leave them to it."

"My treatment was nothing compared to that received by our Lord and His disciples, and that was not His attitude, my Love." Edward's reproof to his wife was gently delivered.

"You are right, of course. Forgive my temperamental state." Her apology included Phillip as well. "But I must ask you not to tempt my husband into danger before his wounds are healed."

"I would do nothing to distress you, Madam, but there should be very little danger in Canterbury. I have received many letters from Society members throughout Kent requesting a preacher."

"But Ned . . ." Durial began, then laid aside her fork with a sigh. "I know I waste my breath. You must excuse me if I withdraw now. I find I cannot keep late hours."

"I shall come with you, Sister." Catherine began to rise.

"No, Cath, please don't trouble yourself on my account. Audrey will help me. You stay and serve our guest."

Catherine left Durial to the ministrations of her maid and served pink pancakes to Phillip and her brother, as the men continued to discuss Phillip's upcoming preaching trip. "My father has a farm at Canterbury I should be happy to see to. And from Tunbridge Wells we could come up through Shoreham," Ned said. "I should much like to visit our parents."

27

"But what of your injuries and—the other objections? I fear I shouldn't have spoken so rashly."

Ned smiled. "My wife is overcareful for my safety. She will get on much better without me here to mess up the house with my books and sheets of music."

Her serving finished, Catherine felt it was time for her to withdraw, but again her attempt to exit was thwarted. "Don't leave us, Cath. If I'm to serve as musician to Mr. Ferrar's evangelistic efforts, I should give him a demonstration of what he's in for. Let's have a bit of music."

That was a request Catherine always granted with eagerness, although she hoped Ned would not choose to sing one of Charles Wesley's hymns. She led the way into the parlor and seated herself at the harpsichord, while Ned lighted the tapers with a stick from the fireplace. The candlelight made shimmers on the holly leaf pattern of her blue damask skirt; the three tiers of Valenciennes ruffles fell gracefully from her elbows as she fingered the keys. The lace was the finest French bobbin work and Catherine spared a thought for her aunt in France who kept her well supplied in fashionable finery.

"What shall I play, Ned?" She ran a scale up and down the keys, the bright silvery tones of the harpsichord responding to her quick touch.

"Here," he set a piece of music before her. "Let's begin with this by our friend Count Zinzendorf. 'Jesus, Thy blood and righteousness . . .'" His rich tenor filled the room. . . . "'Thou hast for all a ransom paid, for all a full atonement made.'"

"Come, come, Phillip. You must join us." Edward placed another sheet of music on the rack. "You sing too, Cath. This old Welsh hymn melody is best with a group of voices."

Catherine hesitated at the words her brother had put before her. Was it a random selection, or did he guess at her spiritual struggles? She forced her fingers to play and hoped her light soprano voice could stay on tune without wavering.

> Guide me, O Thou great Jehovah,
> Pilgrim through this barren land.
> I am weak, but Thou art mighty;
> Hold me with Thy powerful hand . . .

The words sank into her mind as vocalizing the prayer brought its own pledge of faith. Her voice grew stronger on the second verse.

> Open now the crystal fountain,
> Whence the healing stream doth flow;
> Let the fire and cloudy pillar
> Lead me all my journey through.
> Strong Deliv'rer, strong Deliv'rer,
> Be Thou still my Strength and Shield. . . .

She had been so caught by the message of the words and their effect on her spirit, that it wasn't until the repeated refrain that her ear caught the discordant note behind her. "Be Thou still my Strength and Shield." The voice didn't lack strength, just correctness of pitch.

She was caught off guard and gave a gurgle of laughter before she realized what she had done. The dissonance stopped at once. She turned to their guest, afraid she had wounded him by her thoughtlessness.

But instead of seeing pain on his countenance, she met the merriest twinkle she had seen in his blue eyes and a smile so broad it balanced the size of his nose. It was the first open emotion she had seen from him. "Please forgive me, I—" she stammered.

"There is nothing to forgive in your quite natural reaction." The smile continued. "You see now why I hoped your brother would accompany my tour? I fear I take great pleasure in hymn singing, but it must be indulged in only under the harmony from a large congregation." Then the smile broke into a deep chuckle which was considerably more melodious than his singing, and Ned and Catherine joined in the much needed release.

At last Ned spoke, "Catherine, I see I've taken on a much greater challenge than I realized. I fear I shall need help. I doubt the ability of even a great congregation to drown out this fellow's caterwauling. Won't you come with me on his tour? It would be a shame if all the potential hearers of the Word in Kent were to be scared off by the hymn singing."

"O Ned, I'd love to!" Her reaction was instinctive before common sense took over. "But alas, I fear it's impossible. I mustn't leave my school duties, and we can't both abandon Durial." And then fear

29

replaced common sense. "No, I really couldn't. So far on horseback. . ."

Ned put an understanding hand on her shoulder. "We could take the carriage, my Dear. As to the school, couldn't Miss Owen oversee your students for just two weeks? And I've been thinking that our sister Elizabeth would be happy of an excuse to be closer to the London Society. She could stay with Durial."

Catherine laughed in spite of her concerns. "My, how efficient you are. But perhaps Mr. Ferrar does not want his tour so invaded."

Phillip gave one of his small, stiff bows which made the white Geneva bands at his neck fall forward from his black coat. "On the contrary, I would be very honoured to have your company, Miss Perronet." And in spite of his stiffness, his eyes twinkled. "Besides, your brother is sure to need all the help he can get."

"We shall consider the matter further," Catherine said, and turned again to the keyboard where she played a brief melody before stopping to ask, "And have you a new hymn for us to try out, Ned?"

"Not yet ready to show even to so select a company, I fear. I have an image that seems stuck in my head every time I try to write, but I haven't been successful in putting it in words. I see Christ on a great white throne with angels kneeling around Him, each one offering a crown and praising the power of His name. But the wording eludes me. I want to write a hymn of regal power and dignity that will bring honour to His majesty. I pray I will be worthy of the task."

"That is the prayer of each of us, is it not? To be worthy of our task?" Catherine rose from the harpsichord bench and after a few more comments of a general nature, joined her brother in bidding their guest a good-night.

And later, alone in her room, the side curtains of her bed drawing her into her own little world, Catherine pondered Ned's parting remarks to her, "Do come with us, Cath. You need a change of scenery. It will take your mind off more painful things. And you can do some real good."

Catherine doubted just how much actual good she could accomplish. It seemed to her that the female members of the Society who so often accompanied preachers on their journeys went more for their own enlightenment or amusement—or for more subtle purposes, as she suspected of Grace Murray who often accompanied John Wesley. But then she reprimanded herself for being unfair. Women Society members were often invaluable at the services, counseling their seeking sisters in matters men would have no knowledge of.

She was almost to decide in favor of going when the vision of a large bay horse loomed, snorting, before her. She cowered into her pillows. What utter nonsense . . . she should be ashamed. . . . Unthinkingly she rubbed her fingers over her left collarbone and felt the sharp dip there. The imaginary horse snorted again, and the remembered pain in her shoulder was lost in the cries of her little brother who had toddled too close to the stamping feet.

But that was years ago; the crazed horse had been put down, her shoulder rarely ached anymore, and a rambling rose grew over the grave of little David in the Shoreham churchyard. She had overcome her fear sufficiently to ride when the occasion absolutely demanded it, but her greatest victory had been in becoming an expert driver.

So, if they could take the carriage, and Elizabeth could stay with Durial, and Silas Told would agree to allow Miss Owen to take her classes. . . . She must admit there was something that appealed to her in the idea of helping Ned's strangely aloof colleague. As Ned had said after Phillip left that evening, "We're not exactly friends. I certainly like him well enough. He's a fine fellow— don't know that I ever met better—but one can't get close enough to him to feel free to use the word *friend*." Yes, it might be worth knowing what was on the other side of that wall Phillip Ferrar had erected around himself.

Three days later as the carriage rolled eastward along the old Roman Road through the green countryside below the Thames, Catherine was glad of her decision. Whatever else might come of the arguments advanced in favor of her taking this journey, Ned's promise of a change of scene had been gloriously fulfilled. Hedgerows in new leaf sprouted buds that promised busy jam-making in cottage kitchens this summer; and rich, brown earth, yielding to the farmer's plough would, in a month or two, be showing equal promise for a joyous Harvest Home festival in the fall. The fact that few trees had advanced past the bud stage was no hindrance to the flocks of chirping birds building their nests. "O Ned, just listen to that chorus," Catherine said to her brother beside her on the carriage seat. "Surely that will inspire your hymn-writing."

"Pardon?" He looked up absently from his paper.

"What poor company you make, Sir. You are far too busy listening to the tunes in your head to attend either to your sister or to nature's choristers. I find you quite hopeless."

"Phillip!" Edward called to the rider just ahead of the carriage. "You must help me. My sister complains of my company, and I find her incessant chattering an intolerable interruption. Give me your horse."

"Incessant chattering! Sir, I protest. It was the second line I spoke to you in the better part of an hour. And how, pray tell, do you think to go on with your work on horseback?"

"I shall go on very well. Charles Wesley composes nearly all his hymns on horseback; he says the pace of the horse aids his sense of stately rhythm."

"Yes." Catherine guided Old Biggin around a mudhole left by recent rains. "And John Wesley gives all his attention to reading while on horseback. And they are both famous for their continual riding disasters because they never attend to their mounts. This time you're sure to break your arm, and then what will Durial say?"

But her good-natured protest was of no avail, and soon Phillip was sitting beside her on the carriage seat, while Ned, his reins looped across the saddle, followed at a distance. Here was her chance to get acquainted with the enigmatic man beside her; but her reticence took over and she could think of nothing to say that didn't seem unaccountably prying. So in spite of the recent accusations of her being a chatterbox, it was Phillip who broke the silence. "I am pleased you chose to come, Miss Perronet."

"Yes, I am too. But you must call me Catherine. Being traveling companions is almost like being family members."

"I would be honoured—to use your name and to be so considered. You have a large family, I believe?"

Well, if she couldn't ask him about himself, she could use the opportunity to tell him about herself; then maybe he would feel comfortable to be more open. "There were an even dozen of us, Mr. Ferrar."

"No, no. That will never do. If I am to call you Catherine you must call me Phillip. . . . Would you call your brother Mr. Perronet?" He had paused before referring to her analogy.

"No, I wouldn't—Phillip."

"There. Now, tell me more of your family."

"I shall do so, but you must absolve me of all accusations of chattering."

32

He raised his hand in a gesture of absolution.

"Well, Ned was always my favorite brother. With twelve children in the family it would be easy to get lost, be just one of a crowd, but I was never that to Ned. He taught me to climb trees, helped me with my sums—which were always so easy for him and so impossible for me. He took me on long walks in the woods and taught me the names of the birds and flowers. I still keep my scrapbook of pressed flowers and hope to gather some new specimens on this trip."

She paused to observe the clumps of fresh violets growing along the road.

"Ned encouraged my music when I became disheartened. Later I was able to return the favor by sharing the excitement over his compositions and usually being the first to play one of his new hymns." She felt Phillip's urging to continue her story.

"Little Charl was always my special charge, like I was Ned's—I suppose that's the way it works in all big families—each one looking out for the next younger. At least, that's how we did it, whether by rule or by inclination I don't know. Anyway, Charl needed all the attention I could give him—he was forever wandering off and getting lost, or getting hung up on a blackberry bush, or losing a boot in the mud. And it was my job to rescue him. Most of the time I didn't mind, even if it did interrupt my reading.

"I suppose I was bred for Methodist Society work even before there was such a thing, because from my earliest memories I accompanied Mother when she visited the sick and needy in Papa's parish every week. Tuesday, Thursday, and Saturday were her regular visiting days, and at least three of us children always went with her, carrying baskets of garden vegetables, or a fresh cheese, or herbs from the woods—whatever we had at hand or something she knew was needed.

"Dudy and Ned and I, or whoever accompanied her on that day, would occupy the children in the home so Mother could minister to the adults. Then we all joined in prayer before we left—or sometimes in song, especially when Ned was with us. His beautiful voice always made people feel better. I suppose that was one of the reasons—" she stopped abruptly, thankful for the lurch of the carriage that made the interruption seem natural. She had felt so at ease talking to Phillip she had almost said that one of the reasons she loved

33

Charles Wesley was that his was the only other voice she'd ever heard that was as sweet as her brother's.

"Yes?" As the carriage ride smoothed out, Phillip encouraged her to continue.

"So, working with children had been my life since I was old enough to walk and talk. I've always loved it and I can't imagine doing anything else.

"Gracious, I've talked an alarming distance. You must tell me of yourself now, —er, Phillip. What of your family?"

His level gaze that had so encouraged her comfortable reminiscences was withdrawn, and she felt as if the tremulous April sunshine had gone behind a cloud. Throughout her narrative he had remained leaning toward her, focusing on every word; but now he sat stiffly upright and looked straight ahead. It was obvious she had put a foot wrong. "Forgive me if I trespass. I—"

For a moment she thought she saw a flicker of emotion on his stoic features. "No, you have a right to know. I see now my error in not telling your brother. He would not have wanted his sister exposed—"

Before she could press him to complete his muddled remarks, Edward rode alongside them, and Catherine turned to her brother. "How is it progressing, Ned?"

"I don't know. I'm working on the phrase, 'All praise the name of Jesus.' It's the right idea, but it doesn't quite sing. I came to ask if Phillip thought we should put up at the next village? The sky seems to be darkening rapidly."

Phillip looked at the sky. "I had hoped to reach Rochester tonight and preach there in the morning before going on, but perhaps we could stop at Cobham if the inn is suitable for your sister's comfort."

Both men looked questioningly at Catherine, but she made no response. "What do you think, Cath?" Edward asked.

"Hail, I think."

Ned looked at the dark sky. "Perhaps, but I think rain more likely."

"Have you taken leave of your senses? Reign wouldn't suit at all. No wonder you're having trouble with your song."

"Catherine—I'm not talking about my writing. Phillip and I want to know if you wish to put up at the nearest inn. It looks like rain coming."

"Oh, I daresay. Do as you think best. But try 'All hail the name of Jesus' in your song."

By the time they reached Cobham the problematical rain had become a drenching reality and travelers and horses didn't bother to question the advisability of stopping at the inn, disreputable though it looked.

"I do apologize, Miss Perronet. You should never have been brought to such a place." Phillip stood just inside the door surveying the dingy interior.

"Catherine," she reminded him firmly. "And do not worry yourself over the accommodation. I chose to come, and shall make do with what presents itself."

But she soon began to guess how severe a test her brave words were to be put to when, after a brief washing in her damp-smelling room, she joined the men in the inn's only parlor. The room was crowded with ill-clad, unwashed villagers all talking in voices clearly emboldened by the ale they were consuming. "This is intolerable," Edward declared and strode off in search of the innkeeper.

"Catherine—" Phillip took a step toward her.

"Mind your head!" The sharp crack that accompanied her words told her the warning was too late as Phillip struck the low, blackened ceiling beam.

He rubbed his forehead ruefully. "You'd think one of my height would learn."

Ned joined them. "I gave orders for our supper to be served in my room. Its cramped conditions will be preferable to this."

Indeed, Ned's small room, even with the fireplace that refused to draw properly, was an improvement on the cacophony of the public parlor, but the food set before them by a slatternly serving wench couldn't have been worse. The pools of fat floating on the stew had congealed into a stiff, white crust by the time it reached them, and even after Catherine pushed the fat aside and found a piece of meat, it was unchewable.

Ned took a bite of the bread and after no more than three chews grabbed for his cider mug and choked down a swallow of the sour liquid. "I advise you to avoid the bread." He wiped his mouth with the back of his hand, as no napkins had been provided. "In this dismal light I failed to see the mold on it, but the taste was unmistakable."

Phillip chewed stoically on the rubbery meat and soggy vegetables. Then, after a sip of cider, "It's no worse than the orphan asylum. Quite like, if my memory holds."

"Orphanage?" Catherine's fork hit her wooden serving trencher with a clatter.

Phillip nodded without expression. "I started to tell you this afternoon. But I think it best to present you both with the full details now. Then if you wish to turn back in the morning I shall understand."

"Turn back . . .?" Catherine began, but her question was ignored as Phillip turned to her brother.

"Edward, please believe that on my honor as a Christian I would not have embarked on this journey, had I realized the harm it could do to your sister's reputation."

"Nonsense, I am sufficient chaperonage for her good name. Such travels are common practice."

"But not in the company of one with my background. I wish you to know the plain facts. I am a foundling."

There was no reply.

"An abandoned foundling. Which can mean only that my mother was a servant girl—or worse—and my father a care-for-nothing nobleman or a rake. Whatever the case may have been, the fact remains that, except at the very highest and lowest extremes of society, foundling means bastard and therefore disgrace. I know you will not want to expose your sister to such company."

Catherine broke in before Ned could reply, "What contemptible rubbish! I'll hear no more of it, Sir, and neither will my brother."

Ned was thoughtful for a moment as the rain washed against the windows in great, unremitting gulps, and the weak flame fluttered on the grate. Finally he spoke. "God has accepted you. With Him as your Father, there can be no more to say on the matter."

"You are very kind, Edward. But your sister . . ."

"My sister has spoken for herself most adequately."

"Both now, and at some length this afternoon, when I related my childhood to you. I think you should reciprocate, unless to do so would cause you pain." Catherine truly wanted to hear more of his history, and felt in no hurry to leave even so small a comfort as Ned's weak fire for the chill dreariness of her own room.

"The subject is not at all painful to me," Phillip assured her. "I simply fear giving disgust to others."

"Then be at rest, Phillip. Ned is quite right, we share the same Father, so are of the same family. There is no offense possible."

Phillip nodded and stared into the fire. "I always took some com-

36

fort in the fact that Mrs. Ortlund often told me how remarkably clean and well-cared-for was the infant she found on her doorstep in a rush basket. It was most unusual, for a foundling often had little more than a few rags to protect it from the chill fog."

"Mrs. Ortlund raised you?" Catherine asked.

Again Phillip nodded without looking at her. "She named me for a brother who died young, and cared for me. She had been a nurse at the Royal Asylum of St. Anne for Children Whose Parents Had Seen Better Days. The institution was no longer operating by the time I made my unwanted appearance into the world. But she ran a small asylum from the goodness of her heart and her own small living."

The wind and rain that whipped at the old inn made the three occupants of the room draw closer together. "I have never ceased to give thanks for Mrs. Ortlund. Were it not for her, I should have been sent to the parish poorhouse where it is unlikely I would have seen my first year through, amidst the filth, disease, and starvation."

Catherine shuddered.

"I have visited such places as an adult: Pandemonium and vice rule jointly among the paupers, fallen women, neglected children, vagrants, lunatics, aged, and ill. Had the usual fate befallen me, I should have been put in such a place where the best I could have hoped for was some feeble crone who might choose to care for a pewling infant for the short period it could be expected to survive in such circumstances."

"Were there no parish nurses?"

"Yes, but many were as lethal as the parish workhouse. Some are even called 'killing nurses.' More than three-fourths of the infants cared for by parish nurses die every year. I have looked into the subject with some interest—it seems that parish nurses who continue to bury infants week after week, with no criticism and no lessening of the number of children given them, take the hint—society considers it very fit and convenient that such a child should die. After all, it relieves society of the care of an object that at worse is loathed and at best ignored. I thank God that by the large part of such society I was ignored."

All was silent in the room save for the incessant pounding of the rain. Then a violent gust of wind rattled the windowpanes so sharply the inhabitants started. Catherine rose and smoothed her muslin skirt over its quilted petticoat. "It's past time we were in bed. Do you plan to preach in the fields at five in the morning as Mr. Wesley does?"

"I often do. It's a good idea to give the workers the Word of God before they begin their labours. But I fear we would have few hearers in the morning, even if the storm has passed. Let us rise at five and go on to Rochester for our first meeting. There is a small but faithful Society there."

"I will light you to your room." Ned picked up a candlestick.

Phillip's room was next to Edward's and when he opened the door Catherine could see that his fire had gone out. She started toward the stairs, then turned back to say good-night. In the frame of the dark doorway he looked remote and lonely. For a moment she couldn't leave him like that. It was more than she could bear, the thought of his aloneness. She took a step toward him—

"Cath!" Ned called impatiently from the stairway. She gave Phillip a last small smile and rushed to her brother.

Phillip watched Catherine fly up the stairs with a detachment that persisted from his orphanage days. He had learned early that it didn't pay to get too attached to people or things. People moved—went on to school or work; things were lost or stolen—he gave a brief thought for the one thing that had been truly his, the blanket Mrs. Ortlund found him in. He had always kept it carefully folded in the bottom of the chest under his bed in the orphanage. But one day he returned from chapel to find the contents of the trunk spilled on his bed and the blanket gone. He hadn't even reported the incident, as the knowledge that he attached any importance to a worn, faded baby blanket would indeed have made him a laughingstock.

His most determined efforts at detachment had failed him in one tender matter, however—the matter of Sally Gwynne. It was his own fault—he had broken his rule.

It happened without any rational awareness on his part. Indeed, until word reached him and other workers that day at the Foundery that Charles Wesley and Sally Gwynne were wed, he had had no understanding of the depth of his feeling. The fact that every young Methodist who preached in Wales, or met Sally when she visited the Foundery with her father, was more than half in love with the beautiful Welsh girl, was no comfort to Phillip. Nor did the fact

38

that he would never have made an attempt to win her affections—nor have stood a chance had he done so—lessen the intensity of his feelings.

The cut was much sharper, although less deep, than the severing from his curacy had been. But both had produced the same results—an increased determination to remain aloof.

He turned to see if he could fan the few sparks on his grate into life. Then he saw his bag open on the floor. While he was next door in Ned's room a thief had been at work here. Fortunately he always kept his purse with him, and he had little else of value to steal. His two leatherbound books and a linen shirt would fetch a few shillings when resold. But there was little among a clergyman's belongings worth stealing.

Gathering up his scattered goods brought to mind the time he was robbed in the orphanage, and reminded him yet again of the rightness of forming no affections for things or people. There must be nothing in his heart worth stealing, either.

· 3 ·

"PREACHIN' IN THE COCKPIT! Preachin' in the cockpit!" Two urchins ran through Rochester the next morning, publicizing the meeting. And in the amphitheatre usually used for much rougher purposes, the hymn-singing of a curious crowd was attracting newcomers who were willing to stand in the drizzling rain for a fresh entertainment.

Catherine walked among the women on the edges of the crowd, welcoming them, helping them with their children, urging them to join in the singing, and ignoring the rude suggestions of two young ruffians who made no attempt to hide the bottles in their coat pockets.

The faithful of the Rochester Methodist Society sang loudly so those unfamiliar with the songs could follow them. One of the members had requested permission to share his testimony. He took his place in the center of the ring, standing staunch in spite of the jeers of the crowd. "Need a drink, Buddy?" "Haven't seen you at the inn lately; religion got you down?" "Hey, Barber Bolton, how about a shave and a haircut—for a swig of gin?"

Bolton's voice rang above his rowdy audience. "I praise God. When Mr. Wesley were at Rochester last, I were one of the most eminent drunkards in all the town—"

Cries of "'Struth," and "Don't we know it!" and "Miss the old times, Charlie?" interrupted him, but they subsided and Bolton continued.

"Mr. Wesley was a-preachin' at the church. I come to listen at the window, and God struck me to the 'eart. I prayed for power against

41

drinking. And God gave me more than I asked, 'e took away the very desire of it."

An overage egg flew through the air and landed at the speaker's feet. "Run 'em all out of town! They'll ruin business."

Bolton held up his hand. "Yet I felt myself worse and worse, till, on April 25 last, I could 'old out no longer. I knew I must drop into 'ell that moment unless God appeared to save me. And 'e did appear. I knew 'e loved me and I felt sweet peace. Yet I did not dare to say I had faith, till, yesterday was twelvemonth. God gave me faith; and 'is love 'as ever since filled my 'eart."

A combination of Amens and jeers met the conclusion of the speech; but then the audience became unusually quiet as Phillip rose to preach. Catherine breathed a prayer that the service might continue undisrupted.

Phillip opened his Bible and began to read. "For by grace are—"

There was a loud squawking from the back of the crowd and the way parted for two men to enter, each carrying a flapping, screeching rooster toward the center of the cockpit ring. "Now, me fine lords 'n ladies, as so many of you are gathered 'ere a'ready, we'll give you some *real* entertainment. On this side, Chanticleer, my fine red Pyle, and on t'other, Acey Jones' Wednesbury Grey. Fine fightin' cocks both in prime form. Who'll lay odds as to which of these fair-feathered fighters will be first to draw blood?"

Many in the audience surged forward to place bets. Phillip turned to Ned. "Sing loudly and follow me." Holding his Bible aloft like a banner, Phillip led the way through the mob, Ned and Catherine behind him singing the Isaac Watts hymn, "We're marching to Zion."

A vast number of people followed their parade to the market cross in the center of town and more joined them along the way. Catherine hoped that now the chaff had been separated from the wheat and Phillip would have receptive hearers. But as soon as he mounted the steps of the cross, the crowd began thrusting to and fro, and Phillip was knocked from his perch on the highest stone step. Catherine started to cry out for fear he had been seriously hurt, but saw him rise quickly and remount the steps.

The audience continued to shove, but Phillip held his back firm against the stone cross and continued his Bible reading. ". . . For by grace are ye saved through faith; and . . ." Seeing they could not dislodge the preacher by pushing, those who had come for sport—considering field preachers fair game for a rough entertainment—began throwing stones. At the same time, some got up on the cross behind Phillip to push him down. One man began shouting in his ear, making it impossible to continue the Scripture reading. Suddenly the tone of the shout changed to one of pain and the man fell at Phillip's feet, his cheek bleeding profusely where a stone intended for Phillip had struck his harasser.

Then a second troublemaker, far more burly than the first, forced his way toward Phillip. Before he could reach the cross though, a misdirected stone hit him on the forehead and bounced off. Blood ran down his face and he advanced no farther.

A third reached out to attack Phillip from the left. But as he stretched his hand forward, a sharp stone aimed at Phillip, struck the attacker's fingers. With a howl of pain, the man dropped his hand, then stood silent waiting to hear the preacher. As if following his cue, the others became silent and Phillip continued, "By grace are ye saved, through faith. These two little words, faith and salvation, include the substance of all the Bible, the marrow, as it were, of the whole Scripture."

Catherine couldn't believe the change that came over Phillip as he spoke to the vast audience before him. Even in the press of the crowd when she had feared for his life, she had detected no change in his face, no show of emotion. But now, his features took on a glow—an intense shine of joy that she would not have thought possible. And his voice—his tones that were always so controlled, so evenly modulated, so devoid of any betraying feeling—now rang with the passion of truth. She felt as if she could see the Saviour whom he proclaimed.

"And what is this faith through which we are saved? The Scripture speaks of it as a light, as a power of discerning. So St. Paul says, 'God who commanded light to shine out of darkness, hath shined in our hearts to give us the light of the knowledge of the glory of God in the face of Jesus Christ.'"

And as he spoke, the rain, which had been lessening for some time, stopped altogether; the clouds parted, and a shaft of sunlight fell on the fair-haired speaker standing on the market cross. His black cassock fluttered in the breeze and his white satin surplice, remarkably unmuddied from the treatment he had received, gleamed in the sun.

"Faith is a divine evidence and conviction, not only that God was in Christ, reconciling the world unto Himself, but also that the Christ loved me, and gave Himself for me. It is by this faith that we receive Christ; that we receive Him as our Prophet, Priest, and King . . ."

Catherine was so caught up by the preacher and his ringing words that for a moment she lost awareness of the people around her. Then she felt a sharp tug on her sleeve and turned to the woman beside her. "Sister, will ye pray with me? I 'ave need of such a faith."

Catherine led the seeker to the side of the crowd where they both bowed their heads. Catherine prayed first, then the woman; when she looked up, she saw tears running down the woman's wrinkled, weather-beaten face. "Bless you, Sister, I've often 'eard these Methodists at their 'ymn-singing and wanted to join them, but I didn't know how. Now I've got a 'ymn-sing a'goin' in my 'eart."

Catherine introduced the new convert to a local Society member and turned to another who appeared to be seeking. "Would you like me to pray with you?" Perhaps twenty hungry souls were seeking the Saviour around the old stone market cross.

A rough voice interrupted Catherine's prayer. When she looked in the direction of the speaker, expecting more rabble, a surprising sight met her. A man in ragged, dirty clothes with greasy, matted hair hanging beneath a disreputable hat was holding a crisp white linen shirt aloft in one hand and two leather-bound books in the other. "I knowed it was a preacher cove I burgled in the inn last night when I seed 'is Bible an' preacher's garb. But I took w'at I could anyway. I was on my way to sell it for w'at I could w'en 'is words struck me to 'eart. 'ere's yer swag, mister. I repent a' me wicked ways."

Phillip placed a hand on the man's shoulder. "I'll take the books, as I doubt you have use for reading material. But you keep the shirt; you need it worse than I. Let it remind you of the new heart Christ has given you."

A chorus of "Amens" and "Praise the Lords" rose from the believers, turning to calls of "Farewell," and "God go wi' thee," as Phillip and the Perronets continued their journey.

From the carriage, Phillip looked back at the remnant of the congregation with open longing in his eyes. "It is always the same—the wrench at leaving new babes in the faith. How I long to stay among them! I believe this preaching like an apostle, without joining together those that are awakened and training them up in the ways of God, is only begetting children for the murderer. How much preaching has there been for ten years all over England! But where there is no regular preacher, no discipline, no order or connection, the consequence is that nine in ten of the once-awakened are now faster asleep than ever."

"The Society members . . ." Catherine began.

". . . will do what they can to encourage one another in the faith, of course. But they need a shepherd. What hope is there for such as that thief to build a new life without firm guidance?"

"The parish vicar?" Catherine tried again.

"Undoubtedly the holder of at least six livings who visits here once yearly as required by law in order to keep his income. What counsel exists is in the hands of a curate who, without the supervision of his superior, may be as lazy or drunken as suits him."

"Surely you exaggerate. My father . . ."

". . . is a rare example of a godly man. One whose work I would emulate if a place were open to me."

"I understand you were formerly a curate . . ." Her sentence went unfinished as Old Biggin slipped in the deep mud of the rain-soaked road. Ned drew alongside his sister. "We are nearly to the River Medway. I think I should drive across. The waters are sure to be full and swift after the downpour."

The men changed places, and in a few minutes, they approached the raised earthen causeway of ancient Roman construction. At least, that was where the crossing should have been, but it was invisible under the rushing waters. "Can we ride the causeway?" Ned asked the ferryman.

"Yes, Sir, if you keep in the middle."

Ahead of them, Phillip urged his mount to cross the swollen stream. Obedient to her master's voice, Jezreel led the way into the water.

Crossing was much more difficult than they could have imagined. The water rose above the horses' knees and came to the bottom of the carriage, pushing and sucking at the wheels to pull the vehicle sideways. Catherine gripped the seat as Ned urged Biggin forward. "Easy, old boy. One step at a time. Atta boy. Keep going."

Just past the middle a current of water rushed over the causeway with the swiftness of a sluice. Catherine gave a cry of alarm as she saw Jezreel lose her footing. But the horse gave a spring and recovered the roadway, and with two final lunges, she accomplished the crossing and scrambled up the eastern bank.

Biggin, older, and less agile than Phillip's mare, however, was not so lucky. A few feet from shore his right forefoot slipped off the ramp. He fought to regain his footing, but couldn't find a hold in the muddy swirl. He swam valiantly, his muscled thighs straining against the downstream rush.

The carriage, already nearly afloat in the deep water, tilted dangerously, then righted itself and rode the tide behind Old Biggin. Catherine, soaked to her knees in the icy flood, never let go of her hold on the seat, or of her composure, as Ned beside her fought to guide his horse.

Phillip shouted to a group of men on the bank waiting for the ferry. Forming two rows of human pulleys, strong hands reached out for each side of Biggin's harness as he neared shore and pulled the heaving horse up the mirey bank.

Except for a boulder buried under the mud, the rescue operation would have been a complete success. The carriage wheel on Ned's side, however, struck the impediment with a crunch. For a moment the vehicle balanced, suspended on one wheel, then toppled on its side, spilling passengers and luggage into the mud and water.

The rescue party unhitched Biggin, pulled Catherine and Ned to their feet, and sought to retrieve their cases from the muck.

In a few minutes, Ned, Catherine, and Phillip were sitting on tree stumps above the river, surveying the wreckage.

"Compared to the results I feared when I saw your carriage go into the water, I cannot regard the broken axel as so great a disaster," Phillip said.

"We are indeed fortunate," Ned agreed. "Neither of us nor Biggin hurt, and only one bag lost in the river."

"It's easy for you to say 'only one,' considering it was *my* case." Catherine regarded her muddy gown and thought of her other one swirling away downriver.

"Chatham is just ahead. You can purchase some necessities there, while Phillip and I arrange to have the carriage repaired and hire a chaise for the rest of the journey."

"Hire a chaise?" Catherine wiped a sodden curl away from her cheek. "What nonsensical extravagance, Brother. You would be far better served to purchase a saddle for Biggin." Catherine forced a brave smile that showed by its very brilliance how terrified she was.

The other Methodist Sisters rode pillion on circuit. She could do it too. It was high time she laid her fear to rest for once and all.

"But, Cath," Ned placed a hand on her shoulder. "That would mean you must ride pillion. I can afford to hire—"

"No. No chaise." The words were firm, but followed by a small gulp. "I'll be all right. There must be an inn up the road where we can dry out and get warm."

"Cath," Ned tried again.

"I'll be fine," she insisted, more for her own benefit than for her companions'. To give action to her words she stood and began walking up the road. Without thinking, her right hand went to her left shoulder. The cold, wet weather had made the injury ache, as it often did, and brought the old experience vividly alive to her. . . . The big bay horse lowering his head and lashing out with his hind feet, then rearing in front and landing stiff-legged with a jolt that jarred her teeth. The helpless, sick feeling of slipping, at first slowly, then faster and faster, and plunging to the hard earth. The blowing snort from the horse and the cry from her baby brother, and then silence as the pain in her shoulder brought the blessed oblivion of unconsciousness. When she woke they told her about David. . . .

She never saw the horse again, nor her brother. She had probably ridden only ten or twelve times in her life since then, and never pillion. Could she do it now? The answer was there as soon as the question formed: "I can do all things through Christ which strengtheneth me." She gave her shoulder a final rub as she pulled a foot from the mud and set it on the path before her.

The inn they found was a considerable improvement on the one they had stayed in the night before. As the hour was late by the time Ned completed arrangements for the repair of the carriage, and they were wet and cold, they decided to stay the night.

It was to the accompaniment of the dawn chorus that the travelers continued their journey the next day. Since Old Biggin, for all his gentleness, was not really a saddle horse, they decided it would be better to tie their cases on behind Ned and for Catherine to ride pillion on Jezreel. Catherine accused her brother of caring more for his privacy than her comfort, and he replied that she had already informed him of her opinion of his companionship, thank you. In this spirit of raillery, Catherine covered her fears as Ned made a stirrup of his hands and tossed her onto the blanket behind Phillip.

Sitting sidesaddle, she smoothed her round skirt over her petti-

47

coat and placed her left arm loosely around Phillip's waist. "Are you all right?" he asked. "Ned told me of your accident. If I can do anything to make you more comfortable—"

"I thank you for your thoughtfulness, but I assure you I am quite all right."

"Very well. But if at anytime you wish me to stop or ease the pace, please say so at once."

Catherine appreciated his concern, but was determined to conquer her fear. Besides, with this stalwart man in the saddle, and the birds singing them on their way in the fresh spring air, her situation didn't seem so frightful. Even so, she had an idea that it might be a good plan to occupy her mind with conversation.

So, a few minutes later when a gentle mist fell on them through the lightly-leaved trees that arched over the road toward Canterbury, Catherine was reminded of a line from Chaucer, and she quoted, "'When the sweet rains of April fall, they of England to Canterbury wend.' If the rains in Chaucer's time were anything like yesterday, that is surely one of the greatest examples of understatement in the language. Might as well call Noah's forty days and nights of deluge 'sweet rains.'"

"We are not far north of the Pilgrim's Way. The same road Chaucer's pilgrims took is still in use," Phillip said.

"As well as the road the murderers from Henry's court would have taken to commit their foul deed?"

They talked a while of the murder of Thomas a'Becket, whose martyrdom as Archbishop of Canterbury turned the cathedral into the most popular pilgrimage shrine of the Middle Ages, and of Chaucer who immortalized the journey. Then the topic seemed to pall, and Catherine sought another to occupy her mind. "Before our misadventures yesterday, I believe you were about to tell me of your curacy."

The back before her stiffened slightly and she wondered if so simple a topic could have given offense. Then the wide shoulders squared. "I don't know that I was about to tell you, but I shall. My brief curacy in Midhurst was a poor living, but it had for me the feeling of having come home. I thought it was the place God had prepared for me and that I would be there forever, serving Him and those people—belonging to them.

"Forever lasted almost two years. Until the second time the Vicar, on his yearly round of visits to his several livings, was told

48

that his curate was an enthusiast who preached a personal religion from the pulpit, read the prayers with fervor, and had the effrontery to suggest that good Englishmen ask forgiveness for their sins.

"I was given the briefest of hearings and promptly replaced with a young Oxford graduate who was well-known to the vicar at his regular card parties."

His words were astringent, even to the point of often referring to himself in the third person; but Catherine, her sensitivities enhanced by their physical closeness and by her own recent experience of having something dearly longed for snatched from her grasp, found it easy to hear between his clipped sentences and to fill in the spaces with her knowledge of his orphanage background. She knew that for the young man who had never truly belonged anywhere, those brief months had been enough for him to know that what he wanted most in life was to belong somewhere. She knew that they had provided a sudden identification in a life of unbelonging.

She knew that in the months since leaving Sussex the time spent riding circuit, preaching with the band of Methodist ministers in fields or meetinghouses or wherever people would listen to him, had satisfied his desire to share God's Word, but had in no way fulfilled his need to belong. Indeed, it had grown worse, as she had witnessed at Rochester, as each time he would meet new people, new converts would come into the fold, a new Society would be established, and Phillip would have to ride away, leaving the people whose lives he longed to be a part of. He longed to be their pastor and they his people, to marry them, to christen their children, to bury their dead, to attend to all the daily needs of a flock, not just come into their lives for a day or a week and then ride out again.

He told her of the day he left Midhurst, how little Jennie Franks came early in the morning with a drooping bunch of bluebells crushed in her childish hand. Catherine could see him accepting them gravely, as the tribute they were intended to be. She could even see the corn silk pigtails shining in the sun as he patted Jennie's head, and the single tear that slipped from the corner of her eye just before she ran for home.

Jennie had been the first of a long string that morning, old Mrs. Machin with a loaf of fresh bread for his journey, Mrs. Patching with a crock of pickled peaches, the Timmon sisters with a handworked altar cloth—which he had never had a place to use. . .

Catherine could nearly have shed tears with them as she saw that

49

string of loyal, taciturn people, each expressing their love in a tangible way, but without words. Her arm tightened ever so slightly around his thin waist, as they rode in silence for several minutes. Then Catherine reached back and patted the shiny chestnut rump of their mount. "Jezreel's a good horse. It won't tire her too much carrying us both?"

Sitting behind Phillip, she heard rather than saw his rare smile. "It would take a great deal more than your extra weight at this sedate pace to tire Jezreel. She is an excellent animal. I fear you've uncovered my one extravagance, but I'll admit to a great fondness for horses. I can't remember a time when I wasn't hoarding a small pile of farthings for 'my horse.' At least my curacy lasted long enough that I was able to add a few more shillings to my cache and accept farmer Brock's generous offer of sale. I've no doubt the animal could have fetched twice his price at market. Even then she is an extravagance. But I salve my conscience with the argument that nothing can be more important to a circuit-riding preacher than a good mount."

Again Catherine stroked the satiny horsehair. Somehow the information that Phillip was fond of horses increased her determination to conquer her fear, and made each mile she rode a small victory.

They reached Sittingbourne in time for a late afternoon meeting in a green, tree-encircled meadow near the town. Their timing was perfect as the meeting attracted the laborers leaving the fields for their evening meal. Soon a crowd of several hundred was gathered. The rain had ceased, a gentle, setting sun shone on the field, and Catherine hoped the service might proceed without incident.

But Phillip had no more than read his text from Micah 6:8 and begun to preach on what it meant "to do justly, to love mercy, and to walk humbly with our God," when a great shout began on the far side of the field. The rabble from town had brought an ox, which they were vehemently driving among the congregation.

It was impossible for Phillip to preach in such an upheaval, so Ned jumped up beside him on the low stone wall and began a hymn-sing. The efforts of the disorderly were in vain, for the great white ox ran round and round the field, one way and the other, eluding the sticks which would drive him through the middle of the crowd. At length he broke through the midst of his drivers and loped off toward the woods, leaving the worshipers rejoicing and praising God.

The next day, the service at Faversham met more severe resistance. The Society there had arranged for the preaching to take place at a little meetinghouse, but the vast numbers who thronged to the service quickly made it apparent that other accommodations would be necessary. They moved a small wooden table into a nearby field and Phillip mounted it to preach. He had no more than begun expounding to his hearers from his text, "Repent ye, and believe the Gospel," when a young man rushed in, cursing and swearing vehemently. He so disturbed those around him, that they moved to make him go away. "No, Brothers. Let him stay if he will agree to be quiet," Phillip said. The curses subsided to a mutter, and Phillip resumed preaching.

"Repentance means an inward change, a change of mind from sin to holiness, but first we must know ourselves sinners, yea, guilty, helpless sinners . . ."

"That's no way to talk to respectable folk, Parson!" The shout came from a young man dressed as a gentleman but with oddly bulging pockets.

At the sound of his voice another young man nearby cried, "Why, if it isn't my old mate, Bradford White!" He threw out his arms and embraced his friend, bulging pockets and all. Even from where Catherine stood some distance away, the cracking sound was audible. And then the air was filled with the stench of rotten eggs.

The crowd drew back, coughing and choking at the pungent sulphur odor, women put handkerchiefs over their noses, and the young men, dripping a sticky, yellow trail, beat a hasty retreat.

Phillip had no more than begun again on his topic when a mob of ruffians, perhaps inspired by tales of the ox turned upon the congregation in their neighboring town, rushed upon the crowd with a bull they had been baiting. They strove to drive him in among the people, but the beast continually dodged to one side and then the other.

The drivers saw that their sticks and goads were not going to succeed with the beast, so in desperation they tied ropes around his neck and dragged him through the people. By this time the poor animal was tired and bloody from having been beaten and torn by dogs and men, and when his tormenters thrust him in front of Phillip, the greatest danger the bull represented was that of bloodying the preacher's cassock. More than once Phillip put his hand out to thrust the poor creature's head away so the blood would not drip on his clothes.

But in the end, the ruffians almost won the day. They so pressed the bull against the small table Phillip was standing on that it began to rock dangerously. The bull moved away, but was driven again against the table. This time there was the sound of splintering wood and Phillip, going down with his table, fell toward the horns of the bull.

Were it not for the quick thinking and strong arms of those around him who caught Phillip and bore him upon their shoulders, the day might have had a very different ending. When they saw the preacher born aloft, the defeated rabble trudged off, leading their bewildered bull behind them; Phillip found a small rise of ground where he could stand to finish his sermon.

". . .self-will, as well as pride, is a species of idolatry; and both are directly contrary to the love of God . . . Covetousness in every kind and degree, is certainly contrary to the love of God, as is the love of money, which is too frequently the root of all evil . . .

"Beloved, we are to repent, turn from our wicked ways, and seek the Saviour who loves us, who takes us in our sinful state—sin as vile to Him as the stench of those rotten eggs was to us—and cleanses us, washes us free of all stench of sin, and makes our hearts whiter than snow."

Ned again led in singing and groups began praying all around the field that still bore spatters of rancid egg yolk and red drops of bull blood. And then yet another shout interrupted the prayers. This came from the man who had interrupted the service with shouts and curses early on, but now his tone was far different. He declared that he had been a smuggler, and had his swag bag with him to prove his claim. "But I'll never do that no more. I'm resolved to 'ave the Lord for my God."

Even the exhilaration of a victorious service in spite of such obstacles, however, wasn't enough to sustain Catherine's spirits when she saw the night's lodging that had been provided for them by the poverty-stricken Society members. Her room was little better than a cellar. She had to go down three steps and duck her head through the doorway to enter. The initial sensation in the room was one of chill dampness, but after some time, she realized the major obstacle to comfort and sleep was the stuffiness of the cramped quarters. Throwing off her covers, she groped her way across the room to where she could see the dim light of the moon shining against the paper that covered the window. She tore the paper from one of the panes and took a deep gulp of the fresh, sweet air that blew in the opening.

Back in her bed, huddled under her covers, a strange new thought came over Catherine. If the near drownings, stonings, and bull-tramplings, followed by fatigue, starvation, and discomfort of the past days were typical of the experiences of an itinerant preacher and his companions, she certainly did not envy the former Miss Sally Gwynne. With a flash of humor and amazement, Catherine found herself pitying the young woman who was newly wed to one of the most active circuit-riding preachers in the Methodist Society. As she drifted off to sleep in her cryptlike room, Catherine wondered if her bitter disappointment had, in truth, been a blessed deliverance.

· 4 ·

IT RAINED DURING THE NIGHT, so on a washed and shining morning their little party set out on its last lap to Canterbury. Having accomplished one day of pillion riding without disaster, Catherine was now a little more at ease, and still smiling over the Society member whose parting admonition had been, "Don't get carried off by no Frenchies!" She sat in silence behind Phillip as they rode through the bright green and gold morning.

She thought about her companion's silence—so still, so reticent, and yet, one felt at peace in his company even without having a sense of knowing him well. Perhaps it was because he was at peace with himself, if not with his circumstances, and being with him made one more at peace with oneself.

After more time passed she asked, "Have you always wanted to preach?" Rather than an abrupt interruption in the quiet, her soft words matched the rhythm of Jezreel's hoofbeat and seemed a fitting part of their journey to the great church of their faith.

"I had not thought to preach until I came really to understand the basis of my faith while at Cambridge. But from earliest memories I loved the church. Other boys at the foundling school complained about the strict attendance at services required of them, and at Cambridge my fellow gownsmen universally sneered at and slept through the twice-daily chapel. But I felt differently."

The taciturn Phillip found it difficult to speak of his feelings, and Catherine could only guess at all the words encompassed. Phillip had loved the church for more reasons than the spiritual—the peace and beauty there satisfied an aesthetic need deep within him which certainly nothing in the orphanage or his daily school life could fulfill. And something else—perhaps it was the sense of being near God—of belonging to Him, that met his undefined need.

"The orphanage school was a good one?"

"An excellent school—strict and proper. Then I attended Cambridge as a Sizar." And again, it was necessary for his listener to embroider between the spoken words to picture the training in cleanliness and manners far beyond that most boys of his class would have received at home, and the well-grounded, if coldly formal religious training to which his soul had responded with an unaccustomed warmth. And at the university, it supplied the discipline and humility required to fulfill his role as a servant to other students.

"At Cambridge you found assurance of your faith?"

He nodded. "Through reading the works of William Law. Long before that time, Law had been forced to leave Cambridge for refusing the Oath of Allegiance to George I. After I read his *Serious Call to a Devout and Holy Life*, I was privileged to call on him for counsel."

"As did the Wesley brothers, I believe."

"Yes, like so many others who read his excellent book and were privileged to seek out its author, I found the assurance of my salvation." He had found there a place of belonging for his soul. But having his heart set on a heavenly home only increased his feelings of not belonging here. And grasping the warmth and comfort of that hitherto foreign word *home* only increased his undefined longing for an earthly home.

Catherine's thoughts then focused on the scene before them, as the sound of pealing bells rang on the bright air, calling all who would to worship. Through the tree branches, past a field of new-sprouted grain, beyond the medieval stone wall and town buildings, rose the triumphant square towers of Canterbury Cathedral.

As they rode along St. Peter's Place, then turned up the High Street, the church grew before Catherine's fascinated gaze, and she felt her excitement mounting. Here Christian worship had flourished since Roman times; here, on Whitsunday in the year 597, King Ethelbert of Kent was baptized by St. Augustine, an act symbolizing the first official acceptance of Christianity in the Anglo-Saxon realms; here St. Augustine himself became the first Archbishop; here was the Mother Church of English Christendom.

And she was to attend Sunday morning worship on the spot where Christian worship had been offered continuously for 1,150 years.

They tethered the horses by the southwest porch and entered the magnificent perpendicular nave where Catherine's gaze was drawn up, up, up, to the very heavens along with the prayers which were offered there daily to the Glory of God. They took the seats the verger led them to in the choir and Catherine thought of the Old Testament account of how the people under Solomon's direction had built the Temple of God. Here too at Canterbury had the workmen labored, as generation after generation of stonemasons, glassblowers, and woodcarvers plied their humble trades to express their faith.

Throughout the singing of the anthem, the praying of the collect, the reading of the Epistle and Gospel, the preaching of the sermon, the ministry of the sacrament, and the singing of the Gloria, Catherine kept thinking that as God had helped Solomon and all those in the Old and New Testaments to build and spread the faith, as He had helped the Christians of Medieval and Renaissance and Restoration England, so He would help those now striving to do His work. As she looked up the nave to the high altar and above to the ceiling with its pillars and arches spreading like a vast forest of trees with their branches entwined in prayer, her prayer included a special request that Phillip wouldn't be forced to leave his historic faith in order to minister.

"Glory be to the Father, and to the Son, and to the Holy Ghost; as it was in the beginning, is now and ever shall be: World without end, Amen." Catherine sang with the congregation, then knelt for the singing of the Blessing.

After the service, Ned and Phillip chose to climb the tower to the belfry and the view it offered of Canterbury and the surrounding countryside. But Catherine preferred to make her own pilgrimage up the progressive series of stairs to the highest level in the Cathedral where for hundreds of years the shrine of St. Thomas had provided the focal point of the whole building. As she ascended each worn stone step, she took care to place her feet in the deepest of the hollows, stepping where centuries of devout travelers had worn the solid stone away with steps of devotion and penitence.

She was thankful for a faith that didn't rely for its assurance on such outward works, but she was also thankful for those faithful ones who were willing to do what they thought right. At the shrine she walked around the wide barren floor that had once supported Thomas à Becket's tomb. It was moving, especially when she remembered that the golden, gem-encrusted casket had been destroyed during the Reformation.

Surely, Thomas would have preferred this powerful symbolism of the empty space left by a man's death. In a great cathedral of carved marble and jeweled stained glass, what could better express the vacancy left by the death of a man who gave his life for his faith than this expanse of smooth, bare stone?

Thomas à Becket had built the cathedral with his death. His martyrdom had brought pilgrims from all over the world, and much of the splendor of architecture and decoration that enhanced the worship had come from the wealth brought by the pilgrims to the martyr's tomb.

But Catherine thanked God that, no matter how difficult matters seemed for Phillip and other Methodist ministers, Thomas' sacrifice would not be required of them. They might be forced to preach in the fields, they might be forced to live a life of itinerant hardship, they might even be forced to sign the Act of Toleration and declare themselves dissenters. But at least there *was* an Act of Toleration. No longer were men put to death in England for their faith, as St. Thomas was, or the Lollards, or any whose faith happened to disagree with the King's. Dear King George II might have his faults, but he didn't behead those who disagreed with him.

Along the wall Catherine saw statues of great men of history kneeling in prayer—priests and bishops, as one would expect in a cathedral; but even more impressive, Catherine felt, were the generals, dukes, and ministers, the lords temporal who acknowledged their reliance on God as they made decisions and led armies that determined England's destiny.

Before leaving Trinity Chapel, Catherine paused at one more station, the tomb of Edward, the Black Prince. As she looked at the arms of war and arms of peace alternating around the tomb supporting his brass effigy—Plantagenet banners for war and quill feathers for peace—she thought of this excellent prince who more than any other exemplified the ideals of the chivalry of the Middle Ages. Ideals of service, of loyalty, of fearlessness in the cause of right, of integrity in word and deed, of courtesy and generosity, of consideration for those in distress or need. Beside his tomb, the Norman

French inscription read, "Here lies that noble Prince, Mons Edward. . . . Thus the glory of this world passes away."

Catherine descended the stairs on the other side of the chapel, again feeling the swale in the stone made by both the great and the humble, in whose footsteps she walked. And she remembered a couplet John Wesley wrote, after visiting a famous castle that was purported to be the most ancient building in England,

> A little pomp, a little sway,
> A sunbeam in a winter's day,
> Is all the great and mighty have
> Between the cradle and the grave!

Catherine, Edward, and Phillip had just time to take a light refreshment before the service they were to hold for the Society John Wesley had founded and nurtured on his many visits to Canterbury. They left the city through the ancient Quenin Gate, and outside the wall were greeted by a large number of Society members who had gathered to accompany them up the hill to St. Martin's Church.

But before they could reach the church, a crowd of rabble gathered, like flies to a honey sandwich, and followed the Society members up the hill through the grounds of St. Augustine's ruined Abbey. The troublemakers showered cups of water over the marchers, and when that failed to dampen their spirits, they tossed lighted fireworks into the crowd. Fortunately, the water had sufficiently wetted the ladies' skirts and caps and the men's coats so that no serious fires were started. The procession did, however, move considerably faster than usual, to the accompaniment of explosions and shrieks.

By the time they reached St. Martin's church, the rabble had run out of weapons and for the most part lost interest in causing further disturbance. Undoubtedly the presence of several hundred soldiers in the congregation helped to curtail further boisterous activities. Canterbury hosted a major army garrison, situated as it was in a strategic position to guard the English Channel in case of an invasion attempt by England's ancient enemy, France. Indeed, since the recent French attempt to capture Minorca which, along with Gibraltar, gave England naval supremacy in the Mediterranean, Pitt's government was almost neurotic about the fear of a French attack, and so of late the garrison numbers had been greatly increased. Wesley's services had always been well attended by red-coated soldiers and many had been converted by his preaching.

The lusty male voices added much to the singing as Edward led them in one of the hymns newly penned by Charles Wesley, "Oh, for a heart to praise my God, a heart from sin set free. . . ." Canterbury, the oldest parish church in England, was often called the cradle of English Christianity, because here the Christian Queen Bertha and her ladies had faithfully prayed for the conversion of this island every day for forty years before the coming of St. Augustine. Inside was the Saxon font where the newly converted King Ethelbert had been baptized by St. Augustine in 597.

St. Martin's was far too small to hold all their hearers, but the square Saxon tower of stone and Roman brick made a backdrop like a high altar canopy and the grave-covered hillside formed a natural amphitheatre, with the fir trees spreading their branches overhead like the finest Gothic arches. Birdsong accompanied the singing, as more worshipers and curiosity seekers made their way up the hill from town. Catherine turned around and from her vantage at the top of the hill, looked over the heads of the congregation covering the hillside, and through the trees saw the towers of Canterbury Cathedral three-quarters of a mile away.

In spite of their initial ill-mannered rowdiness, the listeners now entered wholeheartedly into the singing, and then gave rapt attention to Phillip's preaching: "If any of you lacks wisdom, let him ask God, who gives to all men generously and without reproaching, and it will be given him. But let him ask in faith with no doubting." As Phillip turned from the words of James to his own exhortation, Catherine thought of her own lack of wisdom and her own doubts. But instead of concentrating on the preacher's words, she found herself focusing on the preacher himself. The long nose with skin drawn tight over the cheekbones, the deepset solemn eyes, the strong jawline and squared-off chin—his features spoke of might and durability as clearly as the ancient stones around him. The preacher stretched out an arm and a long, thin wrist bone extended beyond the white cuff of the shirtsleeve beneath his black cassock. Catherine found the gesture so eminently appealing that she forced her mind back to the words of Scripture Phillip was quoting: "I will

60

instruct you and teach you the way you should go; I will counsel you with My eye upon you. . . ."

Catherine bowed her head as she sent up a prayer that the promise might be fulfilled in her own life. But her prayer was cut short as she became aware of a disturbance that was moving through the congregation like wildfire. "Landed at Dover?" "Less than an hour's march from Canterbury?" "Burning the fields!" A woman shrieked, "Lord, have mercy on us!"

Already the soldiers were coming to attention when a sergeant barked out orders. The company was much hindered by the number of civilians in the way, but in the best order possible, they assembled for command. And everywhere the phrase, "The French have landed!" "The French!" "It's the French—they're coming!"

With imperturbable presence of mind, Phillip tried to calm the consternation, advising the people to depart without panic. But pandemonium reigned. Catherine watched the fleeing backs of the people who moments ago had been worshiping beside her. "Do you think it's true?" she asked Ned. Her voice was calm, but her eyes were wide with apprehension.

"It's doubtful. Such alarms go around regularly, I'm told. More than likely, the rumor was started by one of the rabble, since no army messenger arrived with a dispatch. In this part of Kent small children are taught obedience with the warning, 'And if you don't, the French will get you.'"

"But there *is* war on the continent, these seven years past . . ." She hesitated, for to her *the French* meant Aunt Nicola and a noisy family of cousins living on the Perronet family estate in Nyon; but France was also England's rival and it was just possible. . . .

Phillip joined them. "All the more reason to suppose the French well-occupied on the continent. But the fox is with the hens now—the story of an invasion will spread through the town and tumult will reign for at least twenty-four hours. We may as well go on. There'll be no chance of holding another service for some time."

Back at the Chaucer Inn, Phillip removed his cassock and replaced it with a black frock coat, close-fitting to the waist, with a flared skirt to knee level, its back and side vents making it comfortable riding attire.

Each day's travel made Catherine regret more the loss of her luggage in the flooded river. She had purchased an ivory comb and a boar bristle brush and a few other items of absolute necessity, but

61

chose to hold out until she reached Shoreham and her mother's dressmaker before replacing her wardrobe. She tied a full-length cotton apron over her gown to cover the worst of the spots, and could only be thankful that the day of the accident she was wearing the warmer of her two dresses and her long, hooded mantle. Even if the rain returned, she would have some shelter. But that was her only comforting thought as they set out again on their journey. She had never traveled the road to Tunbridge Wells, the next town where a Society was awaiting them, but she knew it was a long ride, and that their reception at the meetings Ned and Phillip would hold along the way was unlikely to be any friendlier than that they had encountered so far.

As they left Canterbury and rode into the lush green countryside of Kent, Catherine thought that surely this had to be the sweetest, greenest land God ever smiled on. Sprouting fields of hops, rape wheat, and vegetable gardens were beginning to green as April passed into May; fruit orchards showed promise of bloom; and the Hawthorn tree, called the May tree by the poets, graced the landscape with its sweet spring blossoms. The sheep on the hillsides reminded Catherine of the verse, "We are the sheep of His pasture." And here and there the pastoral scene was dotted with red brick, tile-roofed farmhouses and round, cone-roofed oast houses where the locally grown hops were dried for brewing.

They made one detour to spend the night at Vincent Perronet's farm. The stone house was surrounded by rich, black soil and green pastures that fed the red-brown Guernsey cows. The land agent greeted the travelers warmly, and his wife served tea and parkin while Ned went over the account books. Catherine savored the heavy, oatmeal spice cake sweetened with honey, as she listened to Mrs. Adisham's gossip about the tenants and her own brood who were now all married or successfully apprenticed.

"Our Mary was the last to go. She married a ship's chandler over to Dover way. I'd like it right fine to go visit her when her first is born, but Adisham says he can't take me until after the harvest. And I says the child will like to be walking by then and isn't it time he thought about taking it a little easier? His rheumatiz troubles him something fierce when the rains come on. But your father is the fairest of landlords, Miss Perronet, a right finer man to work for there isn't."

When the refreshments were finished, Farmer Adisham conducted his guests on a tour around the farm. "They's good, hardworking tenants," and he pointed to a small cottage nestled in a clump of trees. "But you won't see much labor about today, not with the Maying." He indicated a group of milkmaids walking beside the road, boughs of pink-tinged hawthorn blossoms in their arms.

After taking leave of their guide, they rode through the village of Chartham and saw a cluster of country revelers dancing around a flower-decked maypole to the air of a fiddler. The May Day celebration was one of many customs now vigorously restored, after having been sternly outlawed by Cromwell's Puritans a hundred years before. The maypole, a fifty-foot-high permanent structure on the village green, had been decorated by the young people of the village with ribbons and garlands of flowers and greenery shortly after sun-up that morning. To one side of the festivities sat the floral-crowned May Queen, the most beautiful girl in the village, chosen to represent summer and to preside over all the May celebrations. Near her, cavorting with a band of small children carrying flower-entwined hoops, was another familiar Maying figure—the Jack-in-the-Green, wearing a heavy wicker cage completely covered with greenery, so that only his eyes and feet were visible. On yet another part of the common, a band of Morris men, in their white flower-and-ribbon bedecked suits, danced gaily to the rhythm of the bells attached to their ankles and the tune of the piper who led them.

Catherine's heart soared with delight at the beauty and carefree joy. She would have loved to spend the day celebrating the coming of summer, but their schedule did not call for participating in country festivals, and they must go on.

With such happy scenes and the agreeable weather, the miles at first seemed to pass more quickly beneath their horses' plod. But as mile after weary mile wore on, Catherine began to feel less as if she'd been transported to Paradise. The countryside was no less green and pleasant, but her capacity to appreciate it was fading faster than the afternoon sun.

In all, it took five more days of wearisome pillion riding before they reached Tunbridge Wells. Catherine felt as if she had grown to Jezreel and wondered, if a mythological male with four horse's legs was a centaur, what a female creature might be called.

The hardest day was at Goudhurst. Catherine rose at four

o'clock for private devotions; Phillip held the first preaching service at five o'clock in a field so wet with morning dew Catherine was sure she and all the congregation would catch their death of pneumonia. Then followed three more services throughout the day at neighboring villages, each with some share of rowdyism and of spiritual victory as well.

By that evening, as they rode the last few miles to an inn, Catherine's head, and shoulders, and back ached so, that she wondered if she'd ever feel good again. She did the only thing there was to be done—she hung on and prayed, "Help me to travel in Thy strength, O Lord. Thy strength which is made perfect in our weakness ... and, O Lord, I am so weak."

Catherine was determined not to utter one word of complaint. And when Catherine Perronet was determined, she was very determined indeed.

To her tense and aching body, there came a sense of ease, as she thought of Jesus sitting at the well of Samaria—'Jesus therefore, being wearied with His journey ...' And she prayed, "Yes, Lord, Thou dost know how I feel. Thou wast weary too." And before she knew it, she began singing Martin Luther's words,

> Did we in our own strength confide,
> Our striving would be losing,
> Were not the right Man on our side,
> The Man of God's own choosing.
> Dost ask who that may be?
> Christ Jesus, it is He,
> Lord Sabbaoth His name,
> From age to age the same,
> And He must win the battle.

Phillip had joined her on the last line, as they came near to the inn that promised nothing but poor food and a lumpy bed; but Catherine's spirits were revived.

As Phillip followed Ned and Catherine into the inn, he realized that he was suddenly so tired he could hardly stand up. This had been one of the most demanding and draining days of his life. He was not unused to hard riding after little sleep, nor was he unaccustomed to facing large and hostile crowds; but he had never before had the additional burden—no, challenge—of responsibility for another. And although Edward was always nearby on Old Biggin, it was Phillip who worried about Catherine's physical comfort and mental ease as she rode behind him.

In meetings, he had always been concerned for the souls he spoke to and conscious of his responsibility to God. But over the past days, he had felt a new self-consciousness as he thought about Catherine being in the congregation. It disturbed him that it should be so, and the additional strain fatigued him.

In spite of the meanness of the inn, the landlord Crimpton was able to provide a private parlor where the travelers could eat their brown bread, cabbage, and collops with eggs. As they sat near the fire that evening, Edward, as usual, was bent over a book at a small table with a branched candelabra, leaving Catherine and Phillip in a world of their own, talking softly by the fire. After their brief burst of duet that day, the conversation turned naturally to hymns and hymn writers. Without giving any thought to her words, Catherine said, "Yes, I'm sure the beauty of Charles Wesley's hymns was the cause of much of my attraction . . ." She gave a small gasp as her hand flew to her mouth.

Phillip leaned forward, his elbows on his knees, his level, solemn gaze focused on her. "That day we met at the Foundery, you had been praying in much agony of spirit."

She gave a tiny nod. "I had just heard of the marriage."

He nodded. "And I too."

"You too? . . . You mean, Sally?"

"She was very special. Of course I had no expectations . . ." He tried to keep his eyes free of any flicker of pain that might show how deep the wound had gone.

"So the refused curacy was not your only disappointment that day." Catherine put out her hand in a tentative gesture as if she would touch the creases at the corner of his sad eyes, then hesitated and lowered her arm, her fingers just brushing the back of his hand.

But that brief touch, as light as a butterfly wing, was the most warming human contact he had known. The gentle friendliness of it went all through him.

They continued to sit for some time, the occasional crackling of a log the only sound in the room. Neither one moved, and yet it was as if they had drawn closer together.

At last, Ned closed his book, blew out a guttering candle, stood and stretched with noises that seemed raucous in the quiet of the room. "We must go to bed; we have a full day of riding to reach the Wells tomorrow."

As if to cover the telling intimacy of the quiet, Catherine crossed to her brother with unaccustomed vivacity and gave him a good-night kiss upon the cheek. Ned, his arms still spread out in a stretch, enfolded her in a huge embrace. "Sleep well, Cath." He released her with a brotherly pat on the shoulder.

She turned in a flurry from Ned to Phillip and became suddenly shy. She held out her hand, "Good night, then," and fled from the room.

Phillip was left alone in the suddenly empty parlor, trying to understand the strange emotion he felt. He hesitated to put a name on it since it seemed ludicrous, but . . . why should he feel jealousy at the closeness of brother and sister? What did such a scene have to do with him? Or was that the reason—that he had never been part of such a scene?

· 5 ·

LATE THE NEXT AFTERNOON they arrived at Tunbridge Wells, nestled in a valley of steep sandstone hills. The road into town led down the hill known as Mount Ephraim, the most fashionable residential section of the elegant city. Since the discovery of its mineral water wells in 1606, Tunbridge Wells had grown to be the chief resort of London intellectuals and was second only to Bath as the most popular watering place in England.

Sitting on their mounts, the three travelers watched elegantly clad strollers promenading beneath the grove of trees. The men were outfitted in coats of rich velvet and brocade, heavily embroidered on the wide cuffs turned up to the elbow, waistcoats displaying equally intricate needlework in silver and colored silks, with froths of lace foaming at the neck and wrists. Most men wore braid or feather trimmed tricorns atop their tieback wigs or carefully powdered hair, but some coiffures were sufficiently complicated to make the wearing of a hat uncomfortable, so those gentlemen carried their hats under their arms.

And the powdered and pomaded ladies strolling on the arms of the gentlemen were dressed in sackback gowns of exquisite fabric fastened only at the waist to reveal heavily embroidered stomachers, their V-shape meeting the embroidered petticoat flaring at the hips over an oblong hoop to emphasize the wearer's tiny waist. Triple flounces of lace finished the sleeves which ended at the elbow; lace caps showed beneath the wide-brimmed Bergere hats.

Catherine thought it one of the prettiest scenes she'd ever seen, and she felt only the slightest tinge of envy when she looked down at her own soiled clothes. She had acquired a strong fashion sense from her French grandmother, and although life in a vicarage had taught Catherine the vanity of worldliness, she didn't believe it honored God to look like a dowd. And after almost two weeks in her travel-worn gown, dowd was the only word to express how she felt in proximity to these exquisite creatures of fashion. After one elegant lady in a yellow, ribbed silk gown trimmed with metal lace and artificial flowers eyed her with raised brows, Catherine urged her companions to ride on. Ned and Phillip, who always looked proper in their black cleric's coats with white Geneva bands at the neck, and their neatly tied hair, could have little notion of how she felt.

The ride down the steep hill into town increased her discomfort as she tried to keep from leaning indecorously close against Phillip, and at the same time see the unusual outcroppings of sandstone separating the fashionable houses built along the road.

At the foot of the hill they were met not by a promenade of the fashionable, but by a cluster of small boys and dogs, chasing wildly after a runaway hoop. At first the scene amused Catherine, reminding her of similar scenes at Shoreham vicarage. But suddenly the speeding hoop veered into the roadway in front of them and shouting boys and yapping dogs turned almost directly at Jezreel.

The startled horse skittered sharply sideways and reared with a jerk. Catherine clutched for Phillip's back, but already she had slipped beyond its grasp; and with a cry, she fell to the ground.

Phillip and Ned were beside her in a moment. Ned turned with a sharp command to send the boys on their way, and Phillip knelt beside her. "Catherine, I'm so sorry. Are you hurt? I couldn't hold her steady. Catherine . . ."

Catherine looked at his distressed countenance and a small trill of laughter broke from her. "It is a good thing you didn't hold her. By sidestepping, Jezreel managed to unload me in the only patch of long grass anywhere near this stony road. Very thoughtful of her!" And she drew one of his rare smiles which she had learned to cherish for their scarcity.

"Are you truly all right, Cath?" Ned asked.

"Truly. I wasn't the least terrified, beyond the quite natural fear of falling." She paused to consider. "I realize now that I haven't been afraid for days." With a wide smile she clasped her hands in gladness. "I am entirely recovered." And then she flung her arms out to express a relief beyond words.

Catherine had been a person of few fears. She knew a brief fear of the dark as a child, and she could still remember her father coming in to her room, not hers alone, of course—one was never alone in a family of twelve—but after the others were asleep. And if Father were gone, Ned would come with a simple good-night, to let her know he was there and cared. Therefore, the fear hadn't lasted long.

And then there had been her one fearful experience in the woods, when at the age of twelve she had wandered too far in search of a bluejay and gotten lost. It was long after dark when she heard Ned calling, and the fear fell away as if the woods were lighted.

But her fear of horses had found no such happy ending, until today. She smiled at Phillip, thinking how a fine horse was the one thing that invariably made his cool eyes glow dark and warm. And now she was free of the fear that prevented her from sharing this interest with her new friend. Just as with the help of others, the small Catherine had conquered her fear of the dark and of being lost in the woods, so she had conquered her fear of horses—with the help of Phillip and of God. The God, who at least in this instance, did indeed seem to be still guiding her way.

Phillip remounted and Ned gave her a leg up to her pillion seat. Then, in spite of the increased dowdiness the dark grass stains added to her dress, Catherine Perronet rode in triumph through Tunbridge Wells.

The accommodations offered by Tunbridge Wells were unlike any other they had experienced on the journey, or were likely to on any itinerant preaching tour. The town had changed remarkably since the time of Charles I when his queen, Henrietta Maria, arrived with her court to take the spa waters and had to camp in tents on the common because so few houses or public inns had yet been built.

"Ned, are you quite sure we can afford this?" Catherine was looking at the brocade and gilt Louis XV furniture in the parlor, but her mind was on Phillip's slim purse.

"Perhaps—" Ned began, but was interrupted by a flurry of activity as they were caught between a party arriving at the door and the landlord with the entire staff of the inn rushing to greet the new arrivals who traveled in an elegant, coroneted coach. At the center of the maelstrom was a tiny, sharp-featured woman, her greying brown hair tucked firmly inside a cap of the finest white linen, the severe plainness of her Spitalfields silk gown in no way hiding the excellent quality of the fabric or workmanship.

"Welcome, my Lady. My humble establishment is yours, and I your most devoted servant." The innkeeper bowed so deeply it seemed for a moment he would overbalance and fall on his nose.

The lady began giving orders for the dispatching of her entourage and possessions, all of which were carried out with the greatest alacrity. When the room had been fairly cleared of servants, trunks, and portmanteaux, the noble lady sighted the three travelers who watched from a corner of the room. "Edward Perronet. You may present yourself."

Edward stepped forward and made his bow. "Lady Huntingdon, may I beg leave to present my sister and our companion?"

The lady inclined her head.

"Lady Huntingdon, my sister, Miss Catherine Perronet, and our friend, the Reverend Phillip Ferrar."

"Ah. I recall now, Mr. Ferrar. John Wesley told me you were preaching in this area. I shall hear more of your work. You will join me for dinner." Her gaze included the three of them; then she turned to the hovering innkeeper. "You will provide accommodations for my friends on my account also." She turned back to Ned. "I dine at seven o'clock." Her exit from the room was as straightforward as a military march, the small train on her dress following in obedient folds.

The second assistant to the landlord approached the three still standing in the center of the floor. "May I show you to your rooms?"

In her room, a dismayed Catherine surveyed her attire. Her only comfort was the fact that she had washed and pressed her lawn fichu, so she would have a fresh covering around the neckline of her bodice. But what the countess would say to her soiled skirt, Catherine quailed to consider. She heated her curling iron over a candle and framed her face with small round curls, then drew the remainder of her hair into a bun on the top of her head, to be covered by her ruffled lawn cap.

It was also fortunate that when she entered the Countess' private parlor with Ned and Phillip at the commanded hour, there were sufficient shadows in the candlelit room to conceal the most disreputable of her travel stains. And, as always, Catherine's dignified carriage overshadowed any faults in her attire.

The Countess introduced her traveling companion, her aunt, Lady Fanny Shirley, and directed her servants to set the first course. The roasted pork with turnips suited milady's taste, but the butter pond pudding would not do. "My constitution cannot abide this. Remove it at once." A servant hurried forward. "There is enough butter in that to have drowned the pig, had it been alive. I have come to the Wells to have my health restored, not further endangered by rich puddings."

The offending dish was hastily removed and replaced by jugged pigeons with pease and onions which were much more suited to the Countess' delicate physique. "I more frequently take the waters at Bath," Lady Huntingdon explained to her guests, "but my condition did not respond well to my last visit there, so my physician recommended the chalybeate spring here. You must accompany me in the morning, Miss Perronet. You look entirely too peaked. You want fortifying. You know, after Dudley Lord North discovered these springs early last century, he was miraculously cured from a lingering consumptive disorder."

The other diners made appropriate responses to her monologue. Then she focused on Phillip sitting on her left. "Young man, you are entirely too thin. You must eat more." She carved a thick slice of pork and placed it on his plate. "Preaching the Word of God requires stamina. You must fortify yourself physically as well as spiritually for the slings and arrows of the enemy. Have your services met with success?"

Phillip responded that there had been many victories in spite of the resistence of the rabble. He was about to elaborate when the Countess went on. "This is a benighted area. The season is just beginning, but already you shall see the luminaries of society on the promenade. Dr. Johnson, David Garrick, Mr. Pitt—they come here regularly now that that self-appointed potentate from Bath has undertaken to establish his routines of vice here. I speak, of course, of Beau Nash. Coffee houses, balls, concerts, gambling rooms— that is what Tunbridge Wells offers to kill the souls of those who would drink her waters for the health of their bodies."

The Countess placed a pigeon and another turnip on Phillip's plate. "I thank God that you have come to do battle with the evil one in his very stronghold. But it will not be easy. Not that we are ever to expect the way of our Lord to be easy, of course. But the only established church in the district is the Chapel-of-ease, dedicated to King Charles the Martyr, and it is little attended and is closed altogether between the seasons.

"When I was here with my chaplain, Mr. Madan, he was not allowed to preach in the Chapel-of-ease because of his evangelical beliefs, even though, of course, he is a fully ordained and most godly man. Mount Sion, the Presbyterian place of worship, was placed at his disposal; but such a man is not a dissenter and must not be forced from his own church.

"Mr. Wesley also attended me here once. The Presbyterian place was freely lent for his use, but it was insufficient to contain the numbers who wished to hear. He addressed the assembled multitudes in the open air. This was a new and extraordinary occurrence at Tunbridge Wells, and created no small stir.

"I have been forced to travel without a chaplain this time, Mr. Madan having fallen ill with an ague and Mr. Whitefield not yet recovered from his latest journey to America. But God, in His never-failing graciousness, has provided. You shall preach for me, Sir."

Phillip inclined his head in obedient compliance.

"Tomorrow after we take the waters I shall inspect the subscription list at the assembly rooms to learn who is in town and draw my list. Fanny," and she turned to her aunt, "you shall send invitations to a drawing room."

"Yes, indeed, Selina," Lady Shirley replied.

"Sir Thomas I'Anson shall open his home for me again as he did when last Mr. Madan preached here."

"Yes, indeed, Selina."

The servants entered to remove the dishes. "Nothing sweet," the Countess directed. "You may set a cheddar cheese and some nuts, and perhaps dried apricots if they're nice."

"Yes, Milady, very nice indeed."

She looked at Phillip. "And a dish of sweet whey for this young man, and the other young people. But no nutmeg. My physician warns me it is most harmful to the constitution."

Catherine quickly raised her napkin to her mouth to cover a smile.

Later, when they had obediently consumed the sweetened milk junket eaten with sugar and cream and flavored with rosewater but no nutmeg, and the party was sitting at ease around the room sipping cups of finest Hyson tea with milk to lessen the deleterious effects of its stimulating properties, Catherine had an opportunity to confide in Lady Fanny Shirley. "My portmanteau was lost in a flood. I fear I have nothing appropriate even for drinking the waters in polite company, let alone attending a drawing room in the home of Sir Thomas I'Anson."

"The waters are drunk in dishabille. Have you no morning robe?" Lady Shirley asked in her soft voice.

Catherine would have liked to respond with a laugh, but the Countess had given no indication of favoring such levity in her parlor where she was now engaging Ned and Phillip in deep theological conversation on her strictly-held Calvinist tenets. "Alas, no closer than Greenwich," Catherine said. "One's needs are quite simple on a preaching circuit."

"Yes, I can guess they might be. You are to be commended for your courage in making such a journey. Although I am aware many women do so, I know I should never attempt it. Why, I've heard tell that Mrs. Murray even attended Mr. Wesley into Ireland." She emphasized her words with a small shudder. "But as to your wardrobe, I fancy we can contrive something. You are much taller than I, but perhaps we could let down a petticoat and gather up the overskirt into puffs in the shepherdess style. It was quite the rage when last we were in London, and would look very charming on you—if Selina approves," she added hastily.

Selina approved, and so the next day Catherine appeared on the Pantiles in a charming sprigged muslin dress worn shepherdess style over a fashionably short petticoat. Lady Fanny had even been able to produce new blue ribbons for Catherine's wide straw hat. Fanny had at first suggested pink, but Catherine did not feel that was the most flattering color for her dark complexion, and so was delighted with the light blue.

The colonnaded row of shops, charmingly shaded by lime trees all along one side of the promenade which Catherine and her escorts entered, was the heart of Tunbridge Wells. There a large crowd of the fashionable gathered every morning around the chalybeate spring at the entrance to the square. And, indeed, they were in dishabille, as Lady Fanny had predicted. The men wore long damask dressing gowns which swept the paving tiles, or the shorter banyon, cut similar to a dress coat with flared skirts, but the hem ending well below the knees. But whichever style coat they chose, all the men were wigless, covering their shaved heads either with caps of fabric matching their dressing gowns, or with the more fashionable turbans. The ladies wore simple muslin saques, most of them with long, elegantly embroidered white muslin aprons.

A small group of musicians entertained the visitors as they waited for the dipper to ladle their glass of water from her sunken stall beneath the colonnade. The dipper's appointment, by legal act, was the gift of the Lord of Rusthall Manor, who owned the area; the small sum Edward paid her for their glasses was not for the water but for her service.

Catherine took the glass from her brother and sipped the slightly yellow liquid. "Fa, it tastes like rust."

"Iron water," Ned agreed. "From the forge of St. Dunstan."

Catherine returned her glass to the dipper. "What are you talking about, Ned?" She placed her hand lightly on her brother's arm and smiled at Phillip on the other side of her as they strolled up the shaded promenade.

"It's the source of the amazing properties of the water," Ned continued his story. "In the tenth century, St. Dunstan had a forge nearby. He was visited there one day by a most seductive young lady whom the saint immediately recognized as the devil. The holy man seized a pair of tongs from the fire and gripped the devil by the nose. Whereupon the devil plunged his face into the cooling waters of the spring, thereby imparting to them forever their distinctive metallic tang."

Catherine smiled at her brother's story, then looked up at Phillip, catching one of his brief smiles—which somehow always made her want to cry.

They went up the steps onto the Upper Walk and followed along the houses and shops fronted by rows of Italiante columns, past a general store, the Musick Gallery, the Assembly Rooms where later in the day Beau Nash would preside over the gaming tables, coffee houses filled with patrons bearing the latest gossip, and booksellers, where already a few who had taken their water early were gathering to pen letters or the "water poetry" so popular in the town.

At the end of the walk they turned and left the colonnade for the more open promenade under the lime trees, walking on the flat paving tiles which Queen Anne had paid for when she became impatient with local workmen and which gave the area its name.

They had almost returned the length of the Pantiles to the dipper's stall when a short rotund man in a full-bottomed wig and embroidered red damask coat puffed up the avenue toward them.

"Sirs and Madam," he punctuated each word by tapping on the tiles with his walking stick. "I have the honour of being Squire Penshurst."

Apparently their polite replies to this information did not fulfill his expectations. "Of Penshurst Hall," he added with an additional tap. "I am the local magistrate."

As Catherine wondered if they were to congratulate him upon this achievement, he drew from his pocket a large piece of parchment with an official seal attached to it. "It has come to my attention that you have held irregular preaching services in this vicinity, and as the duly sworn representative of His Majesty's law, it is my duty to inform you that we shall permit no such activities in Tunbridge Wells."

"Sir, it is—" Ned began, but got no further as a small figure in a large, white cap took command.

"Good morning, Squire Penshurst. I see you have met my friends Mr. and Miss Perronet and Mr. Ferrar. I shall present them at a drawing room I am holding at Sir Thomas I'Anson's home tomorrow night." The round figure in the cherry coat put the warrant back in his pocket and bobbed a bow of assent to her ladyship. "And I shall expect to see you there, Squire."

And, indeed, Squire Penshurst was among the elegant assembly that filled Sir I'Anson's drawing room in his Palladian home atop fashionable Mount Ephraim where the Countess of Huntingdon presided as hostess. "Lady Lincoln, and Baroness Banks, may I present our speaker for the evening, the Reverend Phillip Ferrar."

The Baroness extended her hand. "How do you do? Are you connected to the Yorkshire Ferrars, Sir?"

Phillip bowed over the white hand. "I am from London, my Lady."

Catherine who was witness to the small scene, gave a grateful thought to the orphanage matron's careful drilling in manners that could teach a foundling to be at ease in this exalted company.

". . .the Duchess of Richmond. . ." The Countess continued her tour of introduction around the room, then took a seat in the center as Sir Thomas' liveried servants handed round refreshments.

"Mr. Loggan," she signaled a powdered gentleman in a suit of

Genoa velvet with a gold-tissue brocaded waistcoat to take the seat beside her. "I viewed your paintings in London."

"Indeed, I am honored, my Lady."

"Charming. Quite charming. You have an excellent eye. But you must avoid an overuse of too bold colors. You will get nowhere by shocking refined tastes."

"I thank you for your condescension in noticing me, my Lady."

"It is well that you came tonight. You did not attend when Mr. Madan spoke."

"Indeed, my Lady, I was not in Tunbridge Wells at the time."

"Very careless of you, Loggan. You must take more care for your soul. Mr. Madan exhorted with warmth and energy, 'Seek the Lord while He might be found, call upon Him while He is near.' Whilst Mr. Madan was offering that gracious invitation of our Lord, 'Come unto Me, all ye that are weary and heavy laden,' a man in the congregation dropped down and instantly expired."

Mr. Loggan shook out the lace frill at his wrist. "Egad, that must have caused a sensation."

"Indeed, so strong and general an influence on a congregation I seldom remember to have seen. Many were melted to tears, and seemed resolved to fly from the wrath to come."

"Very understandable."

The company having consumed their refreshments, the Countess called for the general attention of her guests and introduced Edward and Catherine who were to present a number by the greatest hymnologist of their day, Mr. Charles Wesley. With her usual grave solemnity Catherine took her seat at the harpsichord and after a few sharp, clear chords blended her voice with her brother's,

> Love divine, all loves excelling,
> Joy of heav'n to earth come down!. . .
> Jesus, Thou art all compassion;
> Pure, unbounded love Thou art.
> Visit us with Thy salvation;
> Enter ev'ry trembling heart.

At the conclusion of the song the Countess introduced Phillip, and Catherine sent him a small smile of encouragement, knowing this audience could be far more daunting than any fireworks-throwing or bull-baiting rabble. Phillip stood at the end of the room, his silver-blond hair and white bands glowing like lights at the top of his tall, black-clad figure. With perfect self-possession he spoke to the distinguished assemblage on the text, "The fear of the Lord is the beginning of knowledge." And every word rang absolutely true because they were spoken by a man whose relationship with Christ was more than head knowledge—it was true fear of the Lord based on reverential awe of His love and greatness.

As Phillip spoke, Catherine looked at him in the elegant drawing room and thought how well he was carrying everything off. The occasion must be a difficult one for him, but he was neither awkward nor exuberant. He brought to the situation the same quiet detachment that he had shown in all other occasions; and now, with the full glare of the most elegant nobility turned upon him, his solemn gracefulness was as perfect as any to the manner born. Amazing in one who had been essentially on his own since childhood. There was a natural excellence in this man that had needed no other guidance than the grace of God.

At the end of the sermon many appeared genuinely moved by the preacher's earnest words. It seemed truly that, "Those who came to scoff, remained to pray," as Wesley had reported of a similar meeting. "I am moved to consider what you say." The artist Loggan shook Phillip's hand. "I would hear more of this."

The Countess was delighted. When the last guest had departed she turned to her speaker and musicians. "A remarkable service. Many were cut to the heart. Truly God was in our midst to wound and to heal. Such happy indications of the approbation of God induce me to hope that He will deign to smile on my humble efforts. I mean to take up the sword for the glory of His great name and the good of the people of this place. Today has given me assurance that He will ultimately crown my efforts with distinguished and lasting success."

She walked the length of the room with her rapid steps, then sat on a straight chair, her back ramrod, her small, pointed chin forward. "Perhaps I shall build a residence here, on Mount Ephraim, that I might work more among these people. But I am forever conscious that every effort is impotent without God's almighty aid. I cry continually to Him for wisdom and strength. What am I, that He should condescend to make me instrumental in communicating any good to others? Is it not a sobering thought? I am humbled in the dust before Him. It is the Lord, *the Lord Himself*, that has done the work. The treasure is in an earthen vessel, but the excellency of the power is of God *only*, and not of man."

She sat for a moment with her head bowed. Then suddenly the head jerked up and the dark, bright eyes snapped. "Miss Perronet, I do not like you riding pillion across the countryside. It isn't ladylike. I understand the gentlemen must go on tomorrow, but you will remain here with me and I shall return you to London at the end of the month."

"Your Ladyship, I thank you for your concern. But my father expects me. I cannot disappoint him."

The Countess blinked as if she could not take in that her plans were meeting disagreement. Her thin cheeks became even thinner and for a moment Catherine feared her response. Then the Countess spoke: "Fine man, your father. Perhaps the most heavenly-minded man I know. Give him my regards."

· 6 ·

THE NEXT MORNING Catherine hoped that her bold behavior had not placed her in the Countess' bad graces, but the ride through the glorious May morning left no doubt in her mind of the rightness of her decision. The road led between ferns carpeting the incline on both sides of the path and across little streams meandering through spinneys of white-barked birches. Birds sang from hedgerows laced with blossoms. Masses of purple and yellow wildflowers colored the fields and wild daisies smaller than farthings grew from the shortest of stems.

"Phillip, pray, stop a moment. I should like to collect some samples for my wildflower book."

He pulled Jezreel to a halt and helped Catherine dismount. "You don't have this variety in your collection?"

"Not this particular shade of lavender." Her long fingers spread the leaves aside and pinched the stems to gather a small nosegay. "One of the things I most look forward to in being at Shoreham again is walking in my dear woods."

As they rode further into Catherine's native corner of Kent, she recognized a growing tranquility, and felt a new contentment in being with Phillip. They could ride for miles with only the briefest of comments on the scenery, then quite suddenly one of them would begin a conversation and they would talk without pause for an equal number of miles. Either way, Catherine found a repose she had never known in the companionship of another. And one of the chief gratifications was her certainty that Phillip, who had such need of fellowship, found equal tranquility in her company.

And whether they were discussing a deep spiritual truth, the meaning of a poem she had read lately, or merely a commonplace observation, Catherine felt she had never been listened to so totally. Phillip's capacity for giving his absolute attention was one of his most endearing charms. Even though she sat behind him and therefore was obliged to talk to the back of his head, there would be the little nod that told her he was listening. And for all his customary silence, his mind was extraordinarily active. Whenever he made a comment, it was incisive and to the point but always spoken with the gentleness that characterized him.

With the hours passing so pleasantly, it seemed impossible that evening shadows should already be lengthening, when the pathway through thick woods curved sharply and Catherine knew they were nearly home. "Whenever I'm away, this is how I think of Shoreham—buried under the trees, so green and protected." Another curve in the path, and she saw ahead of her the dearly loved golden stone vicarage, with its high curving wall around the large garden where Charity Perronet managed to keep flowers blooming from spring to autumn.

The many wings and gables of the house showed where it had been built onto through the centuries: first the low, grey rock, two-room structure; then a red brick wing added at the same time as the square Norman tower was put on the church; and now the lovely golden Georgian wing with the curving fanlight over the door. A symphony of familiar sounds sang Catherine's welcome home: birds twittering in the lime trees, chickens clucking from the hen house, laughter from the inn around the corner, and the voices of children from the vicarage yard.

Then sixteen-year-old John saw the travelers approach and gave a shout which brought family and servants running to meet them. It was Catherine's first visit home since she left to work for the Society in London and now she wondered how she had managed to stay away so long. Her mother, wisps of graying hair escaping from her cap, engulfed them each in her comfortable embrace and warm smile. Vincent, his full-bottomed wig slightly askew, greeted them more quietly but no less warmly, his pleasure shining from his kindly eyes. And Damaris, Henry, William, Philothea, Thomas, and John all had their part in the welcome.

"Betsy, we shall be three more at dinner. Come in, my Dears. You know your rooms. Phillip, Ned will show you. I'm sure you'll want to wash. Philly, you and Tom take cans of hot water up for them." Charity Perronet managed to direct the entire household without ever raising her voice.

All was orderly bustle when they gathered again in the dining room a short time later. Catherine noted Phillip's pause at the door; he hung back as if not sure of his place. Only the slightest tightening of his straight mouth showed his unease; but as he stood aloof, Catherine could see him as he must have been at the orphanage, watching the others, but never fully part of them. Such a contrast to her own family, with a dozen noisy siblings all belonging to each other. Their eyes met and Catherine smiled to let him know she welcomed him as part of the family.

When they had all found a place at the table, Vincent stood and offered grace, remembering the needs of the parish, mentioning each one of his children by name, and including Phillip as well. By the time he concluded with a doxology the roast joint in front of him had cooled considerably, but not the diners' appetites.

Vincent carved the roast while Charity served the potted venison, and hungry eaters passed the currant suet pudding and boiled parsnips with carrots.

"Well, Damaris, are you still the mainstay of the Shoreham Methodists?" Edward asked his maiden sister, who had elected to live at home and take charge of the Society work there.

"It continues to grow remarkably, Ned. We hold preaching in Father's kitchen every Friday night, but we shall soon outgrow even that room."

"One of Damaris' special tasks is seeing to the care of itinerant preachers when they are in the area; so if you find any lacks in the hospitality, Phillip, you must apply to her." The gentle Vincent spoke in a teasing manner, but his pride in his daughter's work showed in his eyes.

"Quite right for the daughter of the man who is often called the Archbishop of Methodism, Father," Ned said.

"And what of your preaching tour, Son? Have you met much resistance?"

Edward recounted many of their hardships at the hands of the rabble.

Vincent shook his head, "So much of that could be avoided if only our preachers would be allowed to use the church buildings."

Edward suddenly struck the table as if he had just come to a hard decision. "As we are all family here, I shall speak my mind boldly on

81

a matter to which I have been giving considerable thought." There was a cutting edge to his voice that made Catherine hold her breath at what his announcement might be. She had noted his sometimes brooding quiet on the trip and knew that although he was the kindest of brothers to her, he was capable of being hotheaded and sharp-tongued when he felt the situation demanded it.

"We must give thought to separation."

"Edward!" Charity's voice was the first to break the shocked silence. "And your father a vicar of the Church of England these past thirty years—twenty-one of them right here in this very church. And you and your brother Charl ordained priests—how can you say such a thing?"

"I am sorry, Mother. But I believe we will come to it. Our brother Charl means to bring it up at the next conference. We should grant license to our own ministers to serve the sacraments."

"You are thinking of becoming a nonjuror, Son?" Vincent asked in his quiet voice.

"I don't know, Father. I can see that I spoke in haste, especially in front of my younger brothers and sister, but the problem is serious indeed. Phillip here is one of the finest men I've ever heard preach; must he spend his life in a cow pasture? He was dismissed from his curacy for enthusiasm and has been without a post these two years, although he has made frequent application. Something must be done. A dissenting chapel must be better than no place at all!" In spite of himself, his voice rose to an impassioned pitch.

"I would remind you, Son, that our Lord had nowhere to lay His sacred head. And His Sermon on the Mount was a pretty remarkable precedent of field preaching. When John Wesley was last here, he told me of the huge multitude he preached to in Moorfields. 'It is field preaching which does the execution still,' he said. 'For usefulness, there is none comparable to it.' What building except St. Paul's Church could contain such a large congregation as a field? One can command thrice the number in the open air that can be held under a roof. And do you not feel the convicting, convincing power of God at work among the people in the fields?"

Edward agreed that was true.

"Then, my Son, do not despise the means which our Lord hath put at your hand. I believe one hindrance of the work of God in York has been the neglect of field preaching; and, I am apt to think that many of the hearers at your meetings have scarcely ever heard a

Methodist before, or perhaps any other preacher. What but field preaching could reach these poor sinners? Are not their souls also precious in the sight of God?"

"Your reasoned words are a help to me. I shall attempt to control my impatience, Father. But I confess to feeling a shadow of bitterness over the situation at times."

"Oh, no, no, my Son. Pray earnestly for the grubbing out of all root of bitterness. You must replace it with love. Love is all."

There was a knock at the door and Betsy hurried from the kitchen to answer it. "It's Mr. Claygate, Sir. Come for the Bible reading. I 'ad 'im sit in the parlor."

"You still hold your nightly Bible readings, Father?" Catherine asked.

"Indeed, Daughter. But I have put the hour back to seven. And a good thing too, or we should have missed this stimulating conversation tonight. Never fear to speak to your family of what concerns your heart, my children." Vincent rose. "Now, let us go to prayers."

Even the generous proportions of the vicarage parlor were crowded as family, servants, and parishioners gathered for nightly Bible reading and prayers. And Catherine was sure that, in spite of all that had been said in favor of field preaching, one of the prayers Phillip would offer would still be for the Lord to open the way to a parish of his own. She too prayed that petition would be granted.

The next morning being Sunday, the village bellringers put to full use the ring of eight bells in the Shoreham parish church of St. Peter and St. Paul. And Catherine entered with the other villagers through the porch, which had been built in the fifteenth century from the root of a huge upended oak, and on through the stone doorway. She took her seat on the second pew where she had worshiped since she was three years old.

As she sang the familiar hymns, listened to the lessons, and knelt for prayers with these people she had grown up among, the conflicts and struggles of the past weeks seemed to slip further and further away. It seemed impossible that there could be such disturbances in God's world. The collect for that fifth Sunday after Easter seemed to hold the key to all problems:

"O Lord, from whom all good things do come; Grant to us thy humble servants, that by Thy holy inspiration, we may think those things that be good, and by Thy merciful guiding may perform the same; through our Lord Jesus Christ, Amen."

While her father preached, she let her eyes wander over the dear church. She had always loved the dark, wood-vaulted ceiling. One of her earliest memories was of peeking up at it when her eyes should have been closed in prayer and counting the golden stars embedded in the wood. One time Ned caught her at her game and reprimanded her later—the stars weren't there to be counted, they were to serve as reminders of the infinity of God, and counting them would spoil everything.

She disagreed, however, and one warm Saturday afternoon when the church was empty, she slipped into its lovely, cool stone interior, lay right down on the flagged floor, and began counting. But she kept getting confused and having to start all over again. In the end, she fell asleep and received a dreadful scolding for not helping Elizabeth peel the potatoes for supper.

Later that afternoon she recounted the memory to Phillip. "I am surprised to hear of the scolding. It seems to me that your family never raises their voices to one another."

"Well, perhaps we only do so in a very restrained way. And then we always say we are sorry as soon as the moment has passed."

They crossed the vicarage garden back to the church. Catherine had volunteered to take the children's service for her father, if Phillip would help her, which he readily agreed to do. She turned to him now against the backdrop of the rambling vicarage and its riotous garden, with their talk of her happy, loving family hanging in the air. She saw him standing there, tall and thin in his dark suit, and thought how austere his life had been.

When she looked at him a short time later as he explained the story of the Good Samaritan to the village children, she saw his face aglow as it was only when he preached, and a great wave of feeling washed over her; it was a feeling she couldn't identify, but that she wanted to clasp to her, in spite of the ache it brought with it.

It was to be a day of strange feelings for Catherine. When her family gathered around the parlor fireplace after Evensong, Phillip was the last to enter. Again he paused just outside the doorway, and she saw him alone, as she was accustomed to thinking of him. Then he entered and sat down and was suddenly so much a part of the family that when young Thomas climbed on his lap and Philothea sat so close as to be leaning on him, he became almost part of the furniture. It was as if in this rural vicarage Phillip Ferrar had dropped into place.

When they had their fill of visiting and cold meats, the family slowly straggled off to bed. Vincent and Charity were the last to leave them. "Thank you for giving us that fine sermon at Evensong. You can come preach for me anytime," Vincent said to Phillip, then kissed his daughter good-night.

Charity also kissed Catherine. "We shall begin our parish visits at nine o'clock in the morning. Old Mrs. Claygate is very poorly, and the Ightham children weren't at the children's service today, and—oh, well, there are so many. My Dear, it will be so good to have you visiting with me."

And then Phillip and Catherine had the fireside all to themselves and for the moment it seemed as if this parish where they were preaching, teaching, and visiting the sick and needy, was their own, as Midhurst must have been for Phillip. Catherine poured out a final cup of tea for her companion who sat with his feet up on the hob, and the very everydayness of it made her feel as if she were a little girl playing house. But she longed for it to be more than playacting.

It seemed to Catherine that this return to her home was to be one of constant revelations and understandings as she accompanied her mother on their round of visits the next morning. She watched as Charity dealt with the needs of the people of the parish, and gradually, it seemed that she was watching a new person—or perhaps, for the first time—a real person in the place of the generalized, comfortable form of "mother." She had always seen her mother as an extension of her father, who found her being in the center of her many children as she directed the household to revolve around Vincent. Father's meals were always on time, composed of his favorite foods, prepared the way he liked them; Father's study hours were always to be undisturbed by children, parishioners, or other clergymen; Father's work must receive her help, visiting the sick, distributing charity from the poor box, arranging flowers on the altar; and Father's children must always be orderly, clean, well-behaved, respectful. Not that Vincent Perronet was a demanding tyrant—a kindlier, softer-spoken soul couldn't be imagined. But this was the natural order of things.

It had given Catherine's childhood a focus, a pattern, a security. Father was the center of the household and the parish, just as John Wesley was the center of the Methodist Society, the King was the center of England, and God was the center of the universe. But now Catherine realized how important a focus her mother was for her own sake—the love and warmth and comfort she shared unstintingly with her twelve children and the three hundred souls in their parish.

Charity Perronet was far more than an extension of her husband; she was a person who chose to be a helpmeet and to fulfill Christ's call to servanthood. And for the first time in her life, Catherine truly saw her mother—saw her with the insight which was like a birth when the infant for the first time sees the world outside. And with it came a new love and appreciation for her mother.

But most important of all, she felt a desire to carry on in her mother's tradition of love and service. She would be the person God created her to be, serving out of love—if only God would show her how and where. "O God," she prayed, "surely Thou wouldst not have given me this desire if Thou didst not have a place for me to use it."

The final stop for mother and daughter was in the center of the village where the Misses Simpson plied their expert needles in the little Tudor shop that was also their home. With her mother's help and the fluttery attendance of the elder Miss Simpson, Catherine looked through the pattern cards and fabrics and chose an open gown to be made from dimity of simple texture but lively pattern, with little bouquets of scattered flowers. The flowers, stomacher, and petticoat reflected Catherine's love of nature as she selected a clear blue like the sky and the bluebells that grew in the woods around Shoreham in the spring.

"You have chosen well, my Dear," Charity told her. "Buying good fabric is never extravagant, because it lasts so much longer. Sometimes I buy French fabric, but only from established shops—one must be careful not to support the runners by buying smuggled products. This lace will make a lovely trimming for the neckline and sleeve flounces."

Catherine hesitated. The lace her mother held was lovely, but many Society members eschewed such marks of worldliness. She had never considered removing it from the dresses she already owned, but wondered about the propriety of ordering it on a new gown.

"There can be nothing displeasing to God in a bit of lace, my Dear. Even your father's best surplice has a trim of lace on it." Char-

86

ity handed the lace to the dressmaker at Catherine's nod. "And now, we must hurry home for tea. I told Betsy to make a special treat."

But even the veiled hint from her mother and the broad smiles from her siblings did nothing to prod Catherine's suspicions that anything out of the ordinary was afoot—not until she had been served a thick slice of seed cake with a dish of sweet tea and Philothea burst out between giggles, "She's forgotten, hasn't she? Cath, don't you truly know what day this is?"

Catherine looked puzzled. "No, I've given it no thought. I lost all account of the days on our travels. It must be May. . . oh, is it truly the twelfth of May? Is it my birthday?"

And then she was obliged to set her tea dish aside very quickly before she was engulfed in congratulatory hugs and birthday kisses from her family.

"And you too, Phillip, you must wish Cath happiness," Philly led their guest forward.

"Felicitations, Catherine."

"Oh, Fah! It won't do if you don't kiss her. Don't be so shy, Phillip." Philothea gave him a sisterly shove that almost landed his lanky form in Catherine's lap.

He bent over gravely, picked up her hand, and brushed it with his lips. "Many happy returns." And suddenly, Catherine felt they would be.

Philothea applauded the performance of the guest she had adopted wholeheartedly as her personal property. "Well done! And when is your birthday, Phillip?"

He withdrew to the back of the company. "I fear I don't have any idea. I have never given the subject any thought."

Catherine chilled with fear for his feelings. She knew how sensitive he was about his foundling status. But she could think of nothing to distract her little sister as Philly insisted.

"Oh, but you must know how old you are?"

"Yes, I know that, I've had the good fortune to accomplish thirty years."

"How odd not to know your birthday." Philothea frowned at the problem. "Perhaps you could celebrate your saint's day. May first is Saint Philip and Saint James' Day—pity Philip didn't get one of his own, the other apostles did. I suppose it was because he was so quiet. If he'd talked more he'd have more stories in the Bible and then they'd have given him his own day." She thought for a moment.

"But don't feel bad, I'm sure he was really a very important Apostle. The collect says, 'following the steps of Thy holy Apostles, Saint Philip and Saint James, we may stedfastly walk in the way that leadeth to eternal life.' Pity it's just past. Will you mind dreadfully waiting a whole year for your birthday?"

Phillip started to say that he wouldn't mind in the least, but Damaris joined in with another suggestion. "Perhaps you could celebrate your spiritual birthday."

Philly thought that a splendid idea. "Oh, yes. 'Ye must be born again.' Father preached on that just two Sundays ago, didn't you, Father? That *would* be a birthday. Do you remember when it was, Phillip?"

"Yes, it was the second Sunday in Trinity. I remember because Trinity term had just begun when I had the opportunity of calling on William Law."

Catherine was happy to steer the conversation away from the uncomfortable subject of birthdays. "How fortunate you were to be able to counsel with a man who has influenced so many."

"Yes, I was perhaps the one man in all Cambridge who prayed in a formal way every day; but Law made me see that giving good words with the mouth, while the heart is far from God, can serve no beneficial purpose."

"And you found assurance of salvation then?" Vincent asked.

"Truly. As soon as I saw that my hope and trust must be fixed solely in my Creator and Redeemer. Law showed me that those systems of divinity which represent an outward atonement in order to make God reconcilable to His creatures, in the same manner that sacrifices were anciently thought to appease the deity—such forms as I had always worshiped in—are totally erroneous.

"When I saw that all was in Christ and His atonement, I knew a great peace."

"Eight Sundays after Easter," announced Philothea who had been looking up Trinity Sunday in the Table of Lessons in the Prayer Book. "So the second Sunday in Trinity is nine weeks after Easter, which will be—" she paused to count on her fingers, "the second Sunday in June. You must remember to celebrate."

He nodded solemnly at the child's earnest instruction.

"Might I have another piece of cake, Mother?" John held out an empty plate.

"Here, have mine." Phillip's response was so natural and the movement with which he placed the cake on the younger boy's plate so rapid, that it was a moment before Catherine realized what had happened. Back in a group, Phillip had reacted as he undoubtedly had at the orphanage to the needs of another. She wondered how often his infinite unselfishness had led him to give his portions of food to another?

"And now, in honor of this day, dear Sister," Edward bowed to Catherine, "I have the pleasure of announcing that I have completed my new hymn."

"O Ned, how splendid! Is it the one you were working on during our trip?"

"Yes, I have seldom had a composition cost me so much effort, but I flatter myself I have captured some of the stateliness I sought." He indicated the harpsichord. "Will you, Catherine? I believe the key of G would suit it best."

She took her accustomed place at the instrument, and as soon as her fingers struck the first few chords of the tune he chose, she felt a thrill at the strength of her brother's composition. He sang it clear through for them,

> All Hail the Power of Jesus' name!
> Let angels prostrate fall.
> Bring forth the royal diadem
> And crown Him Lord of All!

Each of the four verses brought smiles and nods from his appreciative audience until at last Edward concluded with:

> Oh, that with yonder sacred throng
> We at His feet may fall.
> We'll join the everlasting song,
> And crown Him Lord of all!

"O Ned," Catherine was the first to respond. "It's wonderful! So worshipful and majestic! I can feel the greatness of God. It makes me want to shout Glory to Him."

"Catherine, I couldn't imagine you so demonstrative," Edward laughed.

"Well, my spirit shouts, even if I don't," she amended.

Charity dabbed at her eyes with a linen handkerchief, but her words to her son were interrupted by a knock at the door.

Vincent moved to answer it before any of the servants could respond. "Why, Charl, what an unexpected pleasure!"

He stepped back to admit his newly arrived son, but the pleasure that should have accompanied such a visit was quenched by the messenger's words. "Ned, I am sent for you. Your wife is dangerously ill."

· 7 ·

THEY SET OUT AT FIRST LIGHT and by continually pressing their horses and themselves, the riders were able to accomplish the eighteen miles from Shoreham to Greenwich in just five hours. Edward rode always at the front, urging his horse and his companions to greater speed, showing by the sharpness of his voice how near to distraction he was. At Kidbrooke, a mile from Greenwich, he kicked his horse and galloped ahead.

"Go with him, Charl," Catherine told her brother. "I shall be there soon, and he may need your support."

When she and Phillip arrived half an hour later, the stableboy was still cooling the two horses. Joseph helped Catherine dismount, but Phillip stayed in the saddle. "Shall I see you in, or would it be best that I not intrude?"

"Oh, please come in." The thought of his riding off was suddenly more than she could bear. She looked toward the doctor's black carriage waiting by the house. "I don't know what we may find inside. I should be grateful for your support."

And having him beside her did make walking into the unknown easier. The house was ominously quiet. Catherine paused at the foot of the stairs.

"Ned is upstairs." Charl's voice from the parlor startled her. "Is—is she—?"

"Alive. But very weak. She lost much blood."

"The babe?"

Charl shook his head, and Catherine nodded in reply; she feared it would be so.

91

"Thank God Durial's alive. I dreaded the worst." She turned to Phillip. "I must go up to her."

He nodded.

Audrey, hovering outside her mistress' door in case she should be wanted, ushered Catherine into the dimly lit room, where the physician was thoroughly in charge, as he addressed Durial, "You've had a very narrow escape, and you are not to stir from that bed for a fortnight. Do I make myself clear? I shall instruct your cook in making a restorative elixir from the juice of red meat, to be taken morning and night without fail. And I shall call again in the morning."

"Is he just now come?" Catherine whispered to her sister Elizabeth.

"No, no. He sat with her all night, then came back this afternoon. We despaired of losing her."

"What happened?"

"She fell. It was the spring cleaning and she *would* take a hand in turning out the linen closets." Elizabeth moved to the door to see the doctor out, leaving Ned and Catherine alone with the patient.

"Durial, dear, we are so sorry." Catherine moved closer to the bed and received a weak smile from her sister-in-law.

Even in the dim room, Durial's pallor was frightful. She was whiter than her linen sheets, and seemed shrunken into her pillows. "My husband, I am so sorry. If only I hadn't been so headstrong and houseproud. Now I'll never have aught to give you but a clean house."

Ned moved to take her hand in both of his. "No, no, my dear. There shall be others."

Durial moved her head from side to side, slowly as if the movement cost her great effort. "No, Dr. Eltham says there shall be no more."

Edward turned his head so that his wife couldn't see the pain that news gave him, but Catherine saw. After a moment he turned back. "But I shall have your precious self, Durial. Now rest and fret not."

Durial relaxed at his words and closed her eyes. "I shall sit with her," Ned said. "You get some rest, Catherine."

Catherine realized she was still wearing her mud-stained traveling cloak and half-boots, so she went to her room and washed before returning downstairs. The parlor seemed unaccountably chill and empty. "Where's Phillip?" she asked Charl.

"I tried to persuade him to sup with us, but he seemed to think his presence would be an intrusion."

The room no longer seemed merely empty to her—it was desolate.

The room Phillip entered was equally desolate. For the first time, he saw it in its emptiness and shabbiness. Its bleakness brought to mind winter evenings when Matron would send her charges out to take the air after classes. The other children would join in rolling hoops or a noisy game of tutball. But Phillip preferred to stay to himself, breaking up the ice from the puddles on the north side of the building with a stick. What began as a simple time-filler became something of a challenge, and he worked hard to keep ahead of the refreezing.

But he had never learned how to chip at the emotional freeze inside. Keeping to himself had always seemed such a good answer to his fear of abandonment—if there was no one else in his life, if his relationship to God was the only one he relied on, there could be no one to leave him. But these past weeks with the Perronets—with Catherine especially—had produced a hairline crack in the ice. He now wondered whether the infraction should be encouraged.

In not letting others get to know the man inside, he had not gotten very well acquainted with himself—with that emotional, feeling part he had always kept so tightly controlled. Could he be more truly open to God if he were to be more open to those around him? He shivered at the thought of becoming transparent and vulnerable, of being hurt once more, as he had been at Midhurst and then over Sally Gwynne.

Phillip encouraged the uncooperative flame in his fireplace, ate the soup and brown bread Mrs. Watson provided, and turned to his bed, just as he had to his iron cot at the orphan asylum. It had been the last in the row and he found lying with his back to the room was as good as being alone. But now there was no need for that device to achieve solitude.

The next morning Phillip went to the Foundery customhouse to inquire of William Briggs, John Wesley's secretary, if there was any mail for him, or further itineracy assignments. He was surprised to find Elizabeth Perronet also in the office. "I have taken to helping Mr. Briggs with some of his correspondence when I can be spared at home," she explained with a hint of a blush.

"And how is Mrs. Edward Perronet this morning?"

"Her sleep was much disturbed. Doctor Eltham was there when I left. But Ned insisted I should come assist here while Catherine teaches her class. Ned won't leave Durial. I fear he blames himself much for being away when the accident occurred."

"It is said by many that itinerant preachers should not be wed," Phillip nodded.

"Here is a letter come for you last week." Briggs handed the wax-sealed paper to Phillip. "And you will preach the evening service tonight?"

"I'll be happy to. Thank you, William. I hope to hear of your sister-in-law's speedy recovery, Miss Perronet." Phillip took his leave.

In the courtyard he perused his letter. It was from his old friend George Whitefield.

the 9 of 4ʳ, Glous.

My dear Phillip,

As I wish to inform my friends at the Foundery of my recent return from America and report on my work there, but am not assured of my welcome in the Society, nor of my desire to be so, I shall communicate with one whom I have always known to be unfailing in his generosity and fair in his judgment, that he might advise me. I have heard the most disturbing reports while abroad. Can it be that John Wesley preaches universal redemption? That cannot be consistent with the scriptural doctrine of election. Can Wesley have strayed so far?

Although my heart aches to hear that the work may have fallen astray, (although I am assured that that most excellent lady, the Countess of Huntingdon, continues faithful in the doctrines of Calvin) the work in America progresses apace. I had great success in Philadelphia in raising money for my school and orphanage in Georgia which I feel is the heart of my work. I employed that most excellent American, Benjamin Franklin, as a printer, who after my sermon confessed he had been determined to give nothing, since I refused to locate the orphan house at Philadelphia. But upon hearing me preach, he said he began to soften and concluded to give copper. "Another stroke decided me to give silver," he said. And at the finish he emptied his pocket into the collector's dish, gold and all. I should most heartily like to build a school for negroes in Philadelphia.

Dr. Franklin said it was wonderful to see the change soon made in the manners of their inhabitants after my revival services.

I met only one case of rudeness—and that from a nonepiscopal divine. "I am sorry to see you here," he said.

"So is the devil," I replied.

And the Lord continues faithful in that part of the country which they call New England, where my friend Jonathan Edwards is one of the few truly awakened preachers. I am persuaded that there, as in England, the generality of preachers talk of an unknown and unfelt Christ. The reason why congregations have been dead is because they have dead men preaching to them. How can dead men beget living children?

And I thank God, the Harvard Awakening continues, where, to the consternation of much of its faculty, I preached against the liberalism which is making its way into that formerly excellent institution for ordinands. I was told subsequently that the students now are full of God.

Advise me how I shall go on, as regards our friends, and I shall remain,

Yr ever affect,
George Whitefield

His mind on the letter and how he might best advise his friend and hope to heal the rift between these strong leaders of the Methodist party, Phillip went on into the Foundery and back to the book room where the newly arrived printing of Charles Wesley's hymns was causing much interest. Then he realized, to his consternation, he was simply wandering around without purpose, and took himself to his room to prepare for the evening service.

Several hundred ardent voices sang at the leading of a society worker who opened the service that evening. Phillip followed the words of the song with his mouth, but his heart missed his musical companions of the circuit trip.

> Sinners Jesus will receive,
> Sound this word of grace to all
> Who the heavenly pathway leave,
> All who linger, all who fall.

95

Sing it o'er and o'er again,
Christ receiveth sinful men.
Make the message clear and plain:
Christ receiveth sinful men.

His sermon followed the outline of the song,

Come, and He will give you rest.
Trust Him, for His Word is plain.
He will take the sinfulest;
Christ receiveth sinful men.

And at the close of the service, it was apparent that Christ was ready also to receive sinful women, as a wretched-looking female waited at the back of the chapel to speak to him.

"You would have words with me, Sister?" He hoped to make his voice kind to calm the fear in her eyes.

She pushed a scraggle of red hair into her cap with a roughened hand. "Ah, Sir. I was accidentally passing the door, and 'earing the voice of someone preaching, I did what I 'ave never been in the 'abit of doing. I come in."

"You were right to do so. You are most welcome."

"I 'eard you say that Jesus Christ was so willing to receive sinners that 'e made no objection to receiving the devil's castaways. Now, Sir, I am cast down so low that I was returning from seeking work in a bagnio when I passed your door."

"You had gone to sell yourself?"

"That was my attempt. I cannot keep food in my children's mouths. I thought this way to provide for them, but they wouldn't 'ave me. To be turned away from a brothel is in truth to be one of the devil's castaways. Do you think, Sir, that Jesus Christ would receive me?"

"There isn't the least doubt of it," Phillip assured her, and called two of the society women to join him in praying for this soul.

When her radiant face gave assurance of a new cleanness inside, Phillip asked where she lived, so Society members might call on her and her children. Here was a convert he could continue to disciple. It wasn't quite the same as having his own parish, but at least he wasn't required to ride away the next morning.

He felt ashamed that even in the rejoicing over the recovery of a lamb that was lost, his joy was less than complete. He wondered why God would have given him this desire for a people to shepherd, if it was to remain unfulfilled.

And then, the unaccustomed amount of self-analysis he had been undergoing lately led him to turn again to the Great Shepherd for guidance. In the empty chapel he knelt. "Lord, make me more useful for Thy service. I have prayed long for a place of service, but first do what Thou wilt to the server."

He went home still fearful of the vulnerability he had opened himself to, but sure he was on the right course.

The next morning, Catherine, back in the schoolroom, looked at the eleven eager faces in front of her. Well, seven eager, two cautious, and two bored. What did she most want to teach them in the short time she had with them? How could she best prepare them for life? How could she most clearly impart the love of God to them?

Three could barely form their letters; six read stumblingly; two were good readers for their age, but might be forced to leave school at any time as Isaiah Smithson had been, and then would have very little exposure to books or to the Scriptures.

As she looked at them, longing to reach their minds and souls, she was filled with a new awareness of her love for them. And then she knew—she must reach them just as God reached her—in the only way that one personality could reach another—with love.

She smiled at them. Eleven chubby, grubby faces smiled back. Well, nine smiled back; two were making faces at each other.

"Good morning, Children. I am most anxious to hear what you have learned in my absence. Hettie, will you please read for us first."

Hettie stood, smoothed her apron, sniffled, and began reading,

> The eye of God is on Them that do ill.
> Go not from me, O God, my God.
> The Lord will help them that cry to Him.
> My Son, if thy Way is bad, see that you mend it.

"Thank you, Hettie." She called on three more to read aloud; then the scraping of little feet on the wooden floor told her it was time to vary the routine. "All right, class. You may turn to the syllabarium and copy out your letters." Primer pages rustled until all the children had before them a page of five columns of two-letter syllables which formed the basis of reading instruction. "And mind that you make your lines straight."

For a few minutes the heads bent over their slates, until a scraping sound told her someone was not applying his slate for its proper function. "William, you will stand in the corner for ten minutes, after which time I expect your writing instrument to work more smoothly." She had no more than dealt with that than a squeal from Kitty, the smallest girl, told her that Joshua had pulled her long braids again. "Joshua, please present yourself."

Discipline was not her favorite part of the job, but she struggled to put to rest her earlier visions of directing the children with nothing but the power of love as she held the birch rod before her. "Hold out your hands."

At such times she had to rely on the wisdom of John Wesley's injunctions to his teachers.

We must, by the grace of God, turn the bias from self-will, pride, anger, revenge, and love for the world, to lowliness, meekness, and the love of God. From the moment we perceive any of those evil roots springing up, it is our business immediately to check their growth, if we cannot root them out. As far as this can be done by mildness, softness, gentleness, certainly it should be done. But sometimes, these methods will not avail, and then we must correct with kind severity. For where tenderness will not remove the fault, he that spareth the rod, spoileth the child. To deny this is to give the lie to the God of truth and to suppose we can govern better than He.

Wesley's words gave her the courage to administer the full number of lashes. "You may take your seat and resume your work, Joshua." The students worked quietly and Catherine prayed for the balance Wesley wanted them to achieve. He warned that some teachers may habitually lean to an extreme of being overly remiss or severe. If they gave children too much of their own will, or needlessly and churlishly restrained them; if they used no punishment at all, or more than was necessary, all their endeavors could be frustrated.

She pulled the watch from her waistband. The hands had barely moved since last she looked. "William, you may take your seat. And

98

now, class, we shall read together. On the next page of your primer, please listen carefully and pronounce each word as I do."

Durial continued weak, mourning the loss of their child, and Ned stayed close to her side. Phillip departed for a tour of Gloucestershire, and Catherine's students droned on. Duty and routine took over. Each morning brought the splash of cold water in her basin, the rumble of carriages on dry rocks, the scratch of styluses on slates. The Foundery looked as grim to her as when it was used only for metal forging.

Where were the birdsongs? Where were the roses? The scent of new mown hay and the freshness after rain?

"Art Thou there, my God? Dost Thou care? Art Thou still the loving Person who touched my heart and changed my life? Or hast Thou too become only Duty and Routine?"

And in the stillness of her aching heart the answer came, "As I have been, so shall I be." God had promised help for the dry, dull times too, and so she must claim it and simply go on. She looked at her students.

"You may read, Joshua."

"Yes, Miss Perronet. 'Christ is the Truth. Christ is the Light. Christ is the way. Christ is my life. . .' "

At the end of two weeks, a feeble Durial was allowed from her bed for a short time. Ned carried her to a lounge chair in the garden and tucked robes securely around her. Catherine was reading aloud to her sister-in-law from the *Meditations* of John Donne when they heard the clatter of horses' hooves on the driveway. For an instant Catherine's heart leapt—could it be their friend had returned early from Gloucester? She had refused to dwell on the thought, even to admit it to her mind; but in the furthest recess of her heart she knew much of the dryness of the past weeks could be laid to Phillip's absence.

But the newcomer, although clad in the familiar black of the clergyman, was not her Phillip but their brother Charl, just returned from a circuit to the north where he had been in company with Charles Wesley.

"Did you meet with success, Brother?" Catherine asked as soon as the commonplaces of greeting were accomplished.

99

Charl removed his tricorn and ran his fingers through his hair. "I have never met with greater discord."

"O Charl, were you treated rudely by the mob?" Durial asked with quick concern.

"No, no. We met little rowdyism. I speak of the Societies—of the preachers to be exact."

"Discord among the preachers?" Catherine couldn't credit her ears.

"First, there was the matter of James Wheatley—who was accused of embracing the doctrine of polygamy and, we were told, scandalized the Society by practicing it openly."

"Charl, was there any truth to such an accusation?"

"At the direction of John Wesley, his brother and I immediately set up an inquiry into the matter." Charl shook his head. "There was no polygamy, but that would perhaps have been an easier problem to deal with. I heard Wheatly preach with my own ears. I cannot say whether he preached false doctrine or true, or any doctrine at all, but pure unmixed nonsense. Not one sentence did he utter that could do the least good to any soul.

"And there lies the weakest point of our Methodist system of preaching. The majority of those who fill the pulpits are working men who have abandoned their trade to follow what they believe to be their vocation, but without education or preparation or support, except from family or Society."

"What is to be done?" Catherine asked.

"Charles Wesley has declared that every preacher must work at his own trade or business during the week, preparing his sermons as he finds time, and delivering them on Sundays in the neighboring chapels. This way they will at least not lose insight into the standpoint of the common man."

"Well, then, it seems the matter has been taken in hand."

"Yes, but that was not all. We encountered amongst the more prominent of the preachers a spirit of disloyalty to the Church of England which horrified Charles, whose allegiance for the Anglican faith knows no bounds."

"O Charl, not more separatism talk?"

"Of a truth, the remedy is simple, and more and more of our harassed preachers are availing themselves of it. For the sum of sixpence they are furnished with a license which puts them under the protection of the law. Once they are recognized as 'protestant dissenters,' they are no longer at the mercy of the mob. And a similar license will protect their meetinghouses from wreckers and incendiaries. We are beating our heads against the wall in refusing this way."

"But, to leave the church. . ." Catherine shared much of the horror of the idea that her mother had expressed at Shoreham.

Charl laughed. "Cath, you sound like Charles Wesley who said he should rather see his brother in his grave than a dissenter. But it will come to it in time."

Ned then joined them to hear of his brother's journey. But first he took Durial back to her room, and Catherine was left alone in the garden. . . . Alone to consider this further unhappy news. Dissention and faulty standards among the Society preachers, widespread agitation for separatism. What were the answers? Everywhere around her she saw things that were not for the best, in what had been this best of all possible worlds. And Catherine felt afraid. She had conquered her fear of horses, that childhood anxiety that had gripped her so long. But this new fear was much worse— fear of the future was like walking down a long, dark tunnel without a candle. Without assurance of God's guidance, she could feel no assurance of His caring. If no caring, did He then truly provide salvation?

No! She put the question aside as one that came directly from the enemy. She would not doubt that. She would choose to believe, no matter how little she felt the closeness of the Saviour.

And with that determination came the knowledge of what she would do. There was one place she had always felt closer to God than any other. She would go for a walk in the woods.

She ran to her room for her half-boots and a shawl and then, telling Audrey where she was going, she hurried out again into the day which seemed suddenly brighter. Once in the woods there was no possibility of doubting the personal love of a God who created such a world. There was a beauty in the world, a greenness of trees, a trill of birdsong. And her spirits rose higher, as if the trees that shut the world from view behind her shut out the problems too. In the woods were no rowdy crowds, no dissenting preachers, no disobedient schoolchildren, no poverty-stricken families, no disappointed loves. Here there was a coloring of flowers, a sparkle of water, a warmth of the sun.

And inside Catherine, as she responded to all around her, at least

101

for the moment, there were no doubts or fears or anxieties. She knew they would return later when she returned to the real world, but for this brief interval there was now inside her a gurgle of laughter, a prayer of thankfulness, a shout of hosannah.

Had anyone been watching her, however, they would have had no idea this was going on inside the outwardly composed young woman who walked down the wooded path stopping occasionally to pick a specimen for her wildflower press. An especially lovely hawthorn tree brought back to mind the Maying she and her companions had watched on the Kentish village green. She decided to collect a sprig of hawthorn for her book.

The hawthorn branch was just beyond her reach. She stretched her hand to the delicate cluster of berries that would soon turn red, but even standing on her tiptoes they eluded her grasp. Then a gentle breeze, just a small stirring of the air, brought the branch into her hands.

She picked it gladly, freely, as it had been given to her, and savored its beauty in joy. And with that action, a new understanding broke upon her. She had thought she must reach God's will, and had strained her arms and stood on tiptoe to grasp it. But the truth was that He reached down to her. Just as the heaven-sent breeze had placed the hawthorn berries in her hand, so God, in His reaching down to her, had placed and would place all good things in her life, according to His perfect way.

The shadows were falling long across the path. It was time to return. With only the slightest reluctance, she turned her steps back to the world with its challenges and opportunities. "Help me to view them as such, my God, rather than as burdens. Help me, I ask, to serve Thee more gladly. As gladly as Thou gavest me the hawthorn blossom."

At first the faint calling of her name sounded as a rustling in the trees, coming so immediately after her prayer that it seemed as if the voice of God were calling her. And then she thought she had imagined it, recalling her childhood experience when her brother's voice had come to the little girl lost in the woods. But on the fourth call, she knew it was not the wind, not her Creator, nor her imagination. It was a very human male voice. And on the fifth call, she identified the caller. With a cry of gladness, she turned and ran up the path to Phillip.

· 8 ·

PHILLIP STOOD ON THE PATH in a shaft of late afternoon sunlight. For a moment Catherine felt as if she were seeing him for the first time—his striking height, his endearing thinness, his fleeting smile. During the past two weeks she had thought of him with confused emotions, because she hadn't the slightest idea of whether he was thinking of her at all. Indeed, it was impossible ever to guess what he thought, much less what he felt. And now, except for a light in his blue eyes that she hoped she wasn't imagining, his chiseled features were a perfect mask—a barrier between the man inside and the world outside.

Catherine had become part of his outside world; would she ever get inside, behind the mask? She would like to have thrown her arms around him in welcome; but instead, offered him a composed smile. "How pleased I am that you are returned. Tell me about your journey."

They walked up the path toward the house together, Phillip giving her an account of calling on his friend George Whitefield. "He was desperately ill on his voyage from America, but is recovering. He hopes to accompany Lady Huntingdon to London in a few days."

"And what of your services? Had you success?"

"Yes, but the most remarkable victory over Satan was scored before I left the Foundery." Now, as he talked about his work, the stiffness fell away and he talked with animation. "Have you heard of the conversion of Mrs. Smithson? The night before I left, she wandered in off the street while I was preaching—"

103

"Smithson?"

"Yes. I instructed the sisters to call on her. Do you know if any have? Her tale was absolutely remarkable. She was returning from a bagnio where she had sought to sell herself for the sake of buying bread for her children—"

"Had she red hair?"

"It seems so, if I recall—"

"O Phillip," Catherine so forgot herself as to take his arm. "It must be the same. Isaiah Smithson was my pupil, but he had to quit and go to sweeping when his father lost his job. And you say she found the Lord?"

"Indeed, it was a remarkable conversion. She seemed truly a new person."

"Phillip, we must help that family. Do you think the Society might—?"

"Lend to an unemployed man whose children sweep? I believe the Society lending policies to be sounder than that. The Society will lend up to twenty shillings, but the sum must be repaid within three months. It seems most unlikely Smithson could meet those terms."

"But we must do something."

"Indeed we must. Will you call on her with me?"

Catherine readily agreed and they continued on up the path, talking of their work. And Catherine saw no reason to let go of the arm she held.

And the following day Catherine clung to the same arm, as protection from the squalor around her. Chitty Lane off Tottenham Court Road was a row of dilapidated houses that had been turned into one-room dwellings. That they were also warrens of disease showed in the pockmarked faces and emaciated limbs of the children playing in the gutters that obviously were disposal systems for all manner of waste.

"Catherine, I should not have asked you to accompany me. I had no idea—" Phillip began.

"I believe we had this conversation once before, Sir. Surely this is what our Lord had in mind when He reminded us, 'As ye have done it unto the least of these.'"

It seemed impossible to Catherine that such a pocket of misery could exist in the very center of London, almost equidistant between the purity of the Foundery and Aldersgate Street to the east, and the elegance of Mayfair and Park Lane to the west. She turned her eyes away from the sight of a scraggly dog shaking a rat to death, and resisted the impulse to put her hand over her nose.

An urchin directed them down a mud path to an unpainted door hanging crooked on its hinges, then held out his filthy hand for a farthing. It wasn't the dirt on the hand that shocked Catherine, but rather the running sore on his inflamed palm. "Phillip, if that isn't treated, he'll lose his hand."

The stench from the street followed them into the Smithson home where, at least, there was some semblance of order, some attempt to keep the filth at bay with sweeping and scrubbing. With a toddler clinging to her skirt, Elmira Smithson was at work over a stack of linen which she was ironing with alternating flatirons kept hot on the hearth.

Elmira's greeting seemed cheerful beyond all possibility of her circumstances. "The good Jesus you told us about 'asn't left me for one minute," she assured Phillip. "And the Methody sisters brung two loads o' wash. More'n I've 'ad in as many weeks afore."

But her accounting of her blessings was interrupted by a fretful cry from a pallet in a dark corner of the room.

"Are you awake, Isey? We've visitors."

"Miss Perronet!" The fussy voice changed to a whoop of joy.

"Isaiah! I didn't see you there. Are you ill?"

"'s me feet. I got stuck an' the sweep built a fire under me. I wasn't a'feared, t'weren't that. I were stuck."

The sight of Isaiah's badly blistered feet brought tears to Catherine's eyes. His mother attempted to soothe the fever in her son's feet with cool rags. "Have you no salve?" Catherine asked.

Elmira shook her head.

"I shall bring you some first thing in the morning," Catherine promised. "Now, young man, where is the primer I loaned you? Let us see if you have remembered what I labored so hard to teach you."

Isaiah produced the book from under his pallet, in much better condition than Catherine had dared hope for, and they spent half an hour reviewing the answers to the picture catechism, while Phillip instructed Mrs. Smithson from the Bible.

"And what of your husband? Has he found work?" Phillip asked as they prepared to take their leave.

"Da's in the Fleet," Isaiah said, before his mother could answer.

"The Fleet?" Catherine couldn't have kept the horror out of her voice if she'd tried. The Fleet was the largest of London's debtor's prisons, notorious for its dirt, debauchery, and harsh treatment of prisoners—and for the hopelessness of gaining release.

"'e owed Mr. Pinchbeck two quid. When 'e couldn't pay, ol' Pinchy swore out a complaint, swore 'e owed 'im twenty. 'Course they would a taken 'im for the two just the same. Tha's why I went to the bagnio, it's the only place I could think of to earn that kinda money. But they didn't even want laundry done by the loiks of me—let alone any other service."

"For twenty pounds he could be freed?" Phillip asked.

Mrs. Smithson shook her head. "There's the garnish for the jailer and the warden and the guard. Upwards of fifty quid, I should think."

"Fifty pounds!" Catherine was thunderstruck. She knew the graft and corruption in the prison system was unconscionable, but she had no idea of its magnitude. Fifty pounds amounted to the yearly salary of a well-to-do man. It was far beyond anything Smithson or any of his family could hope to raise. Even Catherine, who would gladly have paid his release, couldn't imagine where such a sum could be found.

The toddler began to whimper for some of the thin gruel heating on the hearth beside the flatirons. Catherine was glad that she had brought a basket of bread. Before she and Phillip left, they prayed with the family in a small circle around Isaiah's mat. "I will return with medicine for your feet, Isaiah," Catherine promised from the doorway.

"You must not come here alone," Phillip told her sternly when they were back on their way to the Foundery. "It's not safe. I shall accompany you tomorrow."

And he did, as soon as her class was dismissed the next day. And the next as well. Catherine was pleased that Isaiah's blisters were responding to the calves' jelly salve, but she feared having him fully recovered so that he would have to go back to sweeping chimneys again. "Phillip, I've been thinking about Isaiah. I can't supply the money to get his father out of prison, but I can spare enough to keep him in the charity school."

"What do you have in mind?"

"I'm not sure yet, something like supplying the family with the amount of food his earnings as a sweep would have equaled, perhaps. If it's done through the Society surely they would accept it."

"That is most generous of you, Catherine. I should like to share the responsibility with you."

"Oh, but, Phillip—forgive me, but you have so little."

"On the contrary, I have so much. A visit such as this makes me ever more conscious of it. Please pardon me if I seem presumptuous when I say that it is my observation that children reared by well-to-do parents accept what comes to them as of right—demand it even. One who has received everything from the goodness of another's openhandedness learns appreciation quickly. And since there is nothing I can do to repay those who gave to me, I must give to others."

Catherine nodded. "The theological implications seem boundless."

"God's grace to us all—unmerited favor, you mean?"

"Yes, and adoption—we are all adopted into God's family and made heirs by His love."

For a moment it seemed to Catherine that Phillip was considering his next movement very carefully. Then, decidedly, for the first time in their acquaintanceship, he offered his arm without her making the first move.

And that small linking action stayed with Catherine throughout the evening. Later that night, when reading in her green vellum volume of John Donne, by the light of a branched candelabra, she came upon his Meditation 17. But she found it impossible to think of mankind in general, as the grave image of Phillip Ferrar was fixed in her mind's eye.

"All mankind is of one author, and is one volume: when one man dies, one chapter is not torn out of the book, but translated into a better language, and every chapter must be so translated . . . No man is an island entire of itself." Ah, here was the part she looked for. Phillip was such a remote island, and she had no barque to reach him. With a sigh she returned to her reading, "If a clod be washed away by the sea, Europe is the less, as well as if a promontory were, as well as if a manor of thy friend's or of thine own were. Any man's death diminishes me. . . ."

"And any child's pain," she added. She wished she could take all the urchins in London under her wing, put salve on their sores, teach them to read. But at least she could minister to the one God had placed directly in her path. Tomorrow she would approach Elmira Smithson on the possibility of Isaiah returning to school.

But the next morning Catherine's day presented a full schedule of duties before she could visit the Smithsons. John Wesley was now returned to London, living in his rooms over the Foundery, and he would be preaching at five o'clock in the morning, which meant Catherine must arrive early to be assured of a good seat.

It had been many weeks since John Wesley had filled his pulpit, and yet when he stood before them, it was as if he had never been away. In spite of his forty-six years, his countenance was fresh, his eyes bright and piercing, and his long hair still a rich auburn. But most compelling was the intelligence, energy, and love he radiated to all around him.

After greeting his dear children, he launched quickly into his sermon on Matthew 25:43, "I was sick and in prison and ye visited Me not." And he exhorted his hearers on the importance of not failing in this Christian duty, of not being remiss in this opportunity to show Christian love. "Charity, or love—as I wish it had been rendered throughout Scripture—is love for our neighbor, as Christ hath loved us; it is patient towards all men; it suffers all the weaknesses, ignorance, errors, infirmities, all the forwardness and littleness of faith of the children of God; all the malice and wickedness of the children of the world. And it suffers all this, not only for a time, for a short season, but to the end, still feeding our enemy when he hungers; if he thirst, still giving him drink; thus continually heaping coals of fire—of melting love—upon his head."

Wesley continued, speaking more specifically about prison visitation, and gradually Catherine became sensible of her own negligence. Never had she visited a prisoner. She didn't even know how to go about it.

And then Wesley concluded the service by introducing Sarah Peters who had come to the Foundery looking for volunteers to visit prisons. "This very week in the Fleet," Miss Peters told the congregation, "there are ten malefactors under sentence of death who would be glad of any friends who could go and pray with them."

Quailing inwardly at what she knew she should be required to face, Catherine joined the band of workers around Sarah Peters at the side of the altar after the service. "I shall go with you," Catherine pledged.

She was still shaking inwardly when she turned to leave and saw Phillip among the volunteers. Then she knew she could do it.

Even with the support of Phillip, her Headmaster Silas Told, and two other society members, however, Catherine could not avoid second thoughts that afternoon, when they met Sarah Peters outside the Fleet.

"There are three large wards on the common side," Miss Peters explained. "Here the prisoners are obliged to lie on the floor if they cannot furnish themselves with bedding—this is hired out at a cost of a shilling per week. There are also two smaller wards, including an exceedingly noisome one for women. A number of rooms on the master's side are let out at indefinite charges to occupants who can pay the warden. In some rooms persons who are sick of different distempers are obliged to lie together or on the floor and must pay two shillings ten pence per week for such lodging. But," she hastened to add, "you may be assured we shall in no wise go near cases of small-pox or similar contagion."

As Miss Peters turned to lead the way to the prison gate, Silas Told asked a question, "I have been given to understand that even prisoners for debt must pay garnish to the jailers."

"Yes, that is true. James Oglethorpe who heads a reform committee has made two reports to Parliament on these abuses. We still hope for amelioration. But at present, when taken into custody and sent to the Fleet, every prisoner is expected to pay a total of five pounds, sixteen shillings and four pence in fees. This is divided between the warden, the tipstaff, and the clerk of the judge who ordered the committal."

"But what if they can't pay?" Catherine could think only of Mrs. Smithson's happiness over being given a pitiful pile of laundry whereby to earn a few shillings.

"When the miserable wretch has worn out the charity of his friends, and consumed the money which he has raised upon the sale of his clothes and bedding, and has eaten his last allowance of provisions, he soon grows weak for want of food, with the symptoms of a hectic fever. When he is no longer able to stand, if he can raise three pence to pay the fee of the common nurse of the prison, he obtains the liberty of being carried into the sick ward and lingers on for a month or two on charity rations, and then dies."

"But can nothing be done about it?"

"Oglethorpe's Committee is striving with petitions to Parliament and there is hope of Parliament passing ameliorating legislation. But in the meantime, it seems most fit that we should strive for the souls of these unhappy prisoners. There is little we can do for them here but prepare them for a better world to come. Let us proceed."

Sarah Peters, a seasoned warrior in this arena of graft and corruption, approached the Ordinary, a Mr. Taylor who, but for the fact that he stood without the walls, looked far meaner and more disreputable than any of his prisoners. "You shall not obstruct our entrance today, Mr. Taylor. The God of all compassion shall make an entrance for us so that our acts of compassion and mercy may continue." As she accompanied her brave words with the clink of bribe money, the group was allowed to pass.

Catherine thought she was prepared for the fetid air and squalid, verminous surroundings. But as the great iron bar clanked into place across the heavy oak door behind them, and she knew herself locked inside with desperate murderers and felons as well as with the malignant diseases that ravaged the rag-covered bodies she saw on every side of her, she was gripped with panic.

"You needn't do this, Catherine. Shall I take you home?" With the sound of Phillip's voice, the terror subsided.

"I can do it, Phillip. But stay by me."

He ducked his head in a nod of assurance and she was almost sure she saw a flicker of an encouraging smile cross his face. It was for Catherine as if a brilliant light filled the murky room.

But she had no leisure to consider her own feelings, as the determined Miss Peters shepherded their small party forward to the cell of a prisoner named Lancaster. The turnkey opened the barred door, then closed it behind them.

Sarah encouraged Lancaster to tell his story. He was very young, just above twenty, Catherine judged, yet he told of having lived a life of great wickedness, including having robbed the Foundery of all its brass and candlesticks. "But shortly I shall be with Jesus in Paradise. This morning, about five o'clock, the Sun of Righteousness arose in my dark cell, and I am now so full of God and heaven that I am like a barrel of new wine ready to burst for vent."

The visitors joined him in praising God, and Lancaster gave praise for Miss Peters and her workers who had shown him the way to the light he found.

They visited another cell where six prisoners, all under sentence of death, seemed assured of their acceptance by the Saviour. The workers were about to leave when another prisoner, having bribed the turnkey, entered the cell. His sullen countenance, though, clearly showed he had not come to praise God with them. "Come to scoff at us, are ye? Come to turn us into milksops 'afore we face the hangman? I'll none of your pap!" And his words became abusive.

Phillip stepped forward and in the softest of voices, addressed the man. "My friend, let us tell you what we have come to tell any who will hear."

The prisoner continued to mutter, but seemed less violent, so Phillip continued. "We have come to invite you to the Lord Jesus. To invite you to come as a lost and undone sinner, because Jesus is the sinner's only friend. Jesus, the King of heaven, laid down His life for the chief of sinners, and He died for you too."

As Phillip spoke, the man's countenance softened and his behavior became calm. But there was time for no more as the iron door clanked open and the warden stood before them, filling the passage with his straddle-legged stance, his size increased by the heavy boots and leather jerkin he wore and the black, greasy hair which fell to his shoulders. His hand on his sword hilt, he growled, "The report has been made and the dead warrant just come down. Four of you are ordered for execution. Look to your souls."

As the visitors were ushered from the cell, Sarah Peters assured the condemned men she would return to see them again before they departed this life.

They were almost to the outer door, passing the largest and, therefore, dirtiest and noisiest of the common cells, when Catherine recognized a woman in the corridor before them. "Elmira, I didn't think to see you here." She hurried to Mrs. Smithson.

"I must come to bring Dick 'is loaf." She held up a small hunk of bread. "Some weeks 'tis all 'e 'as to eat if the rations is withheld."

Catherine dug in the pocket she wore tied under her skirt for a coin with which to bribe the turnkey. "Allow me a few minutes longer with my friend."

He jerked his head in assent.

Phillip joined her, as they stood beside the cell bars with Mrs. Smithson. As unobtrusively as possible she slipped the loaf through to her husband and introduced Catherine and Phillip.

Their reception was less than gracious. "What the devil possesses you, Elmiry? Bringin' canters to see me. I 'ope you've not been among the Methodists! I'd sacrifice what's left of my soul rather than you shall go among those miscreants." He shook his fist

111

through the bars. "You're the ones wot filled Isey's 'ead so full of larnin' 'e ain't no good t' sweep."

Elmira moved the visitors to the other side of the passage. "It's th' gin talkin'. 'e didn't use to drink bad, but there's naught else to do 'ere."

"Gin? But where do they get it?" Catherine asked.

Phillip answered. "What isn't smuggled in under the skirts of female visitors is sold right here."

"What? In the gaol?"

"I have read some of the accounts of Oglethorpe's Committee. Upwards of thirty gin shops operate inside the Fleet alone."

Back in her carriage in the fresh air, Catherine knew that never had the sun shown more golden, the flowers bloomed more brightly, nor the trees waved greener in the breeze. She took in great gulps of air, as if she had been holding her breath the entire time she was behind the high stone walls of the Fleet. "Oh, I don't think I've ever truly appreciated freedom before!"

The men agreed with her, and spoke of their determination to work harder in their own fields—Phillip the preacher, who sought to free people from the prison of sin, and Silas Told the schoolmaster, who fought the prison of ignorance. But the metaphor Catherine was living in was the sunshine and the light that had dawned in her world in the darkness of the prison. And that light was Phillip Ferrar. For weeks now he had been central in her thinking—as a dear friend, a special person in the Society work. But now, from the blackness of the Fleet had dawned the light of love.

He had said nothing any gentleman of casual acquaintance might not have said, he had not even touched her, but the simple fact of his presence had been all.

And as she tried to make sense of this, to understand what it would mean in the days ahead, the darkness of the prison experience offered another metaphor. She recognized the inability to see into the future as a kind of blindness. "We see through a glass darkly," as the Scripture said. But now she realized that God had so ordained this in order to develop faith—that one must rely on the heavenly guide as a blind man relies on an earthly guide. But someday it would all be known and all knowledge would be as clear as knowledge of the past now was. Clearer, really, because His perfect light would illumine the whole.

112

She shuddered at the thought of what life without God would be like—like one physically blind walking without a guide. She had experienced a little of that in the days after her crushing disappointment, when she had lost faith in God's guidance. She had been blind, and in a way, she still was. She had no more ability to see the future than before, but she did have faith in her Guide.

· 9 ·

CATHERINE HOPED THAT THE TALL, quiet man on the carriage seat beside her would have a place in that future. The thought of his being taken from her as Charles Wesley had been was more than she could bear.

"Shall you mind that very much?"

Phillip's words so nearly echoing those in her head made Catherine jump. "I beg your pardon. What did you say?"

"I said I have been commanded to bring you and Edward to Lady Huntingdon's drawing room to hear Whitefield preach tomorrow afternoon." He turned his head away from Silas Told who was now reading beside him, and spoke quietly. "Charles and Sally Wesley shall be there. I thought you would want to know."

"You are thoughtful to warn me, but I shall be fine. And you?"

For a moment he looked puzzled, then the level blue eyes so close to hers cleared. "Absolutely fine."

The next day gathering storm clouds darkened patches of London's sky as Catherine and Edward Perronet and Phillip Ferrar set out from the Foundery for Park Lane. It was the first time the three of them had traveled together since their circuit ride and almost the first time Edward had been abroad since Durial's desperate illness. So, whatever the clouds might do to the sky, the renewal of old times and the strong sense of companionship in the carriage could not be dimmed.

The crush of coaches with armorial bearings outside number 14 Park Lane facing on Hyde Park, told the new arrivals that they were hardly alone in their obedience to the Countess' summons. A select circle of aristocratic acquaintances had frequently accompanied the Countess to Whitefield's sermons in London churches years before; but Lady Huntingdon's long retirement from society after her husband's death and her own bouts of illness had prevented any further such activity on her part in the great city until now, when Whitefield's return and the renewal of her energies coincided in perfect timing.

At the top of the pillared portico the door was opened by a liveried butler who announced their arrival, but once into the high-ceilinged, marble-floored reception room, they made no more progress, as the aged widow of the Duke of Marlborough stood in front of them, clasping the hand of her hostess. "My dear Lady Huntingdon, I really do feel so very sensibly all your kindness and attention, that I must accept your very obliging invitation to hear Mr. Whitefield, though I am still suffering from the effects of a severe cold." She waved a white lace handkerchief as supporting evidence.

"My dear Duchess."

The Duchess not only outranked Lady Huntingdon—she was also the only woman Catherine knew of who could outtalk her. "Your concern for my improvement in religious knowledge is very obliging. God knows we all need mending, and none more than myself."

"Won't you come into the drawing room, your Grace?"

The Duchess took two steps at her hostess' bidding, then paused again. "The Duchess of Ancaster, Lady Townshend, and Lady Cobham were exceedingly pleased with many observations in Mr. Whitefield's sermon at St. Sepulchre's Church, which made me lament ever since that I did not hear it, as it might have been the means of doing me some good—for *good,* alas! I do want."

"As we all do, your Grace. And there is the ill-used Lady Anne Frankland." The Countess pointed her fan in the direction of a wan-looking woman. "The poor thing is so unhappy in her new marriage. To think that a great-grandson of Oliver Cromwell could abuse his wife so. Do see if you can comfort her." With that, Lady Huntingdon dispatched her garrulous guest and turned to Catherine. "So you are come. I have been in town these three days. You must call on me more often."

"I should be happy to, my Lady. Of late, I have been much engaged in calling on the sick and imprisoned."

"Yes, indeed. Very worthy work. You must tell me more of it. But we must also carry our message to the wealthy and aristocratic, if the work is to be a lasting one. The influence of money and society is too much overlooked by John Wesley."

The arrival at that moment of two women sumptuously clad in ribbed silk embroidered with silver thread, their skirts spread wide over flattened hoops, proved the success of the Countess' campaign.

"The Dowager Duchess of Buckingham," the butler announced. "And the Duchess of Queensberry."

"Well, Selina, I have brought Eleanor with me to hear your favorite preacher," the Dowager Duchess announced, with a flip of her ivory fan.

The Duchess of Queensberry managed to nod at her introduction, while still keeping her nose in the air. "La, I am exceedingly fatigued. I trust he will not tire me beyond endurance."

Catherine and her escorts started to follow the newcomers up the stairs to the drawing room, but at the entrance of another party the Countess halted them and made her own announcement even before the butler could. "Catherine, this is Sally Wesley; Charles you already know," she dismissed the husband. "You young ladies are to become great friends." And with that decree she waved them up the stairs.

But Catherine could not so easily dispense with the arrival of Charles Wesley. Her first glimpse of the glowing brown eyes, and fair features most frequently described as "angelic" that had so long held preeminence in Catherine's heart and mind, made her catch her breath. But a second, more considered look, told her that the far from classic features of the gaunt man beside Charles had become much dearer to her.

"I am most happy to meet you, Miss Perronet," Sally Wesley acknowledged the introduction, as the ladies led the way up the stairs. "Your brother was so kind in supporting our cause in Garth."

"Yes, Ned has told me of your wedding. I am happy to meet you too." And as she spoke the words, Catherine realized how very much she meant them. Sally was short and vivacious, with dark curls bouncing beneath her lace cap, and snapping dark eyes that made her appear even younger than her twenty-one years. And every time those black eyes fell on her husband of three months, she bespoke how much she loved him.

They barely had time to find seats in the green and rose room

117

when the Countess called on Mr. and Mrs. Charles Wesley to provide music for her guests. Sally, in a flowered dimity dress over a pink petticoat, looked the perfect part of the happy new bride as she seated herself at the harpsichord and filled the room with its delicate music. And then her husband stood by her side, as together they sang,

> Rejoice, the Lord is King; Your Lord and king adore!
> Rejoice, give thanks, and sing and triumph evermore.
> Lift up your heart; lift up your voice!
> Rejoice; again I say, Rejoice!

And it was so obvious that the musicians were rejoicing in their life together, and in the grace they sang of, that the hearts of their hearers were lifted with them. Sunshine streamed through the tall windows of the room as they sang their next song,

> O for a thousand tongues to sing
> My great Redeemer's praise,
> The glories of my God and King,
> The triumphs of His grace!

Catherine's heart could sing along with the musicians—Charles and Sally were so right for each other! After all her struggles over the matter of God's guiding, it was still impossible to know where He was leading her; but that these two were right for each other was indisputable. She must simply trust that God had an equally right answer in store for her life. And seeing that God had led so graciously in the lives of others could help her believe that He would make His way straight before her.

And then George Whitefield stood at the end of the room, beside the east windows. He was of middle height, slender, fair, and good-looking except for a squint in one eye. Nothing about his appearance would predispose his audience to pick out this young man as the one who had brought thousands to Christ on both sides of the Atlantic.

But when he began to speak, they understood. What was remarkable was that he could speak rapidly and yet have every word distinctly heard. "We are all dead in sin and cannot save ourselves. We are saved by the free grace of God, without the assistance of good works which have no share in the matter, though it is impossible for us to have this free grace applied to us without its being followed by good works.

"Good works are, however, the sure tokens of our being born again. By the sin of Adam we are all under sin, and must have been damned but for the free and gracious sufferings of Christ; but though this be our condition, yet everybody that pleases may obtain this free grace by simply praying for it. It is therefore by faith in Christ alone that we are saved, not by our good works."

Clouds alternated with sunshine as Whitefield continued to build the solid doctrinal foundation on which he based every sermon. In a moment when sunbeams and shadows crisscrossed the room, he stretched out his arm at a moving shadow. "See that emblem of human life! It passed for a moment and concealed the brightness of heaven from our view. But it is gone! And where will you be, my hearers, when your lives are passed away like that dark cloud?

"O my dear friends, I see you sitting attentive, with your eyes fixed on this poor, unworthy preacher. In a few days we shall all meet at the Judgment Seat of Christ and every eye shall behold the Judge! With a voice whose call you must abide and answer, He will enquire whether on earth you strove to enter in at the strait gate? Whether you were supremely devoted to God? Whether your hearts were absorbed in Him?"

Now the sun was gone, the room dark, and thunder rumbled in the distance. "My blood runs cold when I think how many of you will seek to enter in and shall not be able. What plea can you make before the Judge of the whole earth?"

The storm was almost overhead. In the eerie light of the thunderclouds, George Whitefield held his arms aloft and cried, "O sinner! By all your hopes of happiness I beseech you to repent. Let not the wrath of God be awakened! Let not the fires of eternity be kindled against you."

Forked lightning streaked past the windows. "See there! It is a glance from the angry eye of Jehovah. Hark—" He lifted his finger and paused. A tremendous crash of thunder shook the room. As it died away the preacher's deep voice spoke from the semidarkness. "It was the voice of the Almighty as He passed by in anger!"

Whitefield covered his face with his hands, fell to his knees in silent prayer while the storm subsided. When the sun shone again in a few minutes the windows reflected a magnificent rainbow. Whitefield rose and pointed at it. "Look upon the rainbow and praise Him who made it. Very beautiful it is in the brightness thereof. It compasseth the heavens about with glory, and the hands of the Most High have bended it."

It was several moments before anyone moved in the room. At last Lord Bolingbroke rose, shook out the lace ruffles beneath the wide cuffs of his green velvet coat, and crossed the room to the speaker. "Sir, I am much moved by your address. Will you call upon me tomorrow morning?"

"I would be much honored, my Lord."

It seemed that Bolingbroke's stamp of approval was what all were waiting for, as now all the guests surged around the speaker. Lord Chesterfield, godfather to the young Earl of Huntingdon, the Countess' son, shook Whitefield's hand. "Sir, I will not tell you what I shall tell others—how I approve of you." He stayed for some time, affably conversing with the preacher.

But the outspoken Dowager Duchess of Buckingham was less enthusiastic as she took leave of her hostess. "I thank your Ladyship for the information concerning the Methodist preacher. But I find his doctrine most repulsive. It's strongly tinctured with impertinence and disrespect toward his superiors."

She turned toward all the room and tapped her walking stick on the parquet floor. "It is monstrous to be told that you have a heart as sinful as the common wretches that crawl upon the earth. I find this highly offensive and insulting. I cannot but wonder that your Ladyship should relish any sentiments so much at variance with high rank and good breeding." With a toss of her head, she exited, the still-fatigued Duchess of Queensberry following in her wake.

As the noble guests made their departure and the room became easier to move about in, Catherine gravitated to Sally Wesley's side, desiring first to compliment her on her excellent musicianship. But they had the opportunity to exchange only a few words before they were joined by the guest of honor himself. "And how is the excellent Mrs. Wesley?" Whitefield asked.

"Very well, Sir, I thank you."

"And how are you getting along in the book I made you a present of?"

"Exceeding well." She turned to Catherine. "Mr. Whitefield

made me a wedding present of William Law's *A Serious Call to a Devout and Holy Life*."

"It is a gift I never tire of giving to others, for I never forget the great longing I had to possess a copy." Catherine was especially interested in Whitefield's words, as she recalled Phillip having told her that the book and its author had a great influence on his life. "I was just leaving for my first term at Oxford," Whitefield continued, "when I called on a friend who kept Gloucester's best bookshop. He showed me the brand-new book which had just arrived that day from London, but allowed me to hold it for a few minutes only, lest my grubby fingers spoil the calf. In those brief moments, though, I read enough to fire me. I still recall the passage.

> He therefore is the devout man who lives no longer to his own will, or to the sway and spirit of the world, but to the sole will of God; who considers God in everything, who serves God in every thing, who makes all the parts of his common life, parts of piety, by doing everything in the name of God, and under such rules as are comfortable to His glory."

"That precise passage provided the recipe I followed for salvation," Charles Wesley said, as he joined them. "Law was counselor-in-chief to both my brother and myself during the years of our Legal night. We often walked from Oxford to London to talk to him. His book convinced me of the exceeding height and breadth and depth of the love of God. The light flowed in so mightily upon my soul that everything appeared in a new view, and I cried to God for help."

The artist Loggan, who at Tunbridge Wells had declared his desire to hear more of the Countess' doctrine, joined them in company with the poet Lord Lyttelton. "And reading that dissenting fellow's book changed your life? Remarkable!"

"The book and its author. They convinced me of the absolute impossibility of being half a Christian. I determined, through His grace, to be all devoted to God, to give Him my soul, my body, and my substance."

"But what did the fellow say to bring on such a determination?" Loggan asked.

Wesley returned Loggan's bow and hastened to answer his question. "With respect to an inward means of atonement, or

121

reconciliation to God, Mr. Law declared his unequivocal belief that through the body and blood of our Lord Jesus Christ alone, and by means of His suffering on the cross solely, mankind can be delivered from a state of sin and misery. That was the good news I had sought for years."

With a deep bow accompanied by a flourish of his green velvet coat skirts, Lord Lyttelton said, "That's William Law, you say? I once took up his book at a friend's house. I was so fascinated I could not go to rest until I had finished it. You can well imagine I was not a little astonished to find that one of the finest books ever written had been penned by a crackbrained enthusiast. Oh," Lord Lyttelton surveyed the circle to whom he spoke, "I daresay, that wasn't very tactful of me, was it?"

Wesley laughed. "Don't give it another thought; if crackbrained were the worst we were ever called, we should be remarkably complimented. But I believe much of Law's greatness lies in the fact that his sensitivity to logic is as marked as his sensitivity to conscience. Many of our number may be crackbrained, but I don't believe the term applicable to Mr. Law."

The poet bowed and the silver thread on his coat shone in the light now streaming in the windows. "Perhaps that is why the book had such a powerful effect upon Dr. Johnson. I recall he told me he had become a sort of lax *talker* against religion, for he did not much *think* against it. He said this lasted till he went to Oxford and there took up Law's *Serious Call*, expecting to find it a dull book as such books generally are. 'But I found Law quite an overmatch for me; and this was the first occasion of my thinking in earnest of religion after I became capable of rational inquiry.' I believe I have his words exactly, as they made a profound impression upon my mind."

The conversation then became general and the Perronet party left a few minutes later, with Sally expressing her warm desire that she and Catherine should meet and visit more during the days she and Charles were to spend in London.

The very next afternoon, just after Catherine had dismissed her students to their noon meal, Sally saw her in the courtyard and called, "Do come up to John's rooms; he has begged that Charles and I make free of them while we're here." Sally led the way to Wesley's apartment and prepared tea for them in the large ivory and blue teapot made especially for John Wesley by Josiah Wedgewood. Catherine read the inscription on the pot,

> Be present at our table, Lord,
> Be here and everywhere ador'd;
> These creatures bless and grant that we
> May feast in paradise with Thee."

Sally poured the tea into little handleless dishes. "Oh, how good it is to be in a well-appointed house. I so long to set up housekeeping."

"Have you and Charles no place of your own?" Catherine tried to keep the surprise out of her voice.

"Alas, no. We have been riding circuit."

"On your honeymoon?" And this time Catherine made no attempt to hide her shock.

"Do not misunderstand. I'm not complaining. I'm most eager to share in my husband's work. And always we have the most sweet fellowship in the sacrament and in prayer. I could ask for nothing more, truly." She paused. "It is just that sometimes the circumstances have been rather, er—uncomfortable."

Such gentle understatement aroused Catherine's sense of humor and soon the tea was cooling in the dishes while the women exchanged stories of their circuit-riding experiences. " . . . and then my mare dropped a shoe, which occasioned so much loss of time that we could not ride across the sands, but were obliged to go round through a miserable road. And then, our guide lost his way, so that we arrived at the ferry too late for the last crossing . . . " Sally paused for a sip of tea while Catherine told of their near-disastrous crossing of the flooded river.

Then Sally took up the conversation. "The next day Charles was preaching to near three thousand when the press-gang came and seized one of the hearers. They even tried to take Charles, but he told them that as a duly ordained minister he was acting under protection of the King's law, and they left him alone."

Catherine then contributed her experience with the military in Canterbury.

"I do not believe Satan likes our work," Sally said. "But a higher One protects us. We were in a Society meeting in a home in Camborne when a member cried out, 'We will not stay here; we will go to Lefroy's house.' That house was in quite a different part of the town, but we all rose up and went, though none of us knew why. Soon after we were gone, a spark fell into a barrel of gunpowder, which was in the next room to the one we had vacated, and blew up the house."

"Such a story builds my faith. I have wrestled long with the matter of God's guidance in our lives."

"And have you reached a conclusion?"

"I am certain He guides . . . if we but have the faith to follow. I think it is now a matter of understanding His perfect timing. Perhaps it is just that I am too impatient," and she spread her hands in a helpless gesture.

Sally laughed, and said, "Oh, how good it is to talk to one who shares my feelings! I have no answers either, but so many questions. And I do know that holding onto the good times—all the times God has answered and fulfilled His promises—has gotten me through the bad times.

"Like the evening Charles was preaching in a barn when he began to sink out of sight before my very eyes. I never knew worse fear. I thought he was to be taken away from me right there. It transpired that the barn had been built on a marsh and the weight of the crowd made the floor sink. No one was hurt, and we continued with a glorious service in the field. That night many even fainted under the sense of Divine love."

Then Sally laughed again and finished her story in a hushed voice, "And that night in the inn, the mattress collapsed right through the bedstead and we were obliged to sleep on the floor." She finished with a blush.

Catherine had promised Durial she would not be late, so with repeated professions of friendship, the women parted, promising to have many more such visits.

But that was not to be; for when Catherine reached Greenwich, she found Durial headachy and fretful, and still struggling to carry on with the housework. For many days Catherine's time was fully consumed and allowed no leisure for anything but duties at school and home. Even her resolution to visit Elmira Smithson had to be postponed.

Phillip, however, was carrying forth his program of prison visitation with success. He had gone back every day since that initial visit to pray with the little band of condemned men. There were now fif-

124

teen who regularly crowded into the murky, fetid room to sit on dirty straw that covered the cold stone floor and listen to the words of comfort Phillip brought them. Lancaster continued to be his strongest support, every day bringing a new prisoner to the group.

But most remarkable of all was Doyle, who had entered spewing curses on that first visit. Following Lancaster's continued witnessing, Doyle had asked forgiveness for his sins and was now a most enthusiastic worker among his fellow prisoners, going from cell to cell, sharing his own clear sense of forgiveness and striving to bring the same to his fellow sufferers.

Today Phillip sat on the straw with the condemned men and listened to Doyle preach. "I say to you, it matters not which side of the walls we be on. It is absolutely impossible to be happy, either in time or eternity, without knowing your sins are forgiven. . . . "

Phillip couldn't help thinking what a shame this man was due to be hanged in two days. If he could have received an education, he would have made a fine preacher. His voice which reverberated so well off the stone walls, could have carried as well in a parish church.

But then, as Phillip rose, and his own voice filled the stone room with prayer, he reflected that the same could be said of himself. He too was preaching in prison when he would sooner be ministering in a church. At the end of his prayer, he looked at the faces around him and had to ask forgiveness that he had complained. For the moment this was his place of ministry, and he would do it to his utmost, with thankfulness to the God who allowed him a place.

He turned to Atkins, a youth of about nineteen. "Are you afraid to die?"

"No, Sir. Really, I am not."

"Wherefore are you not afraid?" Phillip continued the catechism.

"Because I have laid my soul at the feet of Jesus; therefore, I am not afraid to die."

Phillip continued around the room. Next was Gardner, a journeyman carpenter, about fifty, who gave a strong report of what the Lord had done for his soul. And on down the row, to one Thompason, an illiterate young man who, in spite of a severe speech defect, gave assurance that he too was saved from the fear of death, and was perfectly happy in his Saviour.

That evening, Phillip went home knowing that the next night would be his last with those men. Although hardly a humorous situation, he couldn't suppress a small smile at the irony. He had prayed fervently for a congregation he wouldn't have to leave. So he was supplied with a congregation that would be leaving him.

He lit his fireplace, but did not take off his coat. It would be some time yet before the room was comfortably warm, even on a June night. But the flame would be enough to fry a rasher of bacon to accompany his evening tea. Stepping to his cupboard he saw the letter his landlady had laid on his bed.

At first the name Perronet made his breath come in a strange way; but on second look, he saw that the post was from Vincent, not from his daughter. He lit a candle to supplement the dim light from the window and read. The words brought such a surge of hope to his heart he jumped to his feet and circled his small room in five strides before making himself read the letter through a second time.

. . . As the Bishop of Ely is an old friend of mine, I have taken the liberty of writing to him myself to recommend you for this post. I was able to tell him I have personally heard you preach in my own pulpit. Further, with Cambridge in his diocese, he should be well-disposed to your academic credentials.

I wish you well, my Son. May His blessings go with you.

Vincent Perronet

The living at Grantchester was open, and in the gift of the Bishop of Ely. That lovely village on the banks of the Cam, just outside Cambridge, was without a vicar. A vicarage—not just a curacy. It was far more than he had dared pray for.

Phillip's first impulse was to pack clean linen in his bag and set out at once. He smiled for the second time that evening. Such impulsive behavior was unlike him; besides, he could not leave yet. He had a commitment at the Fleet to fulfill first. He cut two slices of bacon from a slab and placed it in a wire rack to cook over the fire. In spite of the excitement in his heart, this night would be spent the same as every other—alone in his room.

But the next night was unlike any other he had experienced. Armed with adequate money for garnishment, Phillip convinced the inner keeper to give the condemned men the opportunity of assembling together in one cell so that they might pass their last hours together in prayer. The men came in quietly and sat on the straw and stone. Nothing in their outward appearance showed that they had but a few hours to live. Phillip began the gathering by reading from the Prayer Book, first the Commination, "Now seeing that all are accursed who do err and go astray from the commandments of God, let us (remembering the dreadful judgment hanging over our heads) return unto our Lord God with all contrition and meekness of heart, bewailing and lamenting our sinful life . . ."

Lancaster led the others with a loud, "Amen."

Then Phillip turned to the Psalm, "Have mercy upon me, O God, after Thy great goodness; according to the multitude of Thy mercies do away mine offenses. Wash me thoroughly from my wickedness; and cleanse me from my sin, for I acknowledge my faults; and my sin is ever before me."

And finally, the prayer, as those who were sitting shifted to their knees: "O Lord, we beseech Thee, mercifully hear our prayers, and spare all those who confess their sins unto Thee; that they, whose consciences by sin are accused, by Thy merciful pardon may be absolved; through Christ our Lord. Amen."

The men then continued in prayer, some extemporaneously, for it seemed that the Lord had opened their mouths and their hearts. Phillip was sure he had never before so truly sensed the reality of God's mercy. Tonight this mercy was enobling these illiterate, condemned prisoners who so wholeheartedly sought it and so fully accepted it.

All too soon the clanking of the iron door brought with it an announcement of the time. The turnkey barked his orders and led the prisoners into the pressyard. But even in the gray of predawn, in the stonewalled yard, with the carts that were to transport them to Tyburn parked by the gate, a solemn joy and peace shone on each countenance. Phillip took Doyle's hand. "My dear Man, how do you find yourself?"

"Find myself! Why truly, Sir, my soul is so filled with light, love, and peace, that I am the same as if I had naught else within me!" He then turned to the jailers in the yard and began telling them of the love of God to him and his assurance of knowing that God for Christ's sake had forgiven all his sins.

But this was cut short, as the jailers began pushing their charges into the carts. Phillip, who had received permission from the warden to accompany the men, was shoved into the first cart with

Doyle and Lancaster as roughly as all the rest. Lancaster sat on his own coffin. Doyle, who could not afford one and so would share a pauper's grave, sat on the rough floor of the tumbril.

The horses started off with a jerk, bouncing the heavy wooden cart on its iron wheels over the rough stone pavement. The procession went down Ludgate Hill and turned into Holborn. Already a crowd had gathered along the street. This was a hanging day and the populace was prepared to enjoy it to the full. Hanging day held the status of a holiday and throughout the metropolis master coachmakers, tailors, shoemakers—any who must deliver orders within a given time—always bore in mind to observe to their customers, "That will be a hanging day and my men will not be at work."

Holborn became Oxford Street, and as the carts approached Tyburn Road the crowds became denser and rowdier.

"Hey, wanta rubber neck, Mate?"

"Swing 'em up 'igh, Charlie, so's they can 'ave a better view!"

"Cooee, they got a parson too! I always knowed they was a thievin' lot!" A tomato squashed through the bars of the cart and red streaks ran down Phillip's sleeve. He suddenly realized that to the observers, he was no different from the prisoners. He felt shame wash over him as he understood that the crowd thought him condemned too.

And then he was ashamed of his shame. Was this not exactly what Christ had suffered for him—to be numbered among the transgressors? And was it not appropriate that he, who but for the mercy of Christ would be condemned eternally for his own sins, should taste just a small portion of what Christ suffered in taking on the sin of others, in identifying with the damned?

The tumbril lurched to a stop. Two carts from Newgate were there ahead of them. A great cheer went up from the crowd as the pealing of church bells, led by those from St. Sepulchre's, announced that the proceedings were to begin. Holidayers passed gin bottles from hand to hand; children clambered atop their parents' shoulders; and the lucky ones with front-row spaces spread picnic baskets on rugs.

And then a louder cheer rose as the first cart opened and the most popular of the condemned, a well-known highwayman called Daring Dirk, stepped out. Highwaymen held the ancient privilege of heading the procession of malefactors, and he was immediately mobbed by spectators striving to obtain a memorial—such as a lock of his hair or a piece of his clothing. With an air of noblesse oblige Dirk pulled bits of lace from his sleeve and buttons from his coat and bestowed them upon the throng.

Jack Ketch, as all public executioners were called after a well-known hangman from the previous century, stepped forward as if to greet the highwayman. But in truth, his hand was not held out to shake, rather to receive his agreed payment from his victim. The larger the bribe, the easier the hangman could make the death, even to pulling on the legs of the victim or to sitting across his shoulders to accelerate strangulation. Dangerous Dirk produced a fat wad; he had no intention of suffering long. Then with a jaunty wave he mounted the scaffold. At the top he turned again and tossed his feathered hat into the crowd with a flourish. The story of his gallant death would be told and retold and his fame as a folk hero was assured.

But in the third tumbril, the mood was not one of such reckless bravado, nor of grim resignation, but rather of quiet rejoicing as Phillip led the men in a hymn.

> Sinners Jesus will receive;
> Sound this word of grace to all
> Who the heavenly pathway leave,
> All who linger, all who fall.
> Sing it o'er and o'er again,
> Christ receiveth sinful men.

The door of the cart opened. Doyle was the first to stand up. Lifting his eyes to heaven, he said with a loud voice so all around could hear, "Lord, didst not Thou die for sinners? Thou didst die for me!" Turning around to the multitude, he prayed extempore. When he was finished, Phillip could not see a dry eye anywhere around him. Then all from the cart went forward together.

Phillip paid Jack Ketch. At the top of the stairs Doyle, Lancaster, Gardner, Thompason turned as one man and cried, "Lord Jesus, receive our spirits!"

· *10* ·

CATHERINE WAS SITTING WITH DURIAL, going over the linen cupboard lists and checking the mending needs when Audrey interrupted with a soft knock. "Mr. Ferrar's below, askin' for the mistress and Miss Perronet. I told 'im Mr. Ned was still on circuit."

"Will you see him, Catherine? I simply must get this chore finished this afternoon." Durial sighed at the mountain of folded linen beside her.

"Gladly." Catherine was out the door before her word was finished.

But at the bottom of the stairs she halted sharply. "Phillip! Are you ill? You look ghastly." She was accustomed to the thinness of his frame and the sharpness of his cheekbones; but the hollowness around his normally bright eyes was alarming. "Audrey, bring a tray of coffee and cold meats to the parlor." She led the way into the sitting room.

"Thank you." Phillip folded his long body into a wing-back chair. "I am not ill, but I have had such an experience. . . . I have just watched four dear friends die," and he told her of the execution.

Catherine poured coffee from the silver pot Audrey set before her on a small table, and considered his account. "Do you not rejoice that their souls are now in heaven?"

"Assuredly I do. I think my grief is more for myself. For them it is a glorious release. I feel bereft. Is that selfish in me?"

If his question had not been so earnest, and at such a sad time, she would have laughed. He was the most unselfish creature she had ever met. "On the contrary, Phillip. It is your great desire to give of

131

yourself in service that causes you grief. Like a mother when her last child marries, you now have no one left to minister to." And with a flash of insight she understood that he was again, but in a different way, suffering the trauma that he had known over the loss of his curacy. Again he had put down roots; and even as shallow as the stone floor of the prison had required those roots to be, the pulling up was painful.

"Phillip," she spoke rapidly in her rush to comfort him, "the Lord will provide a new place of service. He has promised. 'He that walketh in a perfect way, he shall serve Me.' I do believe that, Phillip. He knows your desire. You shall serve Him."

"Thank you, Catherine; I believe it too. And your hopeful words put me in mind of that which I had quite forgotten. I didn't come to mourn with you, but to tell you of the letter I received from your father, and to take my leave."

"Leave?"

"Yes, your father has recommended me to the Bishop of Ely for a living that has come open. I shall leave in the morning for an interview. It is just possible . . . "

"O Phillip! It's more that just possible; it's quite certain!" She jumped to her feet. "Phillip! What a wonderful answer to prayer! Bishop Gooch is an old friend of Father's; I'm certain he will give you a warm interview."

Phillip held up his hand in protest and tried to argue that the matter was by no means certain, but Catherine would not hear of it. She had prayed too long for a place of service for Phillip and had reaffirmed her faith in God's guidance too fully to allow any doubt now.

They talked at length of the vicarage and of Phillip's travel plans. "And when will you return?" Catherine asked.

"If the weather's fine, Cambridge is only three days' ride, then half a day on to Ely. I should be able to accomplish it in just over a week."

"And will you preach on the way?"

"Oh, of course. I haven't thought this through well. Yes, the Cambridge Society has requested a preacher. I shall hold services in Cambridge, Newmarket, Burwell . . . two weeks at least. Will Ned be back by then?"

"I think not. He and Charl have gone clear to Newcastle. But

Phillip, if you are not back by Sunday, you will miss your birthday. I had thought to make you a poppyseed cake."

"My birthday?"

"Yes, don't you remember at Shoreham, when Philothea decreed the second Sunday in Trinity to be your birthday?"

"No, I had entirely forgotten. I shall be sorry to miss the cake."

And that was as personal as his leave-taking was to be—he would miss the cake. The conversation turned briefly back to his prison ministry, with Catherine renewing her vow to aid the Smithson family, and Phillip telling more of Doyle's conversion. In spite of her serene exterior, however, Catherine was troubled inside. She didn't want to talk only of Phillip's work. Did he care for nothing else? No one else? Was his every thought only for those to whom he could minister? As important as his work was, there must be more.

She looked into those steady eyes of his, so revealing and yet so shuttered at the same time. Warm, kind, intelligent eyes that told you nothing about the man behind them, and made no revelation of his emotions.

The fact that she at least partially understood his isolation didn't always make it easy to accept. There were times, like right now, when she wanted to smash the wall he erected around himself so that she could get hold of the real Phillip inside.

There were moments when she wondered if, indeed, he had emotions behind that unrevealing face. But she never wondered for long because, atuned to him as she was, she had learned to read the tiny looks and gestures that gave him away. And she never, not even in her most depressed moments, doubted that, once she reached him, the real Phillip would be worth finding.

And now the tightness around his mouth and the jerky motion with which he placed his tricorn on his head, told her of the importance he placed on this journey.

"God go with you," she called from the doorway, as he mounted Jezreel.

The thought that he was going to interview for a living should have raised Catherine's spirits; but as she turned away from the closed door and crossed the darkened hall, she felt heavyhearted. She searched her mind for a comforting thought, and was horrified at the verse that came to her mind, "And Stephen went out and preached the word of God boldly." No! She would not think about that—about the stones, the mad bulls, the drunken threats Phillip

133

would face. Nor would she think about what preaching in similar circumstances had cost Stephen. That was in God's hands. There was only one thing she could do and that was what she would concentrate on.

Right there in the hall she closed her eyes; and forcing forbidding images away, she deliberately thought about Phillip preaching calmly to the throng, Phillip proclaiming God's love and God's Word, Phillip placing all his faith in the power of God's protection.

She would pray, and continue with her own work. Doing whatever her hand found to do could be a great comfort in times of difficulty. And in Durial's home, there was never any lack of work. Catherine returned to the drawing room to find her sister-in-law hard at work polishing the furniture. "Durial," Catherine protested, "Audrey rubbed the tables with lemon oil not a fortnight ago. Can't you rest?"

Durial ran an impatient hand across her forehead. "With Ned forever away on his preaching trips, someone must keep our home from falling to bits around our ears. The furniture should long ago have been revarnished with alkenet root, rose pink, and linseed oil, but when do you think Ned could have time to see to such as that?"

With a sigh Catherine picked up a rag and the bottle of lemon oil. Monday she would return to her class and would be certain to call on Elmira Smithson.

A few days later when Catherine kept her resolve, the worsening of the Smithson's situation made her almost wish she hadn't called on them. "I ast Dick about lettin' Issay go back to yer school like you said—" Elmira's speech was interrupted by a racking cough that made Catherine put her hands to her own chest in sympathy. "But Dick won't 'ear non o' it. Knew 'e wouldn't—but was good o' you to offer."

Isaiah had returned to sweeping and Elmira was doing a careful job of all the laundry she could take in, even if bending over the tubs of water made her cough worse. Catherine spoke what words of comfort she could, placed two wheaten loaves on the bare table, and gave a boiled sweet to little Susanna before she left.

The days dragged slowly and Catherine was more thankful than ever that she had her faith in God's guidance to cling to. No matter how gray the day, or how dismal the prospects around her appeared, Catherine could say with the psalmist, "As for God, His way is perfect . . . He is a buckler to all those that trust in Him." And then Sally's letter came in the next post.

My Dear Catherine,

How precious my memories of our friendship are to me. What joy to know that one other creature has shared my difficulties and understands my feelings. You will note this letter is sent from Ludlow. I fell ill on the way to Bristol from London, so my dear Charles brought me home to my mother for her excellent nursing while he set about his next preaching tour. My sister Betsy is also a most excellent nurse. Perhaps if I am recovered when Charles returns he might think me strong enough to set up our own home. Write to me of our friends in London. It is beautiful here in Wales, but I miss news of the Society.

Yr Ever faithful friend,
Sally Wesley

The words that fell between the lines of Sally's careful script were the ones that tore at Catherine's heart. Here she was in good health and had only a brother and dear friend to worry about facing the dangers of a circuit. Sally was ill, longing for her own home, missing and fearing for her new husband. Catherine breathed a prayer for her friend and then determined to avoid going the same road herself. No matter how fond her feelings for Phillip, she had no desire to spend her life traveling from one decrepit inn to the next so that a new crowd of ruffians might pitch stones at her husband. Not that Phillip had ever given her the least indication he would make such an offer; but if he did, she knew she must refuse him. Of course, if he found success with the Bishop of Ely . . .

Phillip's great haste to reach the Bishop caused him to plan only one night for revisiting the familiar sights of Cambridge. He tethered Jezreel in St. Andrew's street and, for the first time since his graduation five years before, entered the gates of Emmanuel College. Here he had worked and studied for three years as a sizar, acting as servant first to young Lord Leatham and then to the Hon. Percy Chalmers, noblemen who came to the university to acquire a little civilization and a smattering of classics and mathematics. Since men of independent means who were not destined for the Church or the Bar weren't hindered by any requirement to take examinations or attend classes, Phillip's life had been a constant struggle to please his cavalier masters while maintaining his own academic standards. Examinations were required of one like Phillip who came of the servant class and who would take Holy Orders.

Phillip recalled the nights of study constantly interrupted by demands that he serve liquor, polish boots, and carry notes to ladies. At first he had had only his own determination to carry him through. But then, after acquaintance with William Law's book led him to understand the basis for a devout and holy life, the service ceased to be a yoke and became instead a challenge which he met gladly.

Now he walked across the wide green court toward the colonnade built by Sir Christopher Wren and entered the chapel behind. Emmanuel College, founded in the sixteenth century by Queen Elizabeth's chancellor of the exchequer, had been built on the site of a Dominican friary which was abandoned during the dissolution of church properties by Henry VIII. From the first the college had had a Puritan bias, ties which were strengthened during Cromwell's reign, and which even now, Phillip could sense in the austere white walls, stone floor, and plain glass windows of the chapel. The only contrast came from the well-proportioned carving in the dark wood furnishings.

Phillip left the chapel and walked on beside the herb and rose gardens lining the Elizabethan walls of the court, built largely from the stones of long-crumbled Cambridge Castle. He paused at the doorway of the elegant, unpuritanical Hall and recalled serving his superiors at high table. But for all the nobility that had passed through these doors, the two most famous students had been commoners—William Law and the Puritan cabinet minister, John Harvard, who went to America and founded a college to train clergymen in the colony of Massachusetts.

Phillip smiled as he turned away from Hall. His university years, as his orphanage years, had been marked by his detachment from his fellowmen to the extent that his activities allowed. He had not minded that as a coarsely gowned sizar he held the lowest rank of undergraduate, in the scale topped by the elegantly robed noblemen. They had been years of vast mental and spiritual growth, in the sum, not unhappy to look back upon.

But what Phillip had intended as only a brief walkabout before he settled into a room at The Sun met an abrupt change when he reemerged onto St. Andrew's street and ran almost bodily into a figure from his past. "Thomas Thornton!" Phillip clasped the man's arm as much to steady him from their near collision as in greeting. "Are you still in Cambridge?"

Thornton had been a close friend of Percy Chalmers whom Phillip served at Emmanuel. "Went into the family firm of solicitors in Newmarket. See by your garb you took orders. Seems I recall you had Methody tendencies—didn't become a Jacobite or anything crackbrained, did you?" Thornton looked over his shoulder as if he didn't want to be seen in suspect company should the answer be wrong.

"Oh, I assure you I'm anything but a political rebel. Long Live King George. I *am* with the Methodist Society, however."

"Meeting tonight, but I suppose that's what you're here for."

Phillip assured him he had no idea what he was talking about.

"Big Methody meeting on Christ's Pieces, some Welch fellow, Harris, preaching. Thought I'd look in on the doings. Care to come along?"

Phillip started to refuse. He'd planned on an early evening and riding on at dawn the next morning. But his conscience smote him. In his intense desire to reach Ely, he had forgotten his stated intentions of holding meetings in the area. Certainly he should go with his old acquaintance and lend his support to the preacher.

They arrived at the open green field at the end of Emmanuel Street just as the crowd began singing. It was a new experience for Phillip to stand at the back of such a gathering, and he found the perspective most interesting as he surveyed the farmers and housewives still carrying their baskets of vegetables from the Cambridge market. In spite of a few catcalls, they seemed an unusually peaceable group—until the leader began the third song and complaints began. "What's a' matter—preacher afraid to speak?"

"Yeah, Parson—cat got yer tongue?"

"What is this 'ere? Some 'oity-toity musical society?"

"We want preachin'!"

And then the rumor spread through the crowd—Howell Harris had not arrived as scheduled. It was certain the local vicar would not under any circumstances preach in an open field. Phillip knew what he must do.

137

"Seems I'll have to take leave of your company," he bowed to Thornton. "They need a preacher and that's my calling."

He didn't wait for the startled expression to leave his companion's face. "I daresay, field preaching—?"

As Phillip pushed his way through the throng he breathed a prayer, "O Lord, show me what to say to these people."

The crowd made way for him and he met no obstacle until he reached the wooden platform that the Society had dragged onto the grass to make a speaker's platform. In the very front was a surly young clergyman who would not give way. "My Brother, I have come to offer my services as a preacher, but I see you precede me. Perhaps you would like to address this congregation. I should be happy to be numbered among your hearers," Phillip said.

The cleric gave Phillip a haughty look and stepped aside just enough to allow him to pass. The distressed song leader was more than relieved to introduce the preacher newly arrived from London. Phillip gave only the briefest thought to the tomatoes and peaches he saw in many market baskets before he announced his topic. Arriving as he did without notes or preparation, he had only his Bible with him; but that was enough to carry him through his favorite sermon on 1 John 5:12, "He that hath the Son hath life; and he that hath not the Son of God hath not life."

The crowd was remarkably well-behaved and the few tomatoes and dirt clods that were thrown were poorly aimed. One juicy peach, however, landed squarely on the head of the surly clergyman who was standing so as to block as much of Phillip's access to his audience as possible.

Next morning Phillip put Cambridge and its memories behind him as he set out for Ely. By midday the path across the flat fenland brought him in sight of the cathedral standing on its island like a lighthouse on a hill. Even at this time of day mists from the surrounding waters rose around the building, emphasizing the fact that it was bordered on all sides by wild and treacherous marsh. A hundred years before, Cromwell had completed the plans begun by Charles I to drain the fens and thereby brought hundreds of square miles of land under the plough. So now the fens produced crops of flax, wheat, and hay through which Phillip rode.

For much of the sixteen miles, Phillip meditated on his forthcoming interview and prayed that this would be the answer to his waiting. But then, as Jezreel's hooves clattered over one of the many wooden bridges spanning the drains that crisscrossed the fens, and he saw the eels swimming in the water, his thoughts turned to his surroundings and he gave a smile for the legend which lent the town its name. These eels and all those populating the streams of East Anglia were believed to be the descendants of the monks of the tenth century who had taken wives and were punished by the reformer St. Dunstan, by being turned into eels.

The humor of this bolstered Phillip's flagging spirits, and he sat even taller than usual in the saddle as he rode past the great cathedral and on to the Bishop's Palace. The Bishop's chaplain answered Phillip's knock.

For a moment Phillip couldn't believe what he saw. Just in time he checked his impulse and bestowed a broad smile on the man before him. It was the surly cleric from last night's meeting.

"Phillip Ferrar. I believe My Lord Bishop is expecting me." Phillip offered his letter of introduction from Vincent Perronet.

"Please wait here." The chaplain turned and Phillip noted his hair and clothes were scrubbed clean of any traces of the peaches thrown at the meeting. He ushered Phillip into a richly appointed gallery where he saw a portrait of a dour-looking bishop in a black velvet cape. In contrast to the luxuriousness of the furnishings, the severe austerity of the attitudes around him chilled Phillip. He dared not think what his future held if he met yet another refusal.

The sound of the chaplain's quick step on the polished wooden floor told Phillip he wouldn't have long to wait. "His Lordship will see you now." The chaplain's lips curled in a cross between a smirk and a smile, but his eyes were hard.

The Bishop sat at his desk, light from the leaded window beside him falling on his white hair. A wave of his ringed hand told Phillip to take a seat. The Bishop looked at the papers on his desk and went straight to the heart of the matter.

"You seek appointment to the vicarage of Grantchester. Mr. Perronet is most warm in his support. Why did you leave your curacy in Midhurst?"

The unpleasant must be brought into the open sooner or later. Phillip was glad to have it be sooner. "I was dismissed for teaching Jesus Christ and Him crucified, My Lord."

The ringed hand waved the statement aside. "And what have you been doing since that time?"

"I have been doing itinerant preaching."

"Ah, yes. I have heard of your unseemly enterprise last night. Grantchester is a quiet, well-behaved parrish. I do not believe an enthusiastic vicar would best suit their needs."

The thrust came so rapidly and so quietly that at first Phillip was not aware of the pain from its cut.

"I thank you for the courtesy of your call. But do not let me detain you any longer." Dr. Gooch rose and rang a bell. When the chaplain appeared in the doorway, the Bishop added, "Mr. Flagg will give you a glass of madeira on your way out."

Phillip rose, made a mechanical bow to the Bishop, and left the palace without the support of the offered glass of wine. The complete interview, upon which his entire future hung, had lasted less than five minutes.

As if of their own volition, his feet carried him across the grass to the cathedral. He continued his sleepwalk down the great nave until he stood beneath the glory of the cathedral—one of the wonders of medieval engineering and carpentry—Ely's lantern. Arching his head back, he looked up into the glorious aureola formed from the light shafting downward through the high traceried windows of the octagonal tower. As he looked at the display of pure light which spread from the lantern over the wooden ceiling and throughout the whole church, it seemed that some of that same light touched his soul. The warmth of the light thawed just a drop of all that was frozen within him. But it was enough to allow the Word of God to speak through his numbness, "Cause me to hear Thy lovingkindness . . . for in Thee do I trust; cause me to know the way wherein I should walk; for I lift up my soul unto Thee."

It seemed he had come to the end of the path. But then he looked up into the light and his Guide was there to lead him through the uncharted way. In the great cathedral, Phillip knelt with the light from the magnificent lantern of the tower shining on him like a benediction. And in his pain, he thought of another who had been denied all he had worked for and hoped for, because he did what he believed to be right. Perhaps it was his recent visit to Emmanuel that brought William Law so strongly to his mind as he prayed. Soon Phillip realized he was no longer praying, but instead meditating on Law's life and feeling a great kinship with this man who, after achieving the goal for which he had worked and studied— after becoming a Fellow of Emmanuel, had it taken from him just five years later when he refused to swear the Oath of Allegiance to the new line of German kings after having already sworn fidelity to the old sovereign.

Though a priest of the Church of England, though a man with the highest sense of the responsibilities of the clerical office and the duties of his order, Law gave up all right to conduct a service or to celebrate the Holy Communion, or to preach a sermon, and chose instead to live in seclusion; studying, praying, and guiding souls through his writing and his charities.

As the light from the lantern spread throughout the cathedral along the vaulted arches, so the light of God's leading spread through Phillip's heart and mind. He knew what he would do. He rose to his feet with a much lighter spirit than he brought in with him. He would go to King's Cliffe. William Law would be his counselor.

It was a long ride the next day on across the fenland and finally through the edge of Rockingham Forest to the tiny village where Law lived. It was not until the three symmetrical chimney stacks of the Hall Yard House came into view that Phillip doubted his inspiration to make the trip. What if Law weren't at home? What if he were home, but had no inclination to receive an intruder? What if . . .

Jezreel drew up before the comfortable house built of the local freestone, roofed with greenish slates, and announced their arrival with a whinney. The noise attracted the attention of a black-suited, stout man with broad shoulders and round face who was escorting a bent, ragged man carrying a clean shirt and basket of fresh vegetables across the courtyard. "I shall see you again, my dear Friend. Meditate on the words of our Lord." The merry-countenanced man held the gate for the beggar, then turned to Phillip who dismounted with some chagrin at coming so abruptly into the presence of the esteemed William Law.

Phillip introduced himself, but found it impossible to explain the purpose of his visit, since he didn't understand it himself. Law, however, seemed to find nothing in the least unusual about having a caller he had not seen for more than five years arrive at his gate in search of counsel and comfort.

"Come in, come in. You have had a long ride? I believe our distribution of food and raiment is done for the day. If any other comes one of my house friends can see to it. You have come from London?

141

You must stop here for a time. We get so little word from the great city."

He led the way through the courtyard and into an old wainscoated hall. "My study is upstairs." He waved his hand at an ascending staircase. "But let us go through here first; I should like you to meet my companions." The parlor was unoccupied, so Law went through the back door and into the garden. "Ah, we've found you at last," he called to two women sitting on a garden bench. "Mr. Ferrar, Mrs. Hutcheson and Miss Gibbon, my companions and spiritual pupils."

The ladies put aside their books and came forward to welcome Phillip, and in a moment he was being given as complete a tour of Law's property as if he were expected to take up residence there. " . . . and on the other side of the paddock," pretty, lace-capped Miss Gibbon said, "is the footbridge over Willow Brook. Beyond that are the schools and almshouses which Mr. Law and Mrs. Hutcheson erected and endowed."

"We now have fourteen girls receiving instruction and clothing in our school," the small, plump Mrs. Hutcheson said.

"And there is my oak tree," Miss Gibbon pointed to a small green sprout. "I planted that when I came to reside here, 1744 that was, so it's just an infant yet, but someday it will shade the paddock."

Law's grey eyes and ruddy complexion glowed as he looked at the field washed in the golden light of evening. "It is my habit to take an hour's walk in my fields before supper. Would you care to join me?"

Phillip begged time to stable Jezreel, then joined his host with pleasure. They walked along a footpath bordered on one side with a field of waist-high, dark green grain, and on the other with a brambled hedgerow, lush with ripe berries and vibrant with birdsong. "My favorite form of vesper," Law said, after they had walked for some time with the birds' arias as the only accompaniment to the rustle of their footsteps in the long grass. "You have sought me out for counsel?" Law asked.

And suddenly Phillip found it so easy, so natural to talk to this man. He told briefly of his curacy and rejection, and now his work with the Methodist Society. But through all his words rang clearly his desire for a call from God to a place of ministry—a settled, peaceful place to shepherd a flock. And he told of his latest refusal by the Bishop.

"And would you have acted differently in Cambridge had you forseen the results?" Law asked.

"Fifteen souls sought the Saviour that night. I could do no other, so help me God."

Law nodded, and his open, agreeable countenance took on an expression of nostalgia. "Relinquishing my college Fellowship for conscience sake was a melancholy affair, but had I done what was required of me to avoid it, I should have thought my condition much worse. The benefits of my education seemed at an end, but yet the same education had been more miserably lost, had I not learnt to fear something more than misfortunes.

"If I were not happier now for that earlier trial, I am persuaded it would be my own fault. Had I brought myself into troubles by my own folly, they would have been very trying; but, I thank God, I can think of them without dejection."

A smile broke across his face. "I recall writing something of the like to my brother George shortly after the occurrence. I remember that my most pressing concern was for my mother. I feared she would be overcome in her concern for me. But the Lord was faithful to sustain those dear to me also."

The bell ringers of King's Cliffe church began their ancient custom of pealing the hours of the day as the men turned their steps back toward the house.

"It has always been so. I have found the Lord ever faithful. As we are faithful in our devotion to Him, He supplies our need for others to minister to. That is the key to happiness, meeting the needs of others."

When they returned to the house Law ushered Phillip into a long, low-ceilinged dining room where the table stood by a bow window looking onto the garden. Supper was the simplest meal imaginable, consisting of a few biscuits, cheese, and wine. The household servants then joined Law, his guest, and the ladies for evening prayer and Law's reading of Scripture before the household retired at nine o'clock.

Alone in his room with only the light of the moon shining through his window, Phillip thought of the light that had shined on him at Ely and led him to this house, to this counselor. He was reminded of the Scripture that referred to coming out of the darkness into His wonderful light and he felt assured that William Law would be instrumental in shedding God's light in his life. Perhaps

143

the first spark had been struck. He thought back over their evening stroll in the fields and recalled Law's words of the importance of filling others' needs with oneself. Thinking on this, Phillip felt light and warmth and comfort sink into his soul. He had been so very much alone all his life—isolated in a crowded orphanage. He saw in his own mind the child he had been—the repressed, quiet, good little boy. And he saw the man that little boy had become— quiet, withdrawn, alone, not opening himself to anyone, nor allowing anyone close enough to reach his needs.

Catherine was the nearest to his heart he had admitted anyone. But the thought of allowing her to come closer and then abandon him was too painful to be borne. But here in the Hall Yard House he had found sanctuary.

And the peace of King's Cliffe, the peace William Law practiced with his fellowmen and before his God, permeated Phillip's soul in the following days. Phillip had long known peace in solitude, in the ability to withdraw and be comfortable with himself and with God. But this was a new kind of peace Law practiced, as he lived his devout and holy life in a complete giving of himself.

Law rose early and breakfasted in his room on a cup of chocolate, before appearing in the drawing room to lead family prayers at nine o'clock. He would then invite Phillip to join him in his bedroom upstairs where the morning light fell through the stone-mullioned windows of the bedroom and adjoining study. And throughout the day, William Law put aside his studying and writing to interview each applicant for relief who presented himself at the garden door.

On his third morning there, Phillip sat before the fireplace in Law's oak-beamed bedroom, while Law interviewed the fourth suppliant of the day in his tiny study which he called his "closet." Phillip looked at the hearthstone of the fireplace and noted the hollows Law had worn in places by rubbing his cold feet upon the warm stones. Then he turned to gaze out the windows; through the trees he could just glimpse the school's library, and almshouses endowed by his host. From the next room he heard Law's counsel to the beggar, "My good Man, I shall be happy to meet your needs for half a crown, but see that you spend it wisely. And be assured that I shall do the same. Just as I would not give a poor man money to go see a puppet show, neither would I allow myself to spend it in the same manner. It is a folly and a crime in a poor man to waste what is given him in foolish trifles whilst he wants meat, drink, and clothes. And it would be no less folly, or a less crime in me, to spend that money in silly diversions which might be so much better spent in imitation of the Divine goodness and works of kindness and charity."

Law rose and took the pauper's hand. "And so, my Brother, let us both go forth to serve God and man, in the doing of good. And remember the words of the Holy Scriptures, 'Blessed be the man that provideth for the sick and needy: the Lord shall deliver him in the time of trouble.' Go now and give as it has been given unto you.

"Miss Gibbon will supply you with a loaf fresh from her excellent oven on your way out." Law stepped to the clothespress in his bedroom and drew out a coarse linen shirt that looked to have been worn only once. "And take this in remembrance of Him who said, 'When one asks for your cloak, give him your coat also.'" Law rang a bell and a servant appeared to show the man out. Then he sat in the chair across from Phillip.

"You interview every petitioner personally?" Phillip asked.

"Certainly. It is only by making our labor a gift and service to the poor that our ordinary work is changed into a holy service and made acceptable to God as our devotion. As charity is the greatest of all virtues, so nothing can make it more amiable in the sight of God than adding one's own labor to it."

Phillip shook his head. "And for such as this they call you an enthusiast?"

Law gave his familiar guffaw of laughter. "I believe the term is 'a celebrated enthusiast,' the very worst kind—one who not only teaches the way of salvation, but lives it as well."

In an uncharacteristic show of emotion, Phillip hit the arm of his chair. "But that's monstrous. To call a man an enthusiast is to call him a leper—a man to be carefully shunned." A note of bitterness attended his words.

"My two housemates and I strive to live our lives based on a literal application of the principles of the Sermon on the Mount; so I guess it is appropriate that some should say all manner of evil against us for righteousness' sake—we attempt to rejoice and be glad in it. But I do not live like a nonjuror. I delight in attending every service of my parish church." Just then the bells pealed the hour from their Norman tower across the field. "And at my special request the rector always has the psalms sung. I have always been a high churchman. Through my study and writing, I wish to dispel

145

the prevalent notion that piety is generally accompanied by intellectual weakness."

"*A Serious Call* has done much to dispel that notion."

"The Lord's leading is a great and marvelous thing. I often wonder if I should have written it, had I retained my Fellowship. I left Emmanuel and went as tutor to Mr. Edward Gibbon, brother of my excellent companion. By the by, my old student now has a son of his own, who is showing a precocious interest in Roman history. Shouldn't be surprised if the young scamp might make a name for himself someday. At any rate, the following year I accompanied young Edward to Emmanuel as his governor and wrote the book while there. The Lord has seen fit to bless it in His work."

"Its detractors have said it sets impossibly high standards—that it is practical, but not practicable. But I see that you indeed practice it thoroughly."

"Indeed, the standard is high. But we shall do well to aim at the highest degree of perfection if we may thereby, at least, attain to mediocrity."

The appearance of another applicant for charity, a woman, interrupted their discussion. After a short interview, Law gave her a pail of milk from the four cows he kept, and sent a large kettle of soup to her hungry children. But the soup was not ladled from the pot over the kitchen fire until Law tasted it first himself. After a careful sip of the steaming liquid, he went to the garden door and called, "Miss Gibbon, are there any more leeks in the garden? The broth is a bit weak today."

The additional vegetables strengthened the soup, and the woman went home to feed her children.

"Do you ever turn any away?" Phillip asked.

Law gave his ready, cheerful laugh. "If a rogue came for money, even if I knew him to be a rogue, I would give him money, hoping for the best and believing it my duty to give to all who might be in need. It may be that I often give to those that do not deserve it, or that will make an ill use of my alms, but what then? Is this not the very method of divine goodness? Does not God make His sun to rise on the evil and on the good? Shall I withhold a little money or food from my fellow creature for fear he should not be good enough to receive it of me? Don't I beg of God to deal with me not according to my merit, but according to His own great goodness? And shall I be so absurd to withhold my charity from a poor brother because he

146

may perhaps not deserve it? Shall I use a mirror toward him, which I pray God never to use toward me?"

It was now tea time, but Law, as was his custom, did not join his companions at the tea table. He chose rather to eat a few raisins, standing while they sat. As at all meals, the food was served on wooden platters. Not, Law explained, from any notion about unnecessary luxury, but because it appeared to him that a plate spoiled the knives.

The days at King's Cliffe would forever remain in Phillip's mind as a foretaste of heaven, with William Law supplying the role of the closest he had ever known to an earthly father. But at last the time came when he must leave. On Phillip's last night in Hall Yard House, Law gave a musical gathering. This was Law's most pleasurable recreation, and he had constructed a handsome wainscoted room with a high-coved ceiling, elegantly decorated with festoons of plasterwork, where Miss Gibbon played works of Bach on the organ.

And the next day, beginning his long ride back to London, Phillip thought on all he had learned in his time with that remarkable man. Looping Jezreel's reins over the saddle, he drew Law's book from his saddlebag and read again one of his favorite portions.

All worldly attainments, whether of greatness, wisdom, or bravery, are but empty sounds; and there is nothing wise, or great, or noble, in any human spirit, but rightly to know and heartily worship and adore the great God. That is the support and life of all spirits, whether in Heaven or on earth.

He put the book away and thought of the road ahead of him. Now, after this time of spiritual refreshment, he must return to the real world, to live these principles in the place God had for him. As he guided Jezreel down the road, he thought of the map he sought for his life—looked at his past and thought of the future.

And he could not think of the future without thinking of Catherine. His time with Law had taught him the necessity of giving of himself. For the first time in his carefully detached existence, Phillip was aware of the possibility, perhaps even the necessity, of filling another person's need with himself—his presence and his personality. It was a totally new concept for him. As he had long ago determined that he didn't need anyone, it had never occurred to

147

him that the reverse might be true—that someone could need him, and not just his preaching.

He was trained and experienced in meeting others' needs with Jesus Christ—with introducing them to Jesus as a person—but the idea of filling a need by presenting himself left him shaken.

But, of course, that was ridiculous. Catherine had turned to him as a friend in her disappointment over Charles Wesley, had leaned on him for support in the darkness of the Fleet, had shared her concerns with him for the safety of her brother, but Catherine didn't really *need* him. She had a large family she could turn to; the Society had the deepest respect for her and all the Perronets . . . anyone would help Catherine. Why would she need him? But, then, why had she turned to him?

And what could he offer her? All the new spiritual insights he had gained from William Law did not change the realities one jot. He was still a foundling receiving only a meager stipend from the Society for his preaching, and he had no prospects of ever securing a settled living.

And Catherine would be the first person he must tell of his rejection when he reached London in five days' time. When he thought of the disappointment he would see in her eyes, he shrank from the task.

He couldn't go back; he couldn't tell Catherine. He had failed, had been rejected again. Even the recommendation of Vincent Perronet hadn't been enough. He had hoped so to have this to offer her. Now he would never be able to speak what was in his heart. He would be forever alone.

· *11* ·

IN SPITE OF HER OUTWARD COMPOSURE, Catherine was experiencing inner panic: Ned had returned from his circuit ride with Charl, bringing reports of unrest and division among the Methodist preachers in the north. . . . Sally Wesley was expecting a baby, and she and Charles had taken a house in Bristol—good news except that this would mean he would be severely reducing his itinerant ministry, a move that was causing concern for the work and backbiting gossip among Society members divided in their support of the Wesley brothers. . . . The rift between John Wesley and George Whitefield was openly talked of, and there were rumors of a split between Charles and John. . . . Elmira Smithson's cough sounded worse each time Catherine visited, and there seemed no possibility of freeing her husband from debtors' prison. . . . Durial's sharp tongue was more caustic than ever as she hectored her husband for a settled lifestyle, to give up circuit-riding and spend more time at home with her.

The list went on, but the fact that almost overwhelmed her was Phillip's continued absence. He was never out of her mind and she hated to admit how much she missed him. His kind eyes and sensitive mouth were never out of her thoughts.

When she looked in her own mirror, she hardly recognized the strained, white face and the round, dark eyes with their hollow look of bereavement. She prayed silently, "I do believe Thou wilt take care of all this, Lord. But when?"

On Thursday she returned from the Foundery feeling more wilted than usual. Her students had shown more propensity to

149

wiggle and giggle than to read, and the late summer combination of high heat and higher humidity made the mere thought of labor exhausting. Yet Durial persisted with her housekeeping schedule. With a sigh, Catherine donned a large white apron and joined the entire household staff in the kitchen to help with the preserving.

"There is a peck of plums in the garden that needs pitting," Durial said. "We shall be glad of my special damson jelly this winter."

Catherine pulled a bentwood chair into the shade and began her sticky task. But the peck was less than a quarter done when she heard horse hooves on the gravel. The pale blond head she saw above the hedge made her forget the heat and the plum stains on her hands and apron.

"Phillip! You've been gone so long." As on that spring day in the woods, she ran toward him, and even more fiercely than then, longed for him to open his arms to receive her.

But his bleak face stopped her. "Phillip . . . " It was as if she had run into a wall. Tears threatened to brim in her eyes, but she looked quickly away. If only he would open up to her—*could* open up. "You've had a long ride. Would you care to walk in the garden?"

They walked where they had before, but the glory was gone. Even his long-awaited presence beside her brought no comfort—the set of his shoulders and the jerky motion of his hands told her his news was bad.

He hesitated, and·she knew he wanted to break the news to her gently. But there was no gentle way. "I was refused."

The thin line of his sensitive mouth told her how much he hated saying those words; no matter how calmly he spoke, they had come at great cost. The very briefness of the statement was as final as a locked gate. And it cost her to respond in a likewise unemotional manner, to honor his reticence. For a moment she could not speak. Then, "I shall tell Audrey to prepare some lemonade."

They sat in the shade and sipped cool drinks, but inside, Catherine was seething. Her world had crumbled. This was far worse than the news of Charles Wesley's marriage had been, because she cared far more deeply for Phillip. And now, even if her inklings that Phillip returned her regard had any foundation in truth, she had no hope for a future with him. A few nights ago in a dream, she had viewed herself through the eyes of another. She had been at Shoreham, kneeling in the garden, wearing a blue dress, and holding an infant in her arms. She rose and walked toward the person watching her, cuddling the precious bundle to her breast. When she woke, she knew that she had been walking to Phillip, carrying their child. But now it could not be.

"Would you care for more lemonade?" The words were a mockery, but she must say something.

Before Phillip could answer, a clatter of hooves and flying gravel called them to the front drive. They arrived just as Ned rushed out the front door and Charles Wesley flung off his sweating horse. "My brother intends to ruin himself!" Wesley began his story even as Ned led the way into the parlor.

"You must help me. This insanity must be stopped." Charles drew a crumpled letter from his pocket and handed it to Ned. "He didn't even write to me personally—just sent a copy of a letter to a third person. He intends to marry Grace Murray."

Catherine had never seen the soft-spoken Charles so agitated. He strode around the room spouting disconnected sentences. "The scandal will be unthinkable. It will bring to an end everything we have labored for. She has been promised to John Bennett for months. And now she accepts my brother too! In the past, she has suffered serious mental illness, and I have grave concerns for her balance now." He threw his hands into the air. "It is unthinkable. You must help me. There's no one else I can turn to. This calamity must be stopped."

"Of course we will help you." Ned clasped his friend's shoulders. "What would you have us do?"

"Ride with me. We must go to Newcastle now."

Catherine's heart sank, thinking of the three-hundred-mile ride. "Phillip, you've just returned from a journey, and have not even had a good meal yet." As always, his thinness caught at her heart.

"Durial will set a table for us, and I can supply you with clean linen." Ned flung her objections aside, and within a short time the three men departed. In spite of the lateness of the hour, they were determined not to delay. Catherine felt more alone than ever. She not only was left with the drudgery of her duty and the difficulty of the situations around her; but worse, the one shining hope she had held to for the future had been extinguished. There was no light at the end of the tunnel.

In the month that Ned and Phillip were gone, one island of brightness arose. Catherine's sister Elizabeth, who had been labor-

151

ing so diligently at the Foundery that Catherine had hardly seen her all summer, announced her engagement to William Briggs, John Wesley's secretary.

"O Elizabeth, I am so happy for you." Catherine hugged her sister and then embraced the smiling bridegroom-to-be. "What a perfect couple you will make. I can't fathom why I hadn't thought of the match myself. You'll go to Shoreham to be married by Papa?"

The couple planned to be off the next day so the banns could be published that very Sunday. And then, though happy for her sister, Catherine felt her desolation even more sharply. "When will it be my turn, Lord? In Thy perfect timing, dost Thou have a time for me?" As in answer, she thought of words from Ecclesiastes.

> To everything there is a season, and a time to every purpose under the heaven. . . . A time to weep, and a time to laugh; a time to mourn, and a time to dance. . . . a time to embrace, and a time to refrain from embracing. . . . He hath made everything beautiful in His time; also He hath set the world in their heart, so that no man can find out the work that God maketh from the beginning to the end.

No one can find out the work that God maketh? Then she would have to continue groping her way one step at a time, but with continued faith in her Guide and in His timing.

One thing Catherine refused to give up on was her determination to help the Smithson family. So next Monday when school was dismissed, Catherine took her courage in hand, made sure she had adequate bribe money in her pocket, and hired a carriage to take her to the Fleet. She alighted on the walk outside the huge gray walls which concealed the horror, brutality, disease, and death she knew to be inside. The last time she had stormed these walls, Phillip was beside her. Now he was on his way to the north of England, and she was alone. No, she reminded herself, never truly alone. "For Thou art with me, Thy rod and Thy staff, they comfort me . . ."

Just as Sarah Peters had taught her to do, Catherine ignored the stares of sightseers who gathered daily outside the massive entrance gates to watch and wait and steep themselves in the malevolent atmosphere of the gaol. And she ignored as well the jeers of those who thought she was the wife or sister of a prisoner.

"Got a file under your skirts, 'ave ye?" a watcher called.

"Another Edgeworth Bess a' goin' out the window down bedsheets with yer Jack Sheppard, 'eh?" The rabble roared in delight at this reference to Newgate's most notorious escapee who made his way out to freedom on three daring occasions with the aid of female friends. But the clanking of the heavy doors cut Catherine off from further taunts.

The turnkey took her to Dick Smithson's cell which seemed to Catherine to be even darker and more crowded than before. Smithson sat in almost exactly the same spot, undoubtedly on the same patch of filthy straw where she had seen him months before. He saw her and asked, "What're you doin' 'ere?"

"I'm Catherine Perronet. I was here with Elmira last summer. I used to be Isaiah's teacher."

He nodded slowly and Catherine felt a surge of hope as she realized that he was not drunk. He had probably run out of money to purchase gin. "I 'member. You was with the tall towheaded feller that kept comin' back to sing 'ymns with those fellas they 'anged."

"Yes." She sorely wished for Phillip's company today.

"Must be somethin' to a religion that makes men sing the night afore they go to Tyburn. And that would bring a fella like that one 'ere just to sing with 'em. I 'eard tell 'e rode in the deathcart to the gallows with Lancaster and Doyle."

"News travels in here."

"Ain't nothin' else to do." He shrugged.

"And do you know that Elmira is sick? Her cough is worse every time I see her."

Smithson looked at her with hollow eyes that even in the gloom of the cell showed his fear at the hopelessness of his situation. "I know. Don't know what'll become of the young'uns if she takes poorly."

"Mr. Smithson, would you reconsider my proposal to allow Isaiah to return to school?"

"Might do."

"Would you like me to pray with you, like Mr. Ferrar did with Lancaster and the others?"

But the curl of his lip and the set of his jaw told her she had gone too far. The turnkey returned to escort her out. "Mr. Smithson, think about Isaiah. If he could read and write, he could get a good job as a clerk. I'll return in a few days for your answer."

Before leaving she arranged with the warden to rent a pillow and

153

blanket for Dick Smithson and to have a loaf of bread delivered to him from the jail's bakehouse. And she left an equal amount of garnish for the jailer as well to be certain her instructions were carried out.

At first Catherine was pleased with her visit, and hopeful as to the outcome. But when, on her promised return a few days later, she found Dick Smithson far gone with gin, and unwilling to hear more of her proposal, her heart sank.

And at home Durial's news was no better. A letter from Ned told them that the men had arrived at Grace Murray's orphan house and hostel in Newcastle, where Charles burst in at eleven o'clock in the morning, and cried, "Grace Murray, you have broken my heart!" The letter followed with a tangled account of Charles rushing Grace off to Leeds, where she was to meet both men she had promised to marry—John Wesley and John Bennett; then of their return to Newcastle where Bennett awaited without having seen Wesley.

But the part of the account that worried Catherine most was Ned's report that the coil had produced mass unrest and dissention among the Society in Newcastle. "All in the house were filled with anger and confusion; some threatened to leave the house and preach no more with Mr. Wesley." Catherine foresaw dark days ahead for the Methodists who faced enough opposition from outside, without creating dissention in their own ranks.

That night she went to her room in a cloud of despair. A quick glance at the books on her shelf told her what she wanted to read. Taking her well-worn copy of *Pilgrim's Progress* to a lighted candle by her bed, she turned to the scene of Christian and Hopeful's imprisonment in Doubting Castle, for certainly she felt as much a prisoner of the Giant Despair as Dick Smithson was of his jailer in the Fleet. She read through the scene of Despair exhibiting the bones of doubting pilgrims he had torn limb from limb and thrown into the courtyard and threatening to do the same to his captives in a few days. And later, after Christian and Hopeful prayed, Christian said,

"What a fool am I to lie in a stinking dungeon, when I may as well walk at liberty! I have a key in my bosom called Promise, that will, I am persuaded, open any lock in Doubting Castle. . . ."

Then Christian pulled it out of his bosom, and began to try

at the dungeon door, whose bolt, as he turned the key, gave back, and the door flew open with ease, and Christian and Hopeful both came out.

And Catherine knew that she too held the answer to the despair that threatened to imprison her—a key called Promise. She turned the pages of her Bible.

As for God, His way is perfect . . . He is a buckler to all those that trust in him. . . . It is God that girdeth me with strength, and maketh my way perfect. Commit thy way unto the Lord: Trust also in Him, and He shall bring it to pass. . . . Wait on the Lord, and keep His way, and He shall exalt thee to inherit the land.

Catherine snuffed her candle and slept the best she had for weeks.
The next week when she drew up before the Foundery and found a freshly combed and scrubbed Isaiah Smithson awaiting her, she knew just how Christian felt when he was back again on the King's Highway.

"Isaiah! Your father said you could come to school again?"

"Yup. Da' said you cared enough to sit on the dirty straw with 'im, and then rent 'im a blanket, so 'e figured you was a right'un."

Catherine shuddered at the degeneration in her pupil's speech. "Isaiah, the class is now several months ahead of you. You shall have to work very hard."

"I brung m' book." He held out the primer she had given him. It was dog-eared and dirty, but it would serve.

A fortnight later when Ned and Phillip returned, however, Catherine found that the key of Promise had not yet unlocked the door to solving the Society's problems. The marriage that Charles Wesley felt would be so disastrous for his brother had been averted, but at what cost?

Ned, Durial, Catherine, and Phillip sat before the parlor fire on an early October evening as Ned recounted the events of their trip. He spoke slowly enough that his listeners could grasp the tension and drama of the scenes that had resulted in the marriage of Grace Murray to John Bennett. The incident had caused a grievous rift between the Wesley brothers and a tidal wave of dissention throughout the Society.

"We pushed straight through to Yorkshire. Charles found George Whitefield preaching to the Societies there and enlisted his help. Whitefield at first counseled that Grace's betrothal to Wesley superceded her promise to Bennett. But in the end Charles' arguments prevailed, and Whitefield acted as Charles' assistant at the wedding of Grace to Bennett.

"Oh, no," Catherine said. "That is sure to drive the wedge between Whitefield and John Wesley deeper yet."

"No." Ned shook his head. "That is the one bright note to this affair. John Wesley joined them in Yorkshire two days after the wedding. He had ridden under great strain for almost forty-eight hours and was too exhausted even to take a room of his own. He lay down beside Whitefield on his bed. It was Whitefield's lot to inform John of the marriage of his intended. In Whitefield's anxiety to console his old friend, he wept copiously. Wesley remained dry-eyed, but was so touched with Whitefield's concern for him that he reestablished fellowship with Whitefield. The rift between them was caused by misunderstandings, resulting from their vast geographical separation. When they were together again, the bond reformed."

"So even though John Wesley lost a wife, he regained a friend," Catherine mused. "And how does Charles view his handiwork in preventing his brother's marriage?"

"Charles is certain he had saved his brother from a great wrong, and their lifework from shipwreck."

"And John?"

"Reportedly he has not spoken to Charles since the incident."

"O Ned, what will happen to the Societies if there is a rift between the brothers? I continue to hear whispers at the Foundery about disagreements over standards for preachers, and of fomenting movements to separate—as our brother Charl told us. It frightens me—where will it end?"

Ned made no reply, so Phillip spoke. "It's hard to say. I have always stood firm against separation, and yet, it is a possibility I've considered lately. If I were to sign the Acts of Toleration, I could fill a pulpit in a dissenting chapel."

"But, Phillip, to leave the Church of England—" Memories of her visit to Canterbury Cathedral and all it meant to her rose in Catherine's mind. To leave the Church of England seemed as unthinkable as to leave England itself.

Phillip nodded. "I know. I feel the same way. And any time I con-

156

sider it, I think of William Law. Even though forced into the position, he refuses to live like a nonjuror; though not allowed to minister in his parish church, he never misses a service. Miss Gibbon told me the rector has been known to preach against Law, in his presence; and yet Law continues to sit in the midst of the congregation, saying his prayers and listening to the Bible readings. With his example before me, could I voluntarily take up dissention?"

The question hung in the air, unanswered. But a few days later an unexpected aspect of the matter presented itself. First, Ned received a letter from Charles Wesley with unanticipated good news.

I snatch a few moments before the people come, to tell you what you will rejoice to know—that the Lord is reviving His Church; and that George Whitefield and my brother and I are one, a threefold cord which shall no more be broken. My dear friends, you shall have the full account not many days hence, if the Lord bless my coming in, as He has blessed my going out.

The news that the crisis had passed brought great rejoicing at the Foundery; the next week George Whitefield came to London to give a firsthand account. After the Wednesday preaching service, Whitefield, Ned, Catherine, and Phillip gathered in the apartments the Society maintained for visiting evangelists.

"Edward, let me hear this new hymn of yours that seems to be on everybody's lips since I've returned from America. I should like to hear it sung by the man who wrote it."

Ned stood and sang the first three verses of his hymn, and Catherine and Phillip joined him on the last verse,

> Oh, that with yonder sacred throng
> We at His feet may fall!
> We'll join the everlasting song,
> And crown Him Lord of all.

"Well, Edward, your place in history is secure. I look forward to our singing that around the Throne together in heaven." In spite of his constant squint, which gave his countenance the impression of a frown, Whitefield's eyes sparkled with pleasure.

"I look forward to singing with you anytime," Ned replied. "And

157

now, tell us of the reconciliation you effected between the brothers Wesley."

"I did nothing; the Spirit of our Lord and the love the brothers hold for each other did all. John was with me when Charles arrived at the inn outside Newcastle. At first, he refused to see one he considered to be a Judas. Charles, on his side, declared he would renounce all conversations with his brother except what he would have with a heathen or publican. I simply ignored such inflated stubbornness and constrained the brothers to meet each other."

Whitefield's narrative was interrupted by a servant bringing in dishes of tea. Catherine poured for the company, then urged Whitefield to continue.

"Both brothers were wound up to the highest pitch of emotion and were almost beyond speech; but when they faced each other the tension snapped and they fell on each other's neck."

"And so the Society is safe?" Catherine asked.

"I pray it will be. But the hardest task still remains—to prove to the Methodists that the work of God is not to be interrupted by any private dissention. And also, that though the companionship and love of Grace Murray has been transferred from leader to disciple, the bereavement has left no lasting bitterness behind."

"Can that be done, do you think?"

Whitefield took a deep drink of tea before answering, "In time, pray God." After another pause, made to seem longer by the flickering of candleflame caught in a draught, Whitefield spoke again. "There is much concern of a 'general deadness' in the Society. I have felt it in London, from a few persons who are eager to make mischief. Charles says the same is true in Bristol where he feels almost universal coldness, heaviness, and deadness among the people—they have lost near to a hundred members there alone."

"What the people need," Ned suggested, "is something to shake them up."

Whitefield's next words shook up the company in that tranquil room. "I am concerned about the work here, but my heart is most truly with my work in America. I must return there soon. I dare to believe that my preaching might help create one nation from those thirteen scattered colonies—unite them under God with each other and with the Mother Country. I envision the mighty Atlantic Ocean becoming a highway of exchange for Gospel preachers.

"Phillip," he turned to their silent companion, "will you go with me to help in this work?"

· *12* ·

As WINTER CLOSED IN, bringing with it shorter, darker days and cold winds blowing off the frozen Thames, Phillip wrestled with Whitefield's offer. Could he go on without a parish, without his country, without family? Must he forever be alone?

He spent Christmas Eve alone in his room, in spite of repeated invitations to come to supper at the Perronets after service at the Foundery. He must reach a decision soon. If he was to go, he must make preparations; and if not, Whitefield must be told so he could seek another companion. And whatever he decided, Catherine must be told. . . .

The thought seemed so counter to the new determination he had brought back from King's Cliffe. In the turmoil over Grace Murray, and now as he considered Whitefield's offer, he had made no move to embark on his brave resolve to open himself to Catherine. Indeed, she too seemed more withdrawn than before. For a moment he longed for the days of easy companionship they had shared on their circuit ride.

But before he could decide anything about Catherine, he must know what God desired of him. He picked up his Bible and turned to the Psalms, his heart praying, as David had, for God's guidance,

> Show me Thy ways, O Lord; teach me Thy paths . . .
> lead me in Thy truth, and teach me;
> for Thou art the God of my salvation,
> on Thee do I wait all the day . . .
> teach me Thy way, O Lord,

> and lead me in a plain path . . .
> for Thou art my rock and my fortress;
> therefore for Thy name's sake lead me, and guide me.

And then he turned to the New Testament, where Paul
addressed the believers in Colosse,

> For this cause we also, since the day we heard it, do not cease to
> pray for you, and to desire that ye might be filled with the knowl-
> edge of His will in all wisdom and spiritual understanding.

Phillip desired with all his heart to be filled with the knowledge
of God's will. But as he meditated, a fear gripped him. Had he
somehow, somewhere, missed God's will for his life? Could that
be the source of his conflict now? "My God, please don't let me be
out of Thy will." His heart's cry was desperate.

As he continued in God's presence, he felt that his prayer was
answered with a sense of peace and release; and he was reminded
that the Christian's first responsibility in knowing God's will is
being willing to do it. With that thought came the confidence that
because he was willing, he could also be confident that God would
not allow him to miss His divine will. When William Law had
told him this, he had not realized the immense impact. If he
believed God capable of guiding, he must also believe Him capable
of making His will known. The key was seeking God in prayer.
And then waiting for the answer to be revealed in his perfect time.

A heavy snowfall fell on London, choking the streets and making travel from Greenwich to Moorfields slow and hazardous, so
Phillip did not see any of the Perronets for several days. But on
New Year's Eve, when the Society held its traditional watchnight
service at the Foundery, the entire Greenwich household
attended. And Phillip made no attempt to deny his joy in seeing
Catherine, standing tall and serene and lovely.

Perhaps because so many had been isolated by the recent storms,
there seemed to be a special unity among those who filled the
chapel to sing, pray, and worship God as the year 1750 began. At
midnight, John Wesley served them Communion. Kneeling at the
altar with the others, Phillip felt a special awareness of God's
presence. It was certain to be a momentous year for the Societies,
and perhaps for himself also. Knowing that he must soon make a

decision, he found great comfort in the words of the closing prayer:

Almighty God, who hast promised to hear the petitions of them that ask in Thy Son's Name; We beseech Thee mercifully to incline Thine ears to us that have made now our prayers and supplications unto Thee; And grant that those things which we have faithfully asked according to Thy will, may effectually be obtained . . . to the setting forth of Thy glory; through Jesus Christ our Lord, Amen.

And then they stood and sang the song with which all Methodist watchnights concluded,

> Hearken to the solemn voice,
> The awful midnight cry!
> Waiting souls, rejoice, rejoice,
> And feel the Bridegroom nigh.

With only a parting bow to his friends, Phillip went out into the night of the new year, his confidence in God newly reaffirmed. Whatever the year held, Phillip had courage not to despair.

Catherine's patience in awaiting God's timing was tested as the January snows drifted into February and still there were no answers. She sensed Phillip's difficulty in finding the right answer to George Whitefield's offer. And she knew her hopes for a future with Phillip could bear no fruit until that question was settled.

Only once had her brother broached the subject to her. "Cath, I was thinking of the offer Mr. Whitefield extended to Phillip. If he should decide to go—that is—I understand the orphan house in Georgia is in need of teachers—had you ever thought—"

"A teacher of red Indians? Are you weary of my company?" Though she sought to make her answer light, his question continued to plague her. Her head told her that the discomforts and trials of a circuit ride would be as nothing compared to what must be faced by a missionary to the new world. But no matter how sternly her head lectured her heart, her heart would not listen.

And so she lived from day to day, anxious to hear from Phillip, and yet reluctant to know his answer.

That Thursday she awoke uncommonly early and lay for a moment, wondering what had disturbed her. Then she realized the sparrows in the garden bushes below her window were making an unaccountable racket. She thought a cat must have gotten in among them and pulled the quilt over her head in an attempt to go back to sleep. But when she heard other noise from the stable yard, she pulled a shawl over her shoulders and went to her window to see what was causing the alarm among the animals. There was nothing amiss; when she opened the sash she found it to be unusually mild for the eighth of February. But later that morning the placid Old Biggin was almost uncontrollable as she drove to the Foundry. And her students were no better. If the sky hadn't been such a clear blue, she would have been certain a storm was about to strike. She had never been more relieved to see the hands of her watch approach twelve than she was today. "Your behavior has been most unacceptable this morning. Tomorrow you must be prepared to work harder, or I shall be obliged to have Mr. Told in." The rascals looked duly smitten at her words, but still failed to leave the room in proper orderliness.

And suddenly the noise of the departing children was lost in a great rumbling thunder that shook the building. Catherine turned to place an armful of books on her desk. But the desk was gone. As if the earth had suddenly spun off its axis, all the furniture in Catherine's room slid to the north wall.

The roaring and shaking continued for minutes that seemed like hours. As the earth heaved, the doors and windows in her room burst open. Bricks from the crumbling chimney fell past her window.

Leaning against the undulating wall for support, Catherine felt a kind of terror she had never known. As her knees gave way and she slid to the floor, she relived her childhood experience of falling off a horse; this was much worse because today the earth was not solid. All the fears she thought conquered besieged her again.

Where was Phillip? He had helped her in her anxiety before, but where was he now? When at last the rolling earth subsided, Catherine didn't move. She suddenly realized how much she had come to rely on Phillip in the past months. He was the person she could always turn to, even when the foundations of the earth shook. She had long sensed this, but had never before experienced so deeply her need of his calm stability.

And then as if in answer to the cry of her heart, Phillip rushed into the room. "Catherine, are you all right? I was so afraid I wouldn't find you—that you might be hurt. . . ." He sat on the floor next to her.

"I'm fine, Phillip. Now that you're here." She relaxed in the delicious comfort of resting her head on his shoulder.

In the midst of the rubble they sat together in a calm quiet, until the sound of running feet and excited voices in the courtyard intruded.

"We must help." Phillip got to his feet and extended a hand to Catherine.

"Do you think there's much damage?"

"There's sure to be a great deal in the poorer parts of town. Pray that there won't be a fire."

They were just into the courtyard when the second shock struck, this even harder than the first. Catherine was certain the earth would split apart beneath her feet. But Phillip held her. And even in the midst of the terrified shrieks, the crash of falling bricks, and the roar of the jolting earth, Catherine knew she could not live without this man's support. Even if it meant going to the ends of the earth—even to America. Life without Phillip was unthinkable.

That decision filled Catherine with an unspeakable sense of peace. In the midst of the turmoil around her, her heart was at peace. And she knew she had made the right decision. "My peace I give you, not as the world giveth . . . " Peace was the one emotion Satan could not counterfeit. It was the complete assurance of being in God's will.

And Catherine sorely needed that peace in the days to come, because internal peace was the only quiet available. As John Wesley told a throng of frightened people who crowded into the damaged Foundery in last-minute hope of turning aside the wrath of God by urgent contrition and promises of future piety, "There is no divine visitation which is likely to have so general an influence upon sinners as an earthquake."

Affluent, smug London needed this reminder of the wrath of God and the judgment to come; and Ned had been unwittingly prophetic in saying that squabbling Society members needed shaking up. And now a frenzied, earthquake theology spelled the end of optimism. London's nerves became almost uncontrollable, incited by such predictions as that of Sir Isaac Newton, "Jupiter is going to approach so close to the earth as possibly to brush it."

Whitefield and Wesley conducted all-night services for those too wrought-up to sleep, and those who no longer had a bed to go home to. Phillip held open-air services in Hyde Park. As on their circuit ride, Catherine frequently accompanied him and led the singing. The favorite song was Isaac Watts',

> O God, Our Help in ages past,
> Our Hope for years to come.
> Our shelter from the stormy blast,
> And our eternal Home!
> Under the shadow of Thy throne
> Still may we dwell secure;
> Sufficient is Thine arm alone,
> And our defense is sure.

The crowd sang with a lustiness brought on by desperation, and then listened to the preacher as drowning men cling to a lifeline. Phillip chose Isaiah 2, as his theme: "'The haughtiness of man shall be made low; and the Lord alone shall be exalted in that day . . . for the glory of His majesty, when He ariseth to shake terribly the earth.'"

At the mention of shaking earth, cries of fear rose from the women and shouts of, "Amen," and "'Struth," from the men. Then Phillip read to them from Psalm 46,

> God is our refuge and strength, a very present help in trouble. Therefore will not we fear, though the earth be removed, and though the mountains be carried into the midst of the sea; The Lord of hosts is with us, the God of Jacob is our refuge.

> Come, behold the works of the Lord, what desolations He hath made in the earth. Be still and know that I am God: I will be exalted among the heathen, I will be exalted in the earth.

"Our little philosophies try to explain earthquakes without reference to God, but these are a divine warning that the time has come for Londoners to consider their faults.

"But do not despair—consider these warnings and do not

despair. God has not forgotten how to show mercy. We must be genuinely sorry for our sins. We must repent and turn from our evildoing. We must take our refuge in the Lord of Hosts who is our very present help in trouble."

Catherine saw what a pillar of strength Phillip was, as he led these frightened people to an understanding of the comfort and security God had for them. And she renewed her vow to stay by his side—that is, if he should indicate he desired her to do so.

A few days later, when Catherine and Phillip went to Chitty Lane to call on Elmira Smithson, they were appalled at the desolation the earthquake had wrought in the slum areas of the city. Although an ancient building code required building in brick in order to prevent fire, no one could afford to pay any attention to the code, and the flimsy lath and plaster buildings had crumbled like sandcastles.

Elmira was attempting to shelter her family in a room that now had only three walls. "You must come with us," Catherine said, as she picked up little Susanna and started toward the carriage.

"But where'll we go?" Elmira cried, her voice showing how torn she was between hope and despair.

Catherine stopped. She could think of nothing. She couldn't take them home with her. Durial would never hear of it. The spare rooms at the Foundery were already bursting with now-homeless Society members. There was not an extra inch in Phillip's room.

Then Catherine knew where there was space aplenty. She thought of the elegant homes near Hyde Park that she had seen earlier in the day. "To Park Lane," she said.

The Countess of Huntingdon's butler did not so much as raise an eyebrow at the sight of the dirty, ill-clothed persons who attended Miss Perronet and Mr. Ferrar. "Please come in. I will see if her Ladyship is at home."

Her Ladyship was. "This is most convenient." She bustled into the reception hall wearing a black cloak and a dark straw bonnet over her lace cap. "Lady Fanny and I were just setting out to deliver baskets of food to the needy. It is much better that they should come to me. Rettkin!" The butler materialized out of nowhere. "See that these children are fed and properly clothed. Their mother shall accompany me and direct my charities to the most deserving. I do abhor the thought of bestowing gifts upon the undeserving. You shall be a great help to me in my work, Mrs.—ah, I don't believe we've been introduced."

Her head spinning, as an encounter with the Countess always made it do, Catherine accompanied an open-mouthed Isaiah and his brother and sisters to the housemaid's quarters and saw that they were unafraid in their new circumstances before leaving. "And now you shall have no excuse for coming to school with dirty hands, Isaiah," she said with a smile.

The winter evening was closing in fast when Catherine and Phillip left Park Lane. "I must return you to your brother," Phillip said. "The quake has turned many Londoners' minds to the judgment of God; but an equal number have adopted the philosophy of 'eat, drink, and be merry, for tomorrow ye die,' and the streets are not safe for a woman."

Catherine sighed. "I expect you are right. But I had hoped we might call on Mr. Smithson and inform him of his family's good fortune."

"Tomorrow," Phillip promised.

Catherine had had no time alone with Phillip since the cataclysm, and she longed to speak to him of her new resolve. But it was impossible that she should speak first. He must give her an opening, some encouragement, just the slightest chink in the wall he kept around himself. But Phillip's wall of isolation was perhaps the only one in London not cracked by the earthquake.

The next day Catherine saw that the walls of the Fleet were likewise intact. Outside, the mob listened to a thundering street preacher, "Earthquakes are singled out above all natural phenomena by their majesty and dreadful horror to mark an immediate operation of God's hand exercised in His divine anger.

"Earthquakes are God's instruments. This is why they always strike at populous cities, and not at uninhabited territories, and why they are specially frightful, inasmuch as they are sudden, unavoidable, and threaten us with a peculiarly dreadful form of death."

A high shriek rose above the wailing of the crowd and several women sank to the ground.

"The preservation of London was a miracle. God deliberately refrained from producing the kind of earthquake that would have destroyed London; but damnation will have its numbers, come when it will. . ."

As the lamentation of the mob rose to an even higher pitch, Catherine was for once grateful for the doors of the Fleet which cut her off from the sound.

To her relief, Smithson was sober today and eager for news. "I've 'eard tell such tales about London—tell me what it's like."

Catherine told him some news of London in general, but moved quickly to what he most wanted to know of Elmira and his children. Catherine held her breath after she recounted the role the Countess of Huntingdon played in the story, for she recalled Smithson's earlier resistance to "Evangelical toffs mucking about in his affairs." But today his gratitude was wholehearted.

His appreciation for the care taken of his family even extended to allowing Phillip to read the Bible to him and the others in his cell. Phillip chose Acts 16 and explained, "This is the story of others unfairly imprisoned at the time of an earthquake. 'And when the magistrates had laid many stripes upon Paul and Silas, they cast them into prison, charging the jailer to keep them safely.'"

In immediate identification with the story, the prisoners in the Fleet moved closer to Phillip, who read, "'And at midnight Paul and Silas prayed, and sang praises unto God; and the prisoners heard them. And suddenly there was a great earthquake, so that the foundations of the prison were shaken; and immediately all the doors were opened, and everyone's bands were loosed.'"

"Lor, I wisht the quake 'ad broken the Fleet down," a prisoner said.

"That's th' only way you'll see th' light o' day, Uriah."

Phillip went on, above the comments of his audience, "'And the keeper of the prison awaking out of his sleep, and seeing the prison doors open, he drew out his sword, and would have killed himself, supposing that the prisoners had been fled. But Paul cried with a loud voice, saying, "Do thyself no harm; for we are all here." Then the jailer called for a light, brought Paul and Silas out, and said, "Sirs, what must I do to be saved?" And they said, "Believe on the Lord Jesus Christ, and thou shalt be saved and thy house."'"

The convicts erupted in jeers at Paul and Silas who chose to remain, rather than escape, but Dick Smithson was silent. Indeed, he was so deep in thought when his visitors left that he did not even bid Catherine and Phillip a farewell.

When Catherine arrived home, she found another crisis had descended upon the household. Durial had been listening to a preacher at the Greenwich village green that afternoon. Her high-strung nerves were now at the breaking point as she demanded the family leave London, and nothing Ned could say had any effect in calming her.

"Allow that I know what the preacher said, Husband. And allow me to judge the good sense his words made. Listen to his reasoning. This present earth, a very unsatisfactory second version of the first earth more or less destroyed by the Flood, is going to end in a great conflagration that will burn it right up. The fire will naturally begin at Rome, the headquarters of the Antichrist, but England is sure to be a particularly unpleasant spot because of our extensive coalfields that will burn so easily."

"Durial!" Ned was never a patient man and his wife's vapors drove him to distraction. "If the entire earth and especially all of England is to be burnt up—what can it matter *where* we are living when it happens? My work is here."

"But you can take work elsewhere." Durial's voice rose another pitch. "I do not wish to compare London to Sodom— for London contains many good people; but because of its size it also contains a proportionately large number of evil people. And setting aside all other considerations, London, by reason of its crowded and insecure buildings, is, of all other places, the most dangerous."

Ned turned away.

Durial flung herself across the room at him. "Do not turn your back on me. If our baby had lived—if I could have given you a child—you would not treat me so!" Racking sobs began to shake her body.

Ned turned and took his wife in his arms. "Durial, Durial. I will write to my father. Perhaps he will know of something."

Catherine, who had not intended to eavesdrop on their private quarrel, but had been caught in the entrance hall, fled to her room. It had been a full month since the earthquake; surely the hysteria would soon die down, people would rebuild their chimneys, replace their crockery and reglaze their windows, and the great London earthquake would become nothing but a memory.

Catherine gratefully accepted Audrey's offer to brush her hair for her, since Durial had no call for her Abigail's services at the moment. "Mmm, that feels good, Audrey. Thank you. Please snuff my candles on the way out. I feel as if I could sleep till the day of doom."

Those words were the first thing Catherine thought of early the next morning, when an eruption of the earth broke forth with a thunderous roar and tumultous shaking. Catherine jolted upright with a cry, thinking the powder house on the green had exploded. But as her writing desk lurched, chairs shook, doors slammed, windows rattled, pewter and crockery clattered from their shelves, and the great elm tree outside her window crashed to the earth, sending shards of broken glass flying across her room, Catherine knew London was being visited by yet another earthquake.

· 13 ·

A SHARP CRY, followed by a moaning wail, tore through the house. At first Catherine thought Durial was hurt, and then realized the cry had come from the servants' quarters. She shook the bits of broken glass out of her slippers and off her shawl before donning them and running in the direction of the noise. When she arrived, along with the rest of the household, at Audrey's room, she found the maid sitting in a tangle of bedclothes, smashed crockery, and disordered furniture, cradling an oddly twisted arm and shrieking. "It threw me outta bed, it did. Just threw me out. My arm 'it the trunk, owww!"

"All right, Audrey, you will stop shrieking so that we can see to your injuries." Durial waded through the shambles. Her house-keeping instincts aroused by the disarray, she began giving orders for the care of Audrey and the righting of the room. Catherine smiled. All her sister-in-law needed to take her mind off her troubles was a house to clean. By the end of the day the house would not only be orderly, but also freshly scrubbed, and all the broken dishes replaced and on the shelf.

But not everywhere in London was the damage so quickly repaired. This quake was far more violent than the first, and buildings damaged by the first were leveled by the second. People frightened by the first were terrified now. All over the city, church bells rang of their own accord, adding to the noise and confusion. People had run into the streets in their nightclothes and were still milling about hours later when Catherine arrived at the Foundery. The panic continued for days. In spite of the attempts of Wesley

173

and other clergymen to calm their fears, the people flocked to the prophets of doom who shouted at the tops of their voices on every street corner, "The end of the world is at hand. Prepare to meet thy Maker."

In order to be of more help in the emergency, Catherine moved into London, taking temporary residence with her sister, Elizabeth Briggs, in her newly established home. A small room that Elizabeth usually used for a private sitting room was at Catherine's disposal whenever she could snatch a few hours of sleep.

After a week of such a schedule, John Wesley fell ill, putting an even greater burden on Society members. In spite of the fact that they were working almost twenty-four hours a day in the same building, Catherine seldom saw Phillip. But when she did, his calm self-containment and quiet efficiency reaffirmed her confidence that he was the one God had prepared for her to spend her life with.

After Catherine had spent a particularly tiring day of dispensing soup and changing dirty bandages for the charity school children, Phillip came to her. She gave him a bowl of soup and bandaged a scrape on his hand, as if he were one of her charges.

When he had finished eating she said, "I have heard rumors of damage and riots in the Fleet. Perhaps we should visit Dick Smithson?"

"I would not take you into that danger. There is no knowing what the rabble may be up to."

"Nonsense!" A flicker of a smile crossed Catherine's face; here was her chance to tell Phillip a little of what she felt. "I am more than willing to go anywhere you go, to face anything you face." She said the words with confidence, ignoring the disquiet they caused in her heart.

He looked at her, a questioning wrinkle across his brow. "Catherine?"

The two of them were a small island of quiet in the tumult of post-earthquake London.

She would have liked to remind him of the mad bulls, swollen rivers, and lighted fireworks she had already faced with him. She would have liked to tell him she was now willing to face an ocean voyage, wilderness living, and red Indians with him. But she felt she had said quite enough, so she held out her arm. "Shall we go?"

The fact that the second shock followed exactly four weeks to

174

the day after the first gave rise to alarm in many quarters over what might follow on April 8.

The same preacher they had heard before still held forth from the corner near the Fleet. "What is God going to do next? Will he order winds to tear up our houses from their foundations and bury us in the ruins? Will He remove the raging distemper from the cattle and send the plague upon ourselves? Or—the Lord in His infinite mercy save us—He may command the earth to open her mouth and, the next time He ariseth to shake terribly the earth, command her to swallow us up alive, with our houses, our wives, our children, with all that appertains upon us."

A great weeping and moaning accompanied his words, much stronger in intensity than the first time Catherine heard him.

At first, the prison provost informed Phillip that no amount of garnishment could buy his way in to visit a prisoner in the Fleet. But when Phillip mentioned the name of the man they wished to visit the response changed. "Oh, 'im. Guess that's all right then. Inside with yer." He pocketed the coins Phillip offered.

Inside, a surprise met them. The jail seemed lighter, the air fresher, as if someone had opened all the windows. And then Catherine saw that was precisely what had happened. The dirty panes of glass from the small, barred windows had broken out, allowing fresh air and light into the prison. But more than that, at the end of the hall one section of the wall was broken away, forming a v-shaped passage onto the street. The breech in the wall was well guarded, as a prisoner would have only to scrambled up a small pile of fallen brick and leap through the hole to effect an escape.

"Smithson!" the turnkey shouted.

To Catherine's surprise, one of the guards came forward. "Dick! You've been made a guard? What has happened?"

"It was like in that story you read us from the Bible," he addressed Phillip. "Where the earthquake set the prisoners free. I gave a good piece o' thought to that, and decided they was right to stay. Just 'a cause they was put there unfairly, didn't mean everybody was, and ya can't have murderers runnin' about the streets—wouldn't be safe for the women an' children. So when the quake shook that there 'ole in the wall, I stood in the gap, as ye might say."

"You prevented a jailbreak?" Catherine asked.

Dick's smile was sheepish behind his shaggy beard. "'ad a might 'a trouble convincin' some it were a good idee. So I threw a few bricks 'ere and there to convince 'em."

"And you've been promoted as a reward! Dick, that's wonderful! Will you get paid?"

He nodded. "Yep. Soon's my debt's paid off, I can go 'ome to Elmirey at night."

Catherine's heart sank. It would take more than a year for him to earn enough to pay his debt—unless he demanded bribes from the other prisoners. "Dick, that's wonderful, but you don't want to become like them." She pointed to the hardened jailers standing by the wall.

"No, I'd rather be more like 'im," he nodded toward Phillip. "Thought I might try a piece o' prayin' or 'ymn singin'—course, I can't read the Bible none. Do you ever have any of these Methody Societies of yours in jails?"

Through the break in the wall, they could hear the street preacher still ranting, "The unrighteous are in a deplorable case indeed; they have nothing to feed upon but anguish and despair. You are deservedly alarmed, for aught you know, you may receive a pre-emptory summons that you cannot ploy with . . . to walk into eternity in the twinkling of an eye, whether sleeping or waking, who can tell?

"Surely on the night of Wednesday, the fourth of April, or the morning of Thursday, the fifth of April, London will be destroyed by a third, this time, completely devastating earthquake."

But Catherine could not feel alarmed by the preacher's words. She had just witnessed a miracle, and no fear for the future could diminish that glory. If only she and Phillip could speak of the future—their future. Surely now, with London crumbled around them, they needed each other more than ever before. She knew she needed Phillip; if only he would say he needed her.

As they settled into the relative quiet of the carriage to drive back to the Foundery where Catherine would spend another night with Elizabeth, she thought, "Perhaps now he will speak. We are alone, perhaps now . . ."

And perhaps he did. But Catherine, worn out by the long days of work and emotion with only brief snatches of sleep, fell asleep to the swaying motion of the vehicle. And much to her surprise, she awoke late the next morning, not in the tiny closet off her sister's room where she had been staying, but in her room in Greenwich.

"How did I get here?" she asked Audrey, who was carrying on with her duties in spite of the fact one arm was tied in a sling. Catherine recalled that just a year ago, Ned had been the one with a damaged arm. It seemed as if her life was ever to be punctuated with upheavals, no matter how much she prayed for a more gentle calling.

"Mr. Ned brought you in sound asleep last night. The mistress sent him for you—said it wasn't right for you to be working day and night in London when you needed to be here making your earthquake gown."

"My what?" and Catherine sat upright in her bed.

Audrey handed her a cup of coffee. "All the ladies is makin' 'em. Mistress 'as us all at it—but I'm not much good sewing with only one 'and."

"Audrey, what are you talking about?"

"Earthquake gowns. To wear for the all-night vigil when the final quake comes. Mistress says we'll all go out in the fields— since she can't convince Mr. Ned to take us clean out of London as some are doin'."

"That will be enough, Audrey. Thank you."

Catherine finished her coffee, dressed quickly, and hurried downstairs. Sure enough, Durial had assembled all the female servants in the south sitting room, where each one was stitching intently on a garment of ivory muslin. While they stitched, Durial read to them from a printed Earthquake Sermon, "'If I take the wings of the morning, and dwell in the uttermost parts of the sea, even there shall Thy hand lead me, and Thy right hand shall hold me up.' No distance can separate us, no velocity remove us, from divine vengeance if guilty, nor put us beyond God's protection if righteous . . ." She looked up as Catherine entered. "Hello, Sister. As you see, the next visitation of the Lord's hand shall not find us sleeping. I have ordered a length of muslin for you too."

The sound of approaching horses hooves eliminated the need for Catherine to reply. "Don't put down your sewing, any of you. I shall see to the door," and she fled from the room, wondering what in the world she would do with such a garment. As if it would matter what one wore if they were to be swallowed alive by the earth.

Her heart soared when she saw their visitor. She ran down the steps, and as in all her dreams, Phillip opened his arms and she went into them. For a moment they stood there in the morning sunshine, secure and belonging.

"I have come to speak to you," he said at last.

"Come into the front parlor. Everyone else is in back. You can't imagine what Durial has them doing."

"Making earthquake gowns?"

"How did you know?"

"It's all the rage in London. I called on the Countess this morning and even her household is set about it."

"Has the panic not subsided at all yet?" She led him to a small sofa.

"The Countess said seven hundred coaches have been counted passing Hyde Park Corner with whole parties removing into the country. It is said lodging is unattainable in. Windsor and nearby villages."

Catherine had no desire to continue a discussion of the earthquake, now that she finally had Phillip alone in a quiet room. She looked down at her hands, but couldn't quite suppress the smile on her lips.

Still he hesitated, so she made an opening for him. "You have determined to accept Mr. Whitefield's offer?" Why did those simple words make her think of walking into a dark night?

He gave her a deep, level look, but before he could reply another carriage sounded on the drive. No servants appeared from the sewing circle, so Catherine went to the door. The sight of the beloved figure in a full-bottomed wig brought a joyous cry from her, "Father!" and for the second time that morning, she flew into a caller's arms. "What a wonderful surprise! What brings you to London when everyone else is fleeing the city?"

"That is precisely what brought me, Child. Your mother could not rest until I could bring her my personal assurances that all her children in London are well. We have received the most alarming reports . . ."

And then a small figure bounded out of the closed carriage and threw herself into Catherine's arms as well. "Philothea!"

"Isn't it famous! I convinced Mother that Father shouldn't travel so far alone, and she could spare me much more easily than any of the boys." Then she saw Phillip who had come into the hall

178

to greet the arrivals, and she abandoned her sister for her idol. "I brought you a poppyseed cake. We'll pretend it's your birthday."

Catherine ushered them all into the parlor and turned to summon Durial, when she saw that yet another coach had arrived. Perfect in its shiny fittings and golden coronets on its doors, this coach carried the Countess of Huntingdon.

George Whitefield alighted first and offered his hand to assist Lady Huntingdon; then, as yet another surprise, Charles Wesley emerged behind her. The Countess issued an order to her driver, then led the way into the house, past Catherine who was standing at the door.

"I have come to speak to you," she addressed Phillip. "I do not know what is to be done with that man Smithson. Oh, hello, Vincent. What brings you to London? This is an insane time to be visiting the city—they say it will be level in a short time. But never mind. You're looking well." Without giving Vincent a chance to reply, she went on from her position in the center of the room.

"I paid Mr. Smithson's debts, as you suggested, Phillip, but he has declined my offer of a place on my estate at Donnington Park. What do you say to that?"

Whitefield answered for Phillip, "My Lady, if he feels a calling to minister to those unfortunates in prison, are we to interfere with that?"

"Calling? What does one of his class know of a calling?"

"The disciples were simple men, my Lady. Our Lord called them," Whitefield said.

The Countess tossed her head in the air with a sniff. Just then Ned and Durial entered and the conversation became general. Not even the Countess of Huntingdon was able to upstage a reunion of the Perronet family.

Across the room Catherine sought to catch Phillip's eye. He stood tall and alone in the corner, isolated from all the joyful family greetings. Catherine felt an overwhelming desire to reach him, to tell him she would be his family, that he never need be alone again. But Charles Wesley was beside her and she must speak to him. "What has brought you to London?"

"I received word my brother was gravely ill—at death's door. I came to nurse him, but when I arrived I found him in the quite capable hands of Mrs. Vazielle."

179

"Humph," the Countess said. "Clutches is more like. It will not do, Charles. She must not ensnare him."

Charles nodded. "Indeed, I believe she is a woman of sorrowful spirit."

"She will not do." The Countess issued her edict with another toss of her head and moved on around the room, instinctively playing hostess as if she were in her own London drawing room.

"And how is Sally? I haven't heard from her for months," Catherine asked.

Charles' face became somber. "My dearest is not well. The babe miscarried. It may have been the shock of the first earthquake . . ."

"Charles, I'm so sorry. Is there fear for her health?"

"No, no. The doctor says we may look forward to a full quiver. But this one is mourned."

And Catherine too ached for Sally's empty mother-arms, for the unheard baby laughter, for dreams unfulfilled—an ache of might-have-beens.

And again the question arose in her heart, as she looked at Phillip and wondered if her own dreams must also die before they could be born, "My God, where art Thou? Thou has promised a perfect way—but where? And when?"

Just then Vincent joined her and Charles. "Ah, Mr. Wesley, tell me of the work in your part of the country. Is there still a movement for separation?"

Catherine knew how strongly Charles opposed such ideas and listened carefully for his answer. "It seems the great shaking-up God gave us has not been without its consequence in the minds of the brethren. We had a conference of the northern and midlands Societies just a week ago. All agreed not to separate. So the wound is healed—slightly."

Catherine realized she had been holding her breath awaiting Charles' answer. Now it escaped in a great sigh. It seemed that suddenly, in the very wake of destruction, God was answering all her prayers. Was this His perfect time? The time she had so long awaited?

It seemed even more likely that was to be so as Ned joined them and his father turned to him. "My Son, I have come not only as an emissary from your mother, but also as a petitioner in my own behalf."

"Sir?"

"I think you know from visiting my estate in Canterbury last year that Adisham has been looking for retirement. I can put him off no longer. He must be pensioned into a cottage and the burden of running the farm passed to younger, stronger hands. Would you consider being those hands, Ned?"

"Move to Canterbury? I must give it some thought. I believe Durial would like it above all things."

"And you, Ned? It should give you more uninterrupted time for hymn-writing; and the Societies in Kent are in need of a firm hand among them."

Catherine's head was reeling. This would solve Ned and Durial's problem. But what about hers? She looked across the room at the still-silent Phillip. In the midst of the noisy room he was calm and detached. And yet, he looked sad, as if instinctively missing the belonging he had never known.

She started toward him, but Philothea intervened. "Catherine, I'm longing to hear all about your earthquake adventures! Was it alarming? All we got in Shoreham was a gentle rolling—no more than a rocking chair."

And then Whitefield approached Phillip, and Catherine heard him ask, "And what of my invitation? Have you decided to go to America with me?"

But Phillip's voice was softer than Whitefield's and she could not hear the answer.

· 14 ·

DURIAL WAS AT THE HEIGHT of her glory directing her well-trained servants and seeing to her guests' comfort, and when Ned spoke briefly to her of Vincent's offer, she immediately declared that the entire company should stay to dinner in celebration. Her well-ordered larders were up to any challenge—even to serving the Countess of Huntingdon on short notice. She dispatched Joseph from the stables to London to fetch Elizabeth and William Briggs so that all available family members might be there.

Ned and his father went into the study for further discussion of their plans, and Philothea requested Catherine to show her around the house and garden. As she left the parlor, Catherine heard Whitefield and Phillip discussing the plans for sailing to America, but only one voice was distinct. "America? Nonsense!" And the Countess snapped her fan to punctuate her words.

After giving Philothea a quick tour, Catherine took her sister to the guest room to wash and change for dinner and retired to her own room to do the same. Audrey brought her a brass can of hot water from the kitchen and Catherine reveled in repeatedly splashing her face and arms as if she could wash away the fatigue and strain of the past weeks.

But when she turned to her mirror to arrange her curls she was shocked that her recent fatigue and worry were written so clearly there. What was wrong? God had answered all her prayers—all but one. And surely it was only a matter of time—probably tomorrow Phillip would call and their conversation would be

183

uninterrupted. She had known for weeks what her answer would be; now it only remained for her to voice it. Then she stopped.

Suddenly she knew the cause of the weight around her heart and the hollow feeling in the center of her stomach. She had known peace the moment she acknowledged her love for Phillip. But she had known nothing but internal turmoil, far greater than any caused by the earthquakes, over her decision to go to America. What of her criterion that if a step were directed of God, it would be accompanied by His peace?

Could the fact that she had been thwarted at every attempt to speak to Phillip of her decision to go, and the fact that she felt no peace over the decision, mean she *wasn't* to go? It was true that she felt no real call to the work in America—no intense desire to minister in that field. But wasn't a desire to be with the minister himself enough? Had she mistaken her wish to be with Phillip for a call to be a missionary?

Must she choose between Phillip and God's call? If that were the case there could be no choice.

The arrival of yet another carriage told her the Briggses had arrived. She must go down and take her place in the family circle. Inside, Catherine felt nothing but a gaping hole where her dreams had been, but outside she wore her usual air of calm serenity. Durial's excellent meal choked her, and when she attempted to reply to a remark directed to her, her tight, controlled voice sounded more awful to her ears than if she had shouted.

Across the table Phillip responded to a question from Charles Wesley in his slow, thoughtful voice, then looked across the table at her. For an awful moment their eyes held. Then he gave that tiny, half smile of his and she could sit there no longer.

Summoning all her natural dignity, Catherine asked her hostess to excuse her and walked slowly to her room. Mechanically she went through all the motions of her night-time ritual, then drew the heavy side curtains of her bed around her. She had no sense of God's presence with her in that small enclosure, only her determination to believe that He was still there.

The next morning it seemed a miracle to her that she had slept, that the sun had risen again, that birds were singing. Such things were entirely alien to the desolation inside her. Durial was surprised by her announcement that she did not intend to go in to the Foundery that day.

"Regular lessons have not been resumed yet; I am certain they can get along very well without me."

"A very wise decision, Catherine. I am just surprised you would take so sensible a course. After all, your earthquake gown is yet unfinished. And now we must make one for Philothea too, as Father Perronet does not intend to return to Shoreham before the end of the week. And all the china must be packed—how fortunate that one packing will suffice for earthquake protection and for our removal to Canterbury. I can think of no more satisfactory solution for our needs. Will you live with Elizabeth when we are gone? That seems far the best plan—assuming there remains a London to be lived in, that is."

Durial thrust Catherine's half-sewn gown into her hands and began cutting her final length of muslin for Philothea. "How fortunate that I have just enough fabric left. Now we must decide whether to hold our vigil in the meadows by Hither Green or take to a boat in the Thames. Which do you think would be the best, Ned?"

Edward looked up from the manuscript of a poem he was composing. "Where do you think we'd find a boat? Besides, those gowns will show off to the best advantage in an open field."

Durial was completely unscathed by his sarcasm. "Yes, I suppose that is best. There's always the danger of a great wave swamping a boat. But I did think that in case of fire, the river might be a wise choice."

"Well, to the best of my knowledge, there are no coal fields under Hither Green Meadow, so you should be quite safe there from a conflagration."

The prophets had pinpointed the night of April 4 or early morning of April 5, so all day Wednesday Durial worked everyone around her to a frenzy, storing the last of the crockery and silver, securing the furniture with ropes, and packing huge hampers of food. "If the destruction is great we may have to live in the open for some time. Audrey, you and Joseph fill the pony cart with blankets."

Catherine obeyed, as did all the others, including Vincent Perronet. Hysteria was in the air, and there was no sense in trying to fight it. "Ned," Vincent admonished his son about to depart for the Foundery, "you might bring an extra hymnal or two from the

185

book room, seems we might keep the folks occupied with a candle-light hymn-sing."

Ned agreed, and assured Durial for the seventh time that he would not return late from a visit to John Wesley to encourage him in his convalescence.

By the time Ned returned at five o'clock, Durial had household and carriages in perfect order and all the females of the family and staff properly clad in their earthquake gowns. "Yes, I suppose you must take your cloaks, but it does seem a pity to cover the gowns. Although I imagine by the time it's really cold it will be dark also. But then, if great fires start, you won't need a wrap, will you?"

Catherine was pleased with Ned's news that the Countess would join them at the meadow. She was bringing her household staff and the Smithson family, as something of a celebration for the newly reunited family. But then she was alarmed at his next piece of information. "George Whitefield left yesterday for his parents' home in Gloucester, so she is bringing Phillip in place of her private chaplain."

Catherine climbed into the carriage next to Philothea and was thankful for her sister's chatter all the way to the meadow. The exit route from London was choked with carriages, horseback riders, and pedestrians. Many were well-known to the Perronets and a festival air accompanied the evacuees as they called and waved to their friends. But Catherine sat motionless. Phillip would be there tonight. She was certain he would speak to her, and she would much rather encounter an earthquake than to tell him she couldn't go to America with him.

The sun was setting when they reached Hither Green. Durial selected a pleasant spot near a spinney of trees and directed the servants to spread out rugs on the grass. Catherine remained inside the carriage as long as possible; but when the Countess' party arrived and chose to park not far from them, she could no longer remain hidden. "Come, Cath! Let's go listen to the preachers!" Philothea tugged at her hand.

They walked across the meadow grass, their gowns, devoid of familiar hoops and panniers, swishing around their ankles, and stood behind a crowd listening to a doomsaying preacher. "It says it right here, in the Book of Matthew, 'There shall be earthquakes in divers places. All these are the beginning of sorrows.'" A moan

186

went up from the overwrought audience. "'Then shall they deliver you up to be afflicted, and shall kill you: and ye shall be hated . . .'"

A warm hand touched Catherine's shoulder, and Phillip's deep voice said, "He seems to be overlooking the exhortation to avoid the false prophets that shall arrive at that time."

It was now dark, and as Catherine turned, the glow of the lantern Phillip carried fell on his hair and gentle eyes. She had never guessed that her determination to follow God could teeter so precariously.

"Durial sent me to fetch you. She is serving supper from the hampers."

Philothea hung on Phillip's arm and fairly skipped across the meadow with him, leaving Catherine to walk quietly beside them, wearing the natural calm solemnity of her expression that showed nothing of the pain she was feeling. Was this what it meant to love—to really love? This caring so much you thought you couldn't stand it? And then not being able to do anything about it?

She sat on the rug Durial indicated. She held her plate of food and slipped enough of it to Isaiah Smithson to make it appear she had eaten, and then sent her greetings to his parents who were eating with the servants. And she listened to the Countess holding forth, "England is darkened with clouds of ignorance and sin. If God spares us this night, I shall turn upon our country the light of Divine truth. The church is slumbering at ease, benumbed by the poisonous influence of error. I shall arouse the careless sleepers and apply the Gospel antidote. Throughout England, Wales, Scotland, Ireland, I shall relume the ancient altars and enkindle fresh fires. If we are spared the fires of judgment tonight . . ." But when Ned and her father began gathering the party together to sing hymns, it was more than Catherine could bear. She slipped away to sit in the carriage.

Across the meadow, candles and lanterns were flickering like overgrown fireflies, and the voices of the singers carried to her on the night air, "All hail the power of Jesus' name! Let angels prostrate fall. . ."

They had begun the third song when Catherine heard a soft rap at the carriage door. At first it was so gentle she thought she had

187

mistaken, but then she saw Phillip's dear, craggy profile in the moonlight.

"Catherine, may I come in? I must speak to you." The calmness of his voice sounded as forced as was her effort at sounding cheerful as she offered him the seat facing her.

It seemed he dreaded what he would say as much as Catherine dreaded the reply she must give. He regarded her in silence, a soft glow of moonlight falling through the carriage window. For a moment she who had learned to read him so well saw an opening, a readiness to speak, and then something snapped shut inside.

Now that they were together, they must speak. If only she could reach him, pry open that spring that always closed her out. Phillip seemed to realize how near he had come to letting the barrier down. He put his hands over his face as if he could rebuild the chink he'd let fall from the wall.

At last he took a breath so deep that Catherine felt as if the whole carriage shook. "I shouldn't have come. I don't know why I did. Catherine, I cannot speak. I long to, but I may not. Surely you know how I feel about you, how tenderly I regard you. I had hoped to have something to offer you. But I have nothing."

And the barrier was sealed again.

In the dimness of the night, from the dark of her own pain, Catherine reached out to him and took his hand. "Nothing to offer but your dear self, Phillip."

The term of endearment seem to wound him. He pulled his hand away. "I had hoped to have something of substance—A place to offer you."

"And I had hoped to accept. . ." she said; she could get no further in her own explanation that she must refuse him.

"Catherine, I have refused Mr. Whitefield's offer. Now I have nothing. I tried to accept, but it was wrong. I was considering it for the wrong reasons—to make a home to offer you, not to serve God."

The relief was overwhelming. For long minutes Catherine could only swallow. At last the burning lump in her throat dissolved and she could pray, "Thank You, my God, thank You."

"Catherine, I cannot tell you. . ."

With a sudden force that would make an observer think the earthquake had struck the Perronet carriage, Catherine moved across the seat and into Phillip's arms. "O Phillip, that's the best news I've ever heard. Why didn't you tell me? I had come to the same conclusion. I was determined to go in order to be with you, but then I knew it was wrong. I thought you were going to ask me to go and I should have to refuse you. O Phillip!"

And at last, after months of waiting, he kissed her—or she kissed him. In their close quarters in the dark, it was impossible to tell who made the first move. But as the choir in the meadow sang, "Love divine, all loves excelling, Joy of heav'n to earth come down!" the two in the carriage knew they had known a bit of that divine love on earth.

Then Phillip pulled away. "It's not possible. Life's not really that good—not mine."

"I intend to do my best to see that it is from here on."

"Catherine, in my whole life I've never loved anyone—nor anyone me. I'm afraid I don't know how to go about this."

She traced the hollow of his cheek with a gentle finger. "You're doing very well for a beginner."

But the tender mood was broken as he firmly set her back on her own side of the carriage. "What was I thinking? Forgive me. Catherine, nothing has changed. The fact still remains that I am a foundling without place or prospect. Even if I were such a selfish bounder as to ask you to sacrifice yourself to me, it must be clear to you that the honorable, respected, not to mention well-to-do Vincent Perronet would never give his daughter to one with such a background."

"Phillip, what nonsense! My father believes we are all equal before God, all sons and heirs. There are no foundlings in the kingdom of God."

"Spiritually, I do not doubt that. But in the terms of this world I am a foundling who—"

"A foundling who has found grace in the sight of God and favor in the eyes of the woman who loves him."

This time he came to her across the carriage width and, at long last, everything about him told her that he had come home. Phillip had found a place of belonging as he had never belonged before.

Nothing was solved; but for the moment, having Phillip love her, and loving him in return, was enough. And she had her firm faith that God would guide them, would open a door for them in time. No sooner had the affirmation formed in her mind, than the singers in the meadow began,

A charge to keep I have,
a God to glorify;...
To serve the present age,
My calling to fulfill;
Oh, may it all my pow'rs engage
To do my Master's will!

She turned her head slightly from Phillip's shoulder and looked out the small window. Across the meadow candles and lanterns flickered as the ladies' pale muslin gowns ruffled in a gentle pre-dawn breeze. The night that had been predicted to be filled with terror and catastrophe was flooded with peace and beauty. She turned back to Phillip and closed her eyes.

Perhaps they dozed, because streaks of red and gold were filling the eastern sky when a sharp rap on the carriage door brought its occupants back to the present world.

"Well, it appears the hand of the avenging angel has passed us by. But I must say, if I were the Almighty, I'd be hard pressed to find a reason to spare this lot." The Countess of Huntingdon held the door for them to step out. "I have ordered breakfast served, and I have an announcement for which you might wish to be present."

Everyone looked drowsy after their night's vigil, but not the least bit chagrined that they had spent the night awaiting a calamity which failed to occur. Joseph, Audrey, and Elmira Smithson were passing around cider and pork pie as the morning sun broke over the meadow. Standing in the center of the group, his arms held up to Heaven, Vincent Perronet prayed, "For our deliverance, our Father, we Thank Thee. Help the lives which Thou hast spared to be lived worthily unto Thee. Amen."

And the people who had sung through most of the night responded, "Glory be to the Father and to the Son, and to the Holy Ghost. As it was in the beginning, is now and ever shall be, world without end, Amen."

And then Lady Huntingdon took center stage. "Since the world has not ended, it appears the Almighty intends that we should go on with our work. My chaplain, Mr. Whitefield, is soon to depart for America, and I shall be in need of a replacement for his services. Therefore, I appoint Mr. Phillip Ferrar to fill his vacancy." She looked at Phillip, "You, Sir, are not to go to America. I have determined it will not suit."

190

Catherine gasped and turned to Phillip. The look of astonishment on his face told her he had no idea this was coming.

"This position is, of course, only temporary." Her Ladyship paused. "I have determined to build a private chapel in Tunbridge Wells and install a permanent chaplain there. Mr. Ferrar, you shall have that position."

With the precision with which he did everything, Phillip rose to his feet and bowed to the Countess. "Yes, your Ladyship."

Only Catherine saw the twinkle of amusement behind his smile of pleasure.

"And," the Countess turned a half-circle to take in the entire company, then focused directly on Phillip, "you are to marry this young lady."

The amusement and pleasure on Phillip's face were eclipsed by the look of open love he turned on Catherine as he extended his hand to help her to her feet.

"Yes, your Ladyship," they said to the Countess, but they looked only at each other.

HISTORICAL FOOTNOTE

This book is a work of fiction with a great deal of history woven in. Especially when many of the characters are familiar to the reader, it can be important to separate fact from fiction. The accounts given of: The Wesleys, the Foundery, the Methodist Society, the Countess of Huntingdon, George Whitefield, and William Law are accurate, taken from the journals and biographies listed in the Bibliography.

The earthquakes and reactions to them are matters of historical record; the "earthquake theology" sermons were preached as quoted.

The story of the Perronets is as accurate as I could make it, but here the novelist's imagination was called into greater service, as the references to members of this large family in journals and historical accounts are tantalizingly brief. I have used all I could learn of Catherine—she was indeed on the eligibility list John presented to Charles, but of her later life nothing is known.

Phillip Ferrar is entirely fictional, but is in many ways a composite of the early Methodist preachers recorded in history; most of his sermons are from John Wesley. None of the hardships encountered on the preaching tours are made up. All are taken from the journals of John and Charles Wesley and George Whitefield. As Betty Waller, who previewed the manuscript dedicated to her, said, "And to think, we sit Sunday after Sunday in our nice comfortable pews and don't have any idea what others went through for our faith."

Emmanuel College has made posthumous amends to William Law

for the deprivation of his Fellowship. Only two Emmanuel men have been honored by being pictured in the stained glass windows of Emmanuel College Chapel—John Harvard and William Law. On April 28, 1961, the Rector and people of King's Cliffe held a service to commemorate the two-hundredth anniversary of Law's death. A party of members of Emmanuel, including the master, several fellows and the whole of the chapel choir, went up to King's Cliffe for the occasion.

In spite of Wesley's great desire that the people saved under Methodist preaching would become the "saving salt" for the Church of England, that was not to happen. In 1784 Wesley sat in an Anglican service and heard a tirade against Methodists. That night he sorrowfully recorded in his *Journal*, "All who preach thus will drive the Methodists from the church, in spite of all that I can do." That is what happened after Wesley died in 1791. Not all ties with the establishment were broken, however; for when Wesley's New Chapel, built in 1778, was reopened after complete restoration on All Saint's Day in 1978, H.R.H. Queen Elizabeth II attended. Her comment as she thanked the minister at the door was, "You Methodists do sing loudly."

The church of St. Peter and St. Paul at Shoreham continues to serve its parish under the guidance of the present vicar, Geoffrey Sedgwick Simpson, an American from Vermont. I visited Shoreham on a day filled with sunshine, flowers, and birdsong and suggested to the vicar that he had chosen to serve in Shoreham because he didn't want to wait until the afterlife for heaven.

I wish to express my deep appreciation to John Charles Pollock who read my manuscript for solecisms and anachronisms; and to Cyril Skinner, managing curator, and Douglas A. Wollen, historian, who were so helpful during my research at Wesley's Chapel.

Donna Fletcher Crow
Boise, Idaho
1987

WORD LIST

Abecedarian—an ABC book which also taught prayers and the rudiments of the Christian religion

Bagnio—brothel

Butter pond pudding—steamed pudding served in a pond of melted butter

Cassock—long, close garment worn by clergy

Chaise—a light carriage or pleasure vehicle

Chalybeate—spring water containing salts of iron

Collop—a small slice of meat, such as a rasher of bacon

Commination—a recital of God's anger and judgment against sinners

Curate—an assistant to an Anglican vicar

Dishabille—casual clothing, negligee

Farthing—smallest coin of English currency, valued at ¼ penny.

Fichu—a kerchief of fine white fabric draped over the shoulders and fastened in front to fill in a low neckline

The Foundery—abandoned ironworks John Wesley bought in 1739 near Moorfields and converted into chapels, school, medical clinic, living quarters, etc., for the Methodist Society

Hectic fever—a fluctuating but persistent fever, such as tuberculosis

Infant—pupil in kindergarten or earliest stage of learning

Jugged pigeons—pigeons stewed in an earthenware jug

Lappets—lace streamers falling from cap to shoulders

Lawn—a sheer, plainwoven cotton or linen fabric, as used in the sleeves of an Anglican bishop's robes

Methodist Society—a religious society open to all people, designed to enrich and purify all churches. Societies promoted preaching, fellowship meetings, Sunday Schools, day schools, orphanages, and numerous other services for members' faith, education, health, and well-being

Nonconformist (dissenter)—member of a religious body separated from the Church of England

Nonjuror—Anglican clergyman who refused to take the oath of allegiance to William and Mary and their descendants

Oast house—a conical shaped kiln used for drying hops or malt

Open gown—dress with skirt open in front below waist to reveal an ornate petticoat

Ordinary—a clergyman appointed to give spiritual counsel to condemned criminals; an official position comparable to chaplain

Pannier—hooped petticoat which supports a skirt

Pease porridge—split pea soup

Quid—slang for one pound sterling

Rector or vicar—clergyman of the Church of England who has charge of a parish

Riding pillion—to sit behind the saddle on a small pad

Round gown—dress with skirt closed in front, not showing petticoat

Shilling—British coin equivalent to American nickel

Sizar—a Cambridge student who receives college expenses in return for acting as servant to other students, servitor at Oxford

St. Dunstan—religious reformer who served as Archbishop of Canterbury from 959 to 988

Syllabarium—a section of a primer which began with 2-letter syllables and gradually increased in length until 6-syllable words were taught

Tutball—an early form of cricket

Verger—an official in church who serves as caretaker and attendant

TIME LINE FOR
THE CAMBRIDGE COLLECTION

UNITED STATES	ENGLAND
George Whitefield begins preaching	1738 John Wesley's Aldersgate Experience
French and Indian War	1756
	1760 George III crowned
	1760 Lady Huntingdon opens chapel in Bath
	1766 Stamp Act passed
Boston Tea Party	1773 Rowland Hill ordained
The Revolutionary War	1776 The American War
	1787 Wilberforce begins antislavery campaign
Constitution ratified	1788
George Washington elected president	1789
	1799 Church Missionary Society founded
	1805 Lord Nelson wins Battle of Trafalgar
	1807 Parliament bans slave trade
War of 1812	1812 Charles Simeon begins Conversation Parties
	1815 Waterloo
Missouri Compromise	1820 George IV crowned
John Quincy Adams elected president	1825
	1830 William IV crowned
Temperance Union founded	1833 William Wilberforce dies
Texas Independence	1836 Charles Simeon dies
	1837 Queen Victoria crowned
Susan B. Anthony Campaigns	1848
California Gold Rush	1849
	1851 Crystal Palace opens
Uncle Tom's Cabin published	1852
	1854 Florence Nightingale goes to Crimean War
Abraham Lincoln elected president	1860
Emancipation Proclamation	1863
	1865 Hudson Taylor founds China Inland Mission
Transcontinental Railroad completed	1869
	1877 D. L. Moody and Ira Sankey London Revivals
Thomas Edison invents lightbulb	1879
	1885 Cambridge Seven joins China Inland Mission

BIBLIOGRAPHY

Anthony Babington, *The English Bastille*, New York: St. Martin's Press, 1971.

Esther T. Barker, *Lady Huntingdon, Whitefield, and the Wesleys* Private printing, 1984.

P. Boyle, *The Fashionable Court Guide, or Town Visiting Directory for the Year 1792*, London.

Mabel Richmond Brailsford, *A Tale of Two Brothers, John and Charles Wesley*, New York: Oxford University Press, 1954.

T.D. Kendrick, *The Lisbon Earthquake*, London: Methuen & Co., Ltd., 1956.

Helen Knight, *Lady Huntington* (sic.) *and Her Friends*, New York: American Tract Society, 1853.

"William Law: A Bicentenary," (including the text of Professor Chadwick's Sermon, preprinted from *The Anglican World*), *The Emmanuel College Magazine*, Vol. XLIII, 1960-61.

William Law, *A Serious Call to a Devout and Holy Life*, London: J. M. Dent & Sons Ltd., 1906.

"Law's Serious Call," *The Emmanuel College Magazine*, Vol. XXXI, 1937-8.

The Life and Times of Selina Countess of Huntingdon, by a member of the Houses of Shirley and Hastings, London: William Edward Painter, Strand, 1844.

Ruth McClure, *Coram's Children, The London Foundling Hospital in the Eighteenth Century*, New Haven: Yale University Press, 1981.

T. Crichton Mitchell, *The Wesley Century*, Vol. 2, Kansas City: Beacon Hill Press of Kansas City, 1984.

G. Moreton, *Memorials of the Birthplace and Residence of the Rev. Wm. Law, M.S. at King's Cliffe in Northhamptonshire*, London: The London Printing Works, 1895.

John Pollock, *George Whitefield and the Great Awakening*, New York: Doubleday & Co., 1972.

John Lord Sheffield, *Miscellaneous Works of Edward Gibbon, Esq.*, Vol. 1, London: 1796.

Nila Banton Smith, *American Reading Instruction*, Newark: International Reading Association, 1974.

Richard Tighe, *A Short Account of the Life and Writings of the late Rev. William Law, A.M.*, London: J. Hatchard, 1813.

Silas Told, "An Account of Mr. Silas Told," (reprinted from *Life and Adventures of Silas Told*,) *The Arminian Magazine* Vol. XI, 1788.

Rev. L. Tyerman, *The Life and Times of John Wesley*, Vol. III, London: Hoarder & Stoughton, 1880.

Charles Wesley, *The Journal of Charles Wesley*, Thomas Jackson, ed., Grand Rapids: Baker Book House, from the 1849 edition.

John Wesley, *Journal*, Standard edition edited by Nehemiah Curnock, 8 volumes, 1909-1916.

All Hail the Power of Jesus' Name

God . . . gave Him the name that is above every name . . . Jesus Christ is Lord. Phil. 2:9-11

1. All hail the pow'r of Je - sus' name! Let an - gels pros - trate
2. Ye cho - sen seed of Is - rael's race, Ye ran - somed from the
3. Let ev - ery kin - dred, ev - 'ry tribe, On this ter - res - trial
4. O that with yon - der sa - cred throng We at His feet may

fall, Let an - gels pros - trate fall; Bring forth the roy - al di - a -
fall, Ye ran - somed from the fall; Hail Him who saves you by His
ball, On this ter - res - trial ball; To Him all maj - es - ty as -
fall, We at His feet may fall! We'll join the ev - er - last - ing

dem,
grace, And crown Him, crown Him,
cribe,
song, And crown Him, crown Him, crown Him, crown Him, crown Him,

crown

crown Him, crown Him, And crown Him Lord of all. A - men.

Him,

TEXT: Edward Perronet; adapted by John Rippon
MUSIC: James Ellor

DIADEM
C.M. with Refrain

FICTION FROM VICTOR BOOKS

George MacDonald

A Quiet Neighborhood
The Seaboard Parish
The Vicar's Daughter
The Shopkeeper's Daughter
The Last Castle
The Prodigal Apprentice
On Tangled Paths
Heather and Snow
The Elect Lady
Home Again

Cliff Schimmels

Winter Hunger
Rivals of Spring
Summer Winds
Rites of Autumn

Donna Fletcher Crow

Brandley's Search
To Be Worthy
A Gentle Calling
Something of Value

Robert Wise

The Pastors' Barracks
The Scrolls of Edessa